A QUEST FOR FLIGHT

By

JACK G. SALTER

First published by the Author 2007
ISBN 978-0-9555169-0-0
Printed and bound in the U.K. by
Hobbs the Printers Ltd, Brunel Rd, Totton, Hants

To:

The late D.R. Brinn
A Great Aviator

THE AUTHOR

Jack Salter was born in 1938 and educated at Hamble School. Following which he trained as an aircraft engineer at Air Service Training Ltd., Hamble, and also learnt to fly.

Much of his early flying was of an unusual nature and is featured in three of his books, Praestet Omnibus Prudentia, Vinegar & Honey and Call of the Wing.

He has two daughters who he introduced at an early age to two other passions in his life, piano music and horse riding. And whilst he has held a number of posts, over the years, quite unrelated to aviation his desire to take to the wing remains undiminished.

He lives happily in semi-retirement with his South African wife, Lincia, on the edge of the New Forest and continues to pursue his interest in the whole spectrum of aviation.

The whole problem is confined within these limits viz: To make a surface support a given weight, by the application of power to the resistance of air.

SIR GEORGE CAYLEY (1809)

PROLOGUE

The history of the Herby family's attempts to take to the air goes back to the year 1838 with the birth of George William Herby, son of a mariner, and whose mother of Irish origins was gifted with striking blue eyes and an abundance of humour. A humour that would be tried and tested to the extreme during the forthcoming ambitious adventures of her offspring.

From an early age the young Willy Herby, as he was generally known, displayed an unfailing interest in the flight of birds, and spent endless hours on the cliff tops, fronting his white-washed cottage home, keenly observing gulls perform effortless movements upon the air.

He was fascinated by the ability of the birds to remain motionless in the coastal breezes. And with an eye glued to a telescope, presented to him by father, he studied them at height out over the sea, as they described ever-decreasing orbits and continued soaring skywards till they were nothing more than specks glinting in the sunshine. A notable and intriguing feat in his opinion since it was accomplished with a full spread wing absent of motion.

Initially his interest revolved around the skill and grace with which the birds performed. Then he began to grow curious about the invisibility of the air in which they moved. He came to the conclusion that there was something hiding out there in the void that aided the mobility of the birds but, as yet, was waiting to be explored by man.

At twelve years of age, consumed by an appetite to discover the mysterious agent, he secured a sheet of linen to his wrists and ankles and launched himself from the cliff tops neighbouring his home. And immediately plunged to a sandy seashore some eighty feet in the depths.

A broken leg and sprained wrist did nothing to dampen his enthusiasm. In the time it took his injuries to heal he constructed a framework in the shape of a gull's wing and enlisted his mother's help to stitch Irish linen to it, as a covering. He also made a fan tail, similarly covered, which he explained would be secured to his legs.

Thus prepared he waited patiently for a day when the wind roared in steadily from the sea. He stood on the cliff tops fighting against its force as he slid his arms into the leather harness attached to the underside of the wing and his mother secured the fantail to his legs.

He moved to the cliff edge, his youthful muscles braced against the force of the wind. A force that lessened as he crouched forward and the wing made hesitant attempts to lift him bodily.

Suddenly, without warning, he was hoisted into the air – blown rearwards ten paces – and deposited abruptly and heavily back to earth.

He struggled to his feet, resolved not to be defeated, and limped back to the cliff edge with the wing. He crouched more positively this time, and rather than wait for the wing to lift him he used his feet to push himself into space over the cliff ledge. For a glancing moment he witnessed an expanse of sunlit, blue rambling sea. Then with devastating swiftness he plummeted, involuntarily performed two somersaults, slammed against the cliff face, and tumbled helplessly till the soft sand of the seashore broke his fall.

It was a miracle he was spared from an injury. But he was. And three days later after his mother helped him make a number of repairs to ripped areas of linen with needle and thread he tethered himself to a long length of cord, and secured the other end to a large wooden peg driven in the ground. He was confident he would lift into the air with the capability of a kite.

His mother looked on sympathetically, as ignorant as he was at to what might be the outcome of his latest idea to get into the air. A part of her said there was some logic in his kite theory, whilst another part of her argued that his youthful imagination was running away with him. She felt deeply for his safety, but equally admired his pluck.

As he rather hoped and expected the stiff sea breeze swept him into the air under the canopy of the wing. He rose swiftly, the cord playing out, and mother dropping further beneath him. Then the power of his ascent wrenched the peg from the ground, as the cord reached its limit. Taking him with it the wing reared up, hesitated, fell over backwards and thrust him heavily back to earth into the unforgiving arms of gravity.

The incident resulted in an injury to his spine. An injury that was to haunt him with pain for the remainder of his life, and which he only ever disclosed to his wife, Rosemary, in his later years.

He did, however, grow cautious for a time after his calamitous return to earth. He reverted back to studying the birds through the telescope, fervently hoping he might chance on a clue as to how they mastered the art of flight. And on the rare occasions his father was home from sea they discussed the effects of wind on sail and how it might be compared to a wing in flight.

He also happened to find the skeleton of a gull, during one of his many meanderings along the seashore beneath the cliff tops fronting his home. He raced back to the cottage, driven by a surge of inspiration, and settled down to the finicky task of dressing the skeleton with a silk covering to compensate for the loss of flesh and feather.

But his subsequent attempts to launch it into the air ended in total failure; the mock bird registered immediate disapproval of the air and fell to earth in a fit of resignation.

He placated his disappointment and frustration by concentrating his thoughts on the effects of wind on sail. He made a crude model based on the hull of a ship to which he added a full set of sail protruding from each side of the hull and were set to meet the air at a shallow angle.

Launched from the tether of a hand line and assisted by a steady sea breeze, he was amazed at the speed with which the model rose the heights. Within a matter of seconds it reached the end of the tether and sat on the air, sails rippling noisily, pulling vigorously at the line.

During this time in his experiments he met Rosemary, daughter of a farming family who resided some eight miles inland. The family kept his mother supplied with potatoes; greens, eggs, milk and the odd plucked and drawn fowl.

In the past her parents had delivered the produce but at fifteen years of age they considered her mature enough to make the journey alone in a pony and trap. Part of the deal for the supply of the food was that Willy's mother would make repairs to the clothing of the family. And whilst she worked with needle and thread stitching rents and tears, and fashioning patches, Willy introduced Rosemary to his kite flying and studies of bird flight. She took to it with a buoyant enthusiasm, a shared interest. They grew very close to each other and it culminated in Rosemary carrying his child.

Being of minor age they expected to be descended upon by the wrath of their parents. Quite the reverse, a marriage was hastily arranged through the services of a pastor who was fibbed into thinking the couple was two years older than they actually were.

Rosemary's company and influence brought a new kind of harmony into Willy's life, providing him with a broader and more rational approach to his studies of flight.

The idea struck him when they were strolling along the seashore of an evening.

"Methinks, Willy is a fool!" he shouted and embraced her portly form.

"Why so, Willy?" She smiled at his contagious enthusiasm.

"Because, my dearest, throughout my studies of flight I have never considered the importance of balance." He slapped his forehead with a hand. "Sailing vessels are given ballast for balance, and the sails are trimmed to achieve likewise. And it is obvious a bird must use balance to conduct flight since it too is moving through a sea, invisible as it is. Come – let us hasten home. We must get to work without delay."

By the time Rosemary gave birth to heir son, Samuel, Willy was convinced he had found the key to the door that hitherto had secreted the foundations of flight.

The addition of small weights to the silk covered gull skeleton enabled the bird to take to the air more agreeably, when launched by hand, and settle into gliding flight and whose poise could be enhanced, he discovered, by making minute adjustments to the position of the weights.

Flight after flight, he and Rosemary watched in fascination as the bird flew joyously from the cliff tops out over the seashore to communicate with the invisible agents of the air, slipping, wavering, lurching and, on the odd occasion, becoming too exuberant and spiralling to earth. But, in Willie's opinion, it was always in control of its flight.

For a year he rested peacefully in the knowledge of his discovery and devoted his time to Rosemary and the infant Samuel. There was much to do on the derelict cottage his parents had presented them with as a wedding gift. And winter was coming in.

The completed transformation of their home won considerable praise from family and a handful of friends, and Rosemary would have enjoyed the compliments had she not known of his troublesome spinal injury. She often caught him unaware looking tired, strained, perspiring, his eyes full of pain which he valiantly tried to disguise and dismiss as a minor ailment. She was under no illusion that his suffering was acute at times and to add to her anxiety he refused to consult a physician for reasons he mistrusted such men. He preferred to store his faith in the passing of time and the miracle cures of nature as the best remedies for the ills of mankind.

He constructed another wing using birch wood for the framing to which he fitted a horizontal tail operated by foot stirrups. Rosemary rallied eagerly to his aid spending endless hours stitching linen covering to the frame. His diary records it as one of the happiest episodes in his life when he was able to combine the love of his home and family with his constantly lingering desire to take to the air.

The following Spring they took to the hills further inland with the wing. He was of the opinion the calmer air would increase his chances of success and, what was more, be less strenuous on his ailing spine.

He stood within an aperture positioned midway of the wing span and slipped his arms through leather loops fitted to the underside of the wing. Then ran down the slope of the hill, shouldering the wing, and launched himself into the air. Directly he was detached from the earth he swung his feet back into the stirrups and controlled the fore and aft tilt of the wing by raising or lowering the horizontal fan tail surface: a theory given to a lengthy mention in his written observations of bird flight.

His early attempts in calm air were a success. He graduated from launching from a hill two hundred feet in height to leaping from the summit of Brasher hill that rose to eight hundred feet above the level of the sea. He floated down through the void thinking nothing of the dangers lurking in the daunting, awesome drop. Moreso was the inconvenience of the journey, on foot, back to the summit, carrying the wing, at the termination of each flight.

Figures roaming the downs came to watch him drawn by his courage and his daring, amazing feats of flight and his young, pretty wife who attended his launchings or sat by a picnic hamper nursing an infant.

Spring gave way to summer. The gulls moved inland to begin their ritual of circling over the hills and rising to great heights without the need to elevate their wings. Willy wrote: How I yearn for their skill, their grace and their effortless performance.

The hot, restless summer breezes and vortices, however, were to shatter such hopes and aspirations. Time and time again the unpredictable antics of the wind severely tilted the wing and careered him back into the shoulder of the hill, scattering his admiring spectators.

He struggled on refusing to accept defeat and, after Rosemary had hastily stitched repaired any rents or tears to the linen covering, he leapt, quite undaunted into the air yet again, fighting to disguise his tired and strained limbs and a pain searing through his shoulder joints. Discomforts that were soon forgotten as he floated free and he was filled with a sense of command – of domination. A king surveying his kingdom, a hawk eyeing its prey or, perhaps, an architect admiring the perfected beauty of his creation: a latticework of various colours, in different shades of light, dresses the floor of dale and meadow and shimmers on the crest of the downs. A snaking river is not an intrusion; it merely blends in with the vista and meanders with the gentle flowing elegance as drawn by the brush of its artist...Suddenly, Willy is aware of an eerie silence. No longer is he is moving forward and he is seized by consternation as he notices the wing is carrying him earthwards at an alarming rate. Something is badly amiss and he is helpless to determine what it is. The earth looms! He hastens to free his feet from the stirrups and braces himself.

The redistribution of his weight affects the balance of the wing, tilting it forward. Very gradually the silence is replaced by the sound of air flowing over the wing. The bulbous crown of an oak tree slides rearwards beneath him. Another reaches for his dangling legs. The wing rises slightly. Then slips uneasily backwards. In the next instant he is grappling with the branches and foliage of the tree that served to check his descent and spare him from serious injury.

He did not venture into the air again that summer. He grew very reticent and took to rambling on the hills, alone. At home he sat to the early hours studying the linen-dressed bird, observing it from various angles, and scratching copious notes on parchment with a quill pen.

The devoted, tolerant Rosemary stood by him, confiding in no one, suffering in silence, but using her diary to describe her dilemma during that difficult time in their marriage. "How I miss his cut and dash, and adventurous spirit." She wrote. "No longer are we close enough for me to feel the beat of his heart, or for me to respond to his amorous embraces which, without fail, left me breathless and utterly fulfilled. My pride is in disarray since I am unable to lure him to me – to explore me – to caress me – to express his love for me. Try as I might I am unable to fight this overwhelming force that has imprisoned him in its pursuit to unravel the mysteries of the air.

On a cold, grey afternoon of the following winter, after many weeks of inactivity he took to the hills with the wing. The uninvited Rosemary trailed behind him carrying their warmly clad son, Samuel who smiled defiance at the mournful, wailing lament of the icy wind.

On the peak of Brasher hill Willy attached himself to the wing and trotted off down the slopes to be plucked into the air by the boisterous wind. He struggled for a time to get his feet into the tail stirrups and the wing staggered and lurched until he settled it in gliding flight. Rosemary viewed his courage and gallantry through a film of tears, a congratulatory smile creeping on to her lips as the wing swept earthwards, then rose up with the grace and elegance of a bird reaching majestically for the height. But it was short-lived; the wing suddenly fell over describing the arc of a cartwheel.

"Oh no, Willy!" Rosemary cried out as the wing flicked into a spiral from which it failed to recover. It spun down violently, uncontrollably till it struck ground at the base of the hill.

He was laid to rest in a quiet corner of Ower churchyard in the shadows of a solitary pine tree. All that remains now, barely discernable amongst the overgrown grass, is a small headstone whose inscription, badly eroded by the ravages of weather and time, reads:

GEORGE WILLIAM HERBY
b. 12th May 1838
d. 16th Oct 1857
Beloved husband of Rosemary
And father of Samuel.

"Broken but not destroyed"

ONE

Immediately the boy entered the room the tense atmosphere struck him. A grave expression masked father's face, and mother looked out at the world with angry eyes, having occasion to pout her lips in defiance.

"Sit down, my boy." father said. "Your mother feels we need to talk."

Timothy did so but avoided their dramatic expressions by looking at the only feature in the room that provided any source of comfort: a cheery log fire in the large hearth whose flickering flames reflected on the polished brass casings of the wall-mounted oil lamps.

Father said: "Your mother has decided she would rather not live here any longer. She leaves tomorrow to take up a new residence in Brunton. She suggests you may go with her."

The differences between his parents were not unknown to the boy; it had been going on for several months. He had often arisen of a morning to find father sleeping in his rocker chair by the hearth, and mother had been very difficult to engage in conversation for days. But Timothy had never imagined it would reach a point where a parent would desert the family home.

"What is it to be?" mother demanded impatiently.

He regarded her contemptuously, dumbly daring her to be so callous at such an unhappy hour.

"Since this is our home and where we all belong, I see no reason for leaving it." he said.

"You are not acquainted with the facts, Timothy. Your father and I are…"

"That is enough Rebecca!" father interrupted forcibly. "The boy has suggested you stay. It is not for you to burden him with our petty squabbles."

Mother shuddered at his stern tone, drew herself erect, and pretended his words had fallen on deaf ears.

Father turned and said gently, "Is that your final decision, Timothy?"

"Yes, father."

He rose from the rocker, "Very well. We need not discuss the matter further Rebecca."

She took her leave the following day and, considerate to the end, father carried her trunk to Four Mile Cross to wait for the stage to Brunton. Timothy followed them at a discreet distance and hid in the foliage of an oak to observe her departure, painfully anguished by her abandonment of him and father.

He spotted the coach and six against the skyline as it came over Pilley's ridge, a diminishing form of transport, so claimed a number of village elders, now that mighty horses on rails were conveying increasing numbers of passengers between town and city.

Presently it came clearly to view lead by the pounding hooves of the six mounts, its carriage rocking and swaying, the large wooden spoke wheels crushing the earth bare highway into clouds of dust, and heralding its arrival with a rousing series of blasts from a coachman's horn.

It drew to a halt before the figures of mother and father in a flurry of tinkling brass traces, straining leathers and grating brake blocks. Whereupon mother, without the hint of a farewell to father, climbed immediately up the step into the carriage leaving father to lift her trunk on to the roof rack with the aid of a coachman: to which the carriage groaned and sagged a little in response to the additional weight. A mount raised and shook its head vigorously. Big, fine beasts they are, gleaming with sweat, their eyes hooded by large black blinkers.

Under the combined threat of a verbal command from the driver, and his whip, they lunged forward, hastened into their stride by the shrill, curdling call of the horn, leaving the solitary figure of father by the wayside. A pitiful sight that Timothy would never forget.

He clambered down from his hiding place in the tree and raced to join him. Father's grim expression vanished. He rested a hand on Timothy's shoulder and led him home.

Timothy never really grew accustomed to mother's absence; it created a huge vacuum in his life. She had been part of the cottage as far back as he could remember, always there to see him off to school and always there to greet him on his return. Whereas father's employment on the Hadley Estate took him away from the cottage for long periods.

He could not deny, however, that mother's departure returned a welcome peace and tranquillity to the cottage. No more grim, strained faces. No more tense, uneasy silences. He grew closer to father and took on more responsibility for the chores in and around the cottage, accompanied as he, was in father's absence, by their two dogs, Jeppy, a black Labrador and Sniffy, a golden retriever.

Mother had never taken kindly to them; she would not dream of them sharing the hearth on a bitterly cold night. And if father insisted, which he had on numerous occasions, she retreated angrily from the room and retired to their sleeping quarters behind a securely locked door, causing a tense silence to descend on the cottage in the days to follow.

Equally she would not be trifled by the care of the horses. Father used Yorkie for his duties about the estate. Timothy had received Paddy from father as a birthday gift.

He had always shared a close affinity with the animals. But when mother abandoned the family circle the importance of their friendship grew. Many an evening found him sprawled before the glowing logs of the hearth talking to the dogs whilst waiting for father to arrive home. There were times when his thoughts drifted off to happier days. Days when all of them, including mother, ventured on to the nearby downs to launch one of father's kites.

He recalled the feel of the scorched grasses against the soles of his bare feet, up there on the hills. And the view of mother sitting by a picnic hamper, reading a book, attired in a long cotton dress and a posy of flowers, picked by father, adorning the brim of her wide-brimmed bonnet. She rarely exhibited any interest in the kite flying. Though, for Timothy, it would not have been the same without her, as too had the dogs not been in attendance. They were an integral part of the family despite the fact the dogs were roused to a mixture of fear and anger each time a kite rose into the air, and hovered at the end of the line like a threatening alien.

Three summers past he had been a mere novice fighting to master the art of flying the kites: silk covered diamond shapes, trailing long ribbon tails that cavorted erratically in the air at his unsteady and inexperienced hand upon the line.

But over the years father's patient, thorough instruction had instilled in him an artful skill to fly any of the kites using the minimum of assistance from the wind. The latest addition to the kite collection was an unusual construction invented by father himself. It consisted of two slightly convex surfaces, measuring six feet in span, which were separated by twelve struts and diagonal runs of bracing cord. Adjustable surfaces at the rear extremities of the lower surfaces had enabled father, after numerous experiments, to demonstrate the kite's ability to tilt and turn in flight. And the addition of a horizontal tail made it perform with more dexterity. The real poise and harmony came when father fitted a lead weight to provide the kite with the correct balance in flight.

Unlike the other kites it was not controlled by a line. It was launched by hand and, of its own free will, flew a steady graceful trajectory to the lowlands four hundred feet in the depths. The sound of the door latch being lifted interrupted Timothy's trail of memories. The dogs stirred, wagging their tails in eager anticipation. The door creaked open and father came in, his presence adding to the warmth and security of the room.

After supper that evening he announced his intentions to construct a full-scale version of their latest kite and partner it into the air. Timothy gaped at him in astonishment; he did not doubt father's skill in handling the kites but he had never envisaged it would lead up to anything quite spectacular as manned flight. In his opinion, if such a feat was humanly possible, it would only be accomplished by personages of scientific learning.

Further proof of father's intent to take up the challenge of manned flight came when he unrolled a number of plans on the kitchen table. Detailed drawings revealed a host of dimensions and a description of the materials to be used. He also disclosed he had been collecting lengths of spruce, and rolls of calico, over the months, and stored them in the hay-loft of the stables.

Evidently the full-scale kite would be constructed in the shelter of the stables, and the horses turned out to weather the winter in the open, rugged, as they would be, to lessen the discomfort of the cold winds and icy nights.

Timothy pored over the drawings and pondered on the many impossibilities of such an enormous undertaking. No man, to his knowledge had ever taken to the air in flight. So what chance had father, a humble estate employee, of conquering the evasive knowledge of bird flight or of solving the qualities of the invisible air in which flight might take place.

Taking him completely by surprise father invited him to his sleeping quarters and opened the lid of a trunk deposited in a closet. "In here, my boy, you will find all the information I have collected, and written, on the subject of flight. You are welcome to read it at any time you choose."

The offer had the immediate effect of humbling the boy and making him realise just how much he had underestimated father's commitment to his quest for flight.

Hereafter he raced home from school, completed the chores which included preparing supper for father's homecoming, then settled at the kitchen table, in the light of an oil lamp, and delved in to father's collection of papers.

The trunk opened up a mine of information – a whole new avenue of knowledge. His reading took him out and beyond the restrictions of life on the estate to meet other pioneers of flight, messrs. Cayley, Stringfellow, Hargrave, Ader, Lilienthal and Pilcher and of whom two had perished in their quest for flight. In fact Mr Pilcher had succumbed earlier that year according to a newspaper cutting. Another, dated three years past, reported Mr Lilienthal's tragic end following fatal injuries incurred during experiments with flight in a country overseas.

Another fatal end printed on a very old and faded newspaper cutting arrested Timothy's attention with a jolt. It briefly described the death-plunge of a Mr. George, William Herby during one of his many attempts to emulate the flight of birds, by launching himself, attached to a bird-shaped wing, from the heights of Brasher hill in the West Country. A wife and infant son survived him.

Timothy was intrigued by the surname and intended to ask father if there was a family connection.

Rolls of dried cracked parchment, covered in sketches and the scratched writing of a quill pen, accompanying the report of George, William Herby's demise, expounded on the importance of balancing a craft of the air and compared it to the trim and balance of a sailing vessel. The drawings displayed a bird in various postures of flight and notes adjacent to the drawings explained how the bird attained such postures.

The link between father and George William grew more evident when Timothy came across a collection of papers written by father on flight. By comparison, father's notes and observations were more extensive, more detailed. They embraced the complete anatomy of a bird ranging from the digestive tract to the minor and major pectoral tendons used to raise and lower the wing. There was also a suggestion that the wing was equipped with two types of feather serving different functions... Timothy paused to massage his tired eyes. It was all so incredibly exciting and absorbing, difficult to comprehend in many respects because everything was cloaked in theory, nothing substantial. He shook his head and carried on reading.

Father's attention to detail in his notes came through again and again. He recorded the snaring of a song thrush for the purpose of measuring it wing span and wing area. He then weighed the bird to calculate the weight the wings would need to lift into the air. On another page he mentioned the finding of a bird carcase up in the woods and how he had discovered the bones in the structure were hollow. By way of a foot note he added: There can be no doubt that the hollow bones make for a significant reduction in weight and proceeds to explain why our feathered friends conduct their flight with such ease and precision.

Other papers covered the unusual construction of the most recent kite, the reason for the curved wing surfaces, the lengthy experiments to obtain the correct combination of movement on the adjustable areas of the wing to activate a tilt and turn, and the function of the hinged tail surface which was to pitch the kite fore and aft. The final part of the paper covered the calculations to determine the exact spot on which a weight would be fitted in order to balance the kite in flight.

Timothy grinned to himself; it had never occurred to him that father had been researching the possibility of flight for so long, and with such dedication. Family life, as he had known it, had only ever centred around father's employment on the estate, mother's duties in the home and his own progress at school. Apart from a number of annual social functions, arranged by the squire and lady Hadley, life was routine and a little tedious.

Two weeks after making his intentions known father began the first job of altering the stables to accommodate the construction of the full-scale kite. The horses were rugged up and turned out each night. A work bench was installed and equipped with an assortment of tools some of which were borrowed from the local smithy and carpenter. And father dug a fire pit and suspended a cauldron of water over it.

Work on the kite began in earnest. A fire was started under the cauldron and as soon as the water boiled and saturated the air with vapour father spent many hours steam-bending the lengths of spruce into the skeletal outlines of the wings. A hazardous task as Timothy was to learn to his cost when attacked occasionally by the scalding steam, as was father. But it did not deter them; if anything it had the effect of strengthening their will and resolve, and nourishing their pride and growing sense of satisfaction at what was emerging from the chrysalis of their endeavours.

Father worked like a Trojan. He rarely arrived home from the estate much before mid evening and after a brief supper retreated to the stable to continue the work on the kite, toiling to the early hours long after ordering Timothy to his bed. At weekends they worked all day apart from a couple of respites to take food. They fitted two spars running the entire span of each wing and followed this by slotting curved sections of wood on the spars at equi-distance. Timothy erred with two he fitted. Father did not complain; he quietly insisted they be removed and reset. They were to become known as the wing ribs.

A solid wooden section joining the bottom wing puzzled the boy until father explained the reinforcing was necessary to support his weight when he accompanied the kite to the air.

At times the ravages of the winter chills forced them to retreat from their labours and seek the heat of the hearth in the cottage to thaw their numb fingers and toes, and satisfy their raging appetites on steaming bowls of broth and home-baked bread. Often on such occasions, in the stillness and warmth of the flickering hearth fire and the soft glow of the oil lamps, with the dogs sprawled before his feet, Timothy found his thoughts dwelling on mother's absence. He missed her badly at certain intervals of the day. And to know she was lingering nearby would have done something to mitigate her loss from the family circle. To hear the bustle of her dress, to catch a glimpse of her brown eyes or the wrinkling of her nose in moments of anger would have done much to soothe the restless insecurity and private grief he suffered as a result of her painful desertion.

He got the impression father missed her too, but stalwartly buried her loss by bending his energies to the construction of the kite: an example Timothy knew he would need to follow if he were to cultivate the sterling qualities of the Herby family. Particularly when father disclosed of an evening that George, William Herby, mentioned amongst his collection of papers, was in fact, his father and Timothy's grandfather.

The revelation filled Timothy with a surge of pride. "What actually happened, do you think, on that fateful day, father?"

After a brief pause for thought he said: "I can only surmise, from a note in your grandmother's diary, that what little control he had over his wing was wrested from him."

"But why did he fail? And Mr. Lilienthal? And Mr. Pilcher?"

He smiled wryly, "I have my suspicions, my boy. But until I put my own theories to the test, I am as much at risk as they were."

"Are your theories much different to theirs, you think?"

Father paused to put a taper to his pipe. "If you have gleaned anything from my collection of papers you will observe Grandfather Willy and others write about the importance of balance and give no mention of control. Presumably because they opined that balance combines the two function. Your grandfather's wing used a tail surface to raise or lower the wing fore and aft. There is not, however, amongst his notes, any suggestion what he would do if the wing became the victim of athwartships tilt."

Timothy said; "Are you saying there is a difference between balance and control."

"Difference in as much they must be treated separately."

Jeppy lay stretched across his feet feinting sleep, eyes closed, an ear cocked. Sniffy squatted before the hearth baring her breasts to the heat. A lamp flame flickered nervously as an unseen draught of air made its way into the room.

"How can you be sure they are of separate uses, father?"

He drew thoughtfully on his pipe before he said, "As sure as the many birds I have observed through the telescope as they circled over the summit of Pritchards and Hadley during the summer months. They gave the impression of twisting the extremities of their wings to achieve turning flight. And which I have since proved by the use of the adjustable surfaces on the model kite to entice it to perform a turn in flight."

Timothy said: "If balance and control serve a different function, how do you regulate the balance?"

He grinned over the bowl of his pipe, "Do you not recall the lead weight I fitted to the model kite, and how steadily and gracefully it flew with the weight located in a certain position?"

Timothy did remember. Especially the number of times he clambered down the hill to retrieve the kite after each flight and father moved the lead weight countless times before he decided the kite was able to conduct balanced flight.

Work on the full-scale kite continued. The completed skeleton framework of the wings were set upon trestles and dressed from the rolls of calico, stretched tight and secured by an odorous glue that, rather oddly, carried the pungent smell of swine manure.

Then they embarked upon fitting the struts, numbering sixteen in total, to the bottom wing by slotting and pegging them at measured distances along the spars. Wooden brackets, surrounding the pegs, were employed to prevent the pegs working loose in flight.

Attaching the top wing to the top end of the struts entailed relentless clambering up and down wooden steps to affect the connection of the individual pegs and brackets. Timothy had the job of holding a lighted oil lamp close enough for father to perform the work, in plunging winter evening temperatures. Which coated the stable roof with a heavy layer of frost that, in time, succeeded in penetrating the roof to nip at the tip of finger and toe.

Constructing the moveable surfaces for the wings progressed under similar conditions with father getting him involved more seriously by explaining and teaching him the uses of the various tools.

Timothy did not succeed too well at first. He sawed wood unevenly, and planed and chiselled erratically. He misread father's drawings. But father, patient as always, persevered with his shortcomings in much the same way as when he had taught him to fly the kites.

Introducing the surfaces to the snug fit of the wing cutouts, and setting them upon piano wire hinges, father displayed yet again his exemplary store of patience and an ability to tackle intricate work with calm efficiency. Sharp contrast, Timothy thought, to mother's moods of late when she hustled and bustled every chore in haste, setting the world alight with anger if it did not go to her liking and piling the blame on him and father for its failure. Timothy smiled reflectively; he remembered how her irksome rages unsettled him and how he had drawn comfort from father's rational unspoken response to her outbursts that had the effect of driving her into a corner and depriving her of an adversary with whom to continue her verbal assault.

The more he worked alongside father on the kite under his gentle, patient, constructive supervision the more the urge grew to measure up to him.

Making up the horizontal tail surface and attaching it to two spars protruding from the rear of the centre section, using a spigot joint to raise and lower the surface, was relatively easily compared to the rigging of the wings after the connection of numerous diagonal runs of twine between the struts.

Specially angled sections of wood were wedged between the bottom surface of the wing tips and the trestles. To obtain what father referred to as, the correct inclination. And glass tubes of water were placed at measured distances along the top of the wing to check the symmetry of the slope.

Hour after hour father walked back and forth checking the slope of the water against lines of twine held vertical by weights, suspended from the wings, making adjustment to the slope by increasing or slackening the tension of the diagonal runs of rigging between the struts.

It puzzled Timothy as to why father tortured himself with so much precision; the bird wing as he knew it was subtle and flexible and mastered the art of flight with supreme agility. He raised the issue with him and he said, "The bird uses the beat of its wing for propulsion, my boy. And until we learn the secrets of that movement we must content ourselves with a rigid wing. Bearing in mind our straight wing is more practical to construct."

"Why all the fuss and bother with the inclination, father?"

"I happened to spot a pigeon up in the woods some months past and observed it conducted gliding flight employing a high upward tilt of its wings which, I am sure, had the effect of stabilising the athwart ships balance. Then I experimented by adjusting the inclination on the model kite and deducted there was an improvement in levelling the wing if it became disturbed by the forces of the air." He resumed his attention to the rigging and Timothy trailed behind him, finding it difficult to understand his line of reasoning. There might be some grains of truth in what father said, but what proof was there whilst the mysterious moods and traits of the invisible air remained unknown.

Neither could he dispute father's practical skills and his knowledge relating to his duties on the estate. However, at no time in the past, had he demonstrated any flair for the academics. The academics belonged to the intellect of mother. Her writing flowed from a stylish, disciplined hand. She was well read in Latin and English literature. And her understanding of mathematics warranted applause, particularly as she was a lady, and without her outstanding knowledge and, at times, bullying Timothy was only too aware he would not have won the distinction of gaining first place in his school examinations for two years in succession.

What motivated the suggestion, he did not know. Suddenly it was there challenging him during his pondering on the disparity of his parents as he followed father and his relentless adjustments to the rigging. Might it be, that father had a gift denied to him and mother. The gift of imagination, an ability to look into the unknown, the unseen, armed with the flimsiest of evidence and theory, and visualise and reasonably formulate an idea of what one might expect to find during the voyage of discovery.

The possibility thrilled him. No longer need he agonize over the roles and talents of his parents. Mother's superiority had been impressed on him by her dominating attitude. Now it was all changed. He saw his parents as equals. It cheered him up no end and did much to sweeten the bitter pill of mother's desertion.

In his mind father began to figure as a man of importance: a constructor, a pioneer: an eminence far removed from his humble employment on the Hadley estate, and the five years he had served with the colours. Timothy felt he had a duty to measure up to him but realised it would not be easy.

Father had a clear mental picture of how an object reacted as it passed through the intangible agency of the air. Whereas he could not digest or comprehend any of father's theories because he could not accept the air was anything more than an empty space. Occasionally it made its presence known by breathing hot on bare limbs in summer, nipping icily in winter, raising a spiral of dust off a sun-baked roadway or whisking a gathering of fallen leaves skywards in the surge of an up current. But on each and every occasion he regarded it as abstract and unreal.

He encountered no such difficulty with the kite. It was a fact, a reality, a growing work of art conceived from the union of wood and cloth, in the womb of the stable.

They had worked solidly on the kite for six weeks when father called a temporary halt to their labour. A shaft of sunlight, through an open door, coned an area of clean white calico and drew attention to particles of dust clinging to a number of wing struts. The whole construction gave off a pleasant scent of new wood, fresh calico, the greasy drift of wax that thinly coated the wing rigging, the creamy pigment of paint and the sweet tang of varnish. The curious Sniffy ran his nose along a wing trestle and before he chanced to cock a leg father hastened him on his way. Father gave a wing a friendly pat of the hand in farewell, led the way to the cottage and said: "By way of a change, my boy, you shall write up the journal this evening."

The journal recorded the daily work on the kite. Timothy laid it on the kitchen table, located a vacant page and sat pondering on what he should report. Father's shadow fell across the empty page, "Read and observe what I have written on previous occasions." he said. "It will give you a clue as to what is the most important and informative."

Timothy nodded and continued playing with the pen. After a long pause a sprinkling of ideas began to float across his mind and convert themselves to words under the guidance of the scratching noise of his pen on paper. The daylight faded. Father lit the stuttering oil lamps and settled in his rocker by the hearth. He put a match to his pipe that gurgled and crackled in the stillness of the room before releasing miniature clouds of smoke which scented the room with briar and honey.

Timothy handed him the journal for his opinion of what he had written. Whilst waiting for the verdict he helped himself to a plate of bread and cheese and pickled onion, and sat enjoying the peace and tranquility in the dim light of the lamps, the smell of the burning tobacco and the view of the dogs sprawling before father's feet. If only mother was there to complete the family unity, he thought.

He managed to hide his most personal feelings about her loss, from father. As the weeks passed and there was no news of her it pained him to think that she would not be coming back. The prospect of not ever seeing her again saddened him deeply.

Intentionally or otherwise father had an uncanny knack of jerking him out of his gloomy reflections. He complimented him for his written observations in the journal and announced they would benefit from deserting the cottage for a couple of days. Timothy would partner him on an inspection of all the land owned by the estate.

They arose at first light the following morning, fetched the drowsy horses from the paddock and tacked up. Paddy, a Grey Connemara, measured thirteen hands and whose sloping shoulders made for a comfortable ride. Yorkie, father's mount, a Cleveland Bay stood higher at fifteen hands and displayed a broad deep girth, well developed loins and, because of his stamina, could maintain a steady pace over long distances. They set out from the cottage, dogs in pursuit, and rode steadily to the summit of Hadley hill's eastern face to be greeted by the rising sunlight drawing the dew off the lowlands in a veil of mist. Father halted and stood in the stirrups. To which Paddy's ears went up and an excited quiver ran through his withers. Yorkie remained motionless perhaps aware that it was friends of his breed toiling in the shafts of a carriage mending its way down the long winding highway to Four Mile Cross.

Paddy chafed at the bit and tore impatiently at the ground with a hoof. Timothy reined him short, knowing full well what was passing through his mind and his own for that matter. But which father had not condoned in the past. A challenge made all the more enticing by the distant curdling call of the coachman's horn.

"Come my boy." father shouted. "Let us ride with it for a spell. You to the right and me to the left."

They hastened down the hill. Paused at the base to let the coach thunder past, trailing a cloud of dust. Then chased after it. Paddy soon got into the strides of a gallop, snorting wildly, straining hard against the leathers and head harness leaving Timothy to grip in tight with his thighs and pivot evenly to the motion of Paddy's unleashed power and energy.

An amused gentleman viewed them from the rear external seat of the carriage. Beside him a young lady smiled from the shadows of her winged bonnet. Timothy thought she was rather pretty. He glanced over his shoulder to see Yorkie gaining on him, eyes large and bright, nostrils fully open his large yellow teeth grappling with the bit. Trees and hedgerows lining the highway gave way to open heathland. Paddy surged ahead taking them past a gathering of faces peering from the window of the carriage and, presently, past the exposed figures of the driver and coachman whose stern expressions indicated they were not well-pleased with Paddy's challenge to a race.

For Timothy it was enough; they had clearly demonstrated their superior turn of speed; what more need they prove. Paddy however did not concur; he enjoyed to the full this rare opportunity to stretch his legs and show off his paces. He willfully ignored commands from rein and heel to moderate his pace, and careered ahead seemingly oblivious to a copse of trees bearing down on them at great speed.

Much to his growing concern Timothy realised he was mustering all his reserves of strength in an attempt to break the disobedient mount out of the gallop. To which Paddy pulled harder, stronger and tossed his head defiantly. Timothy's enjoyment faded; he could not decide whether his misbehaving mount was the result of the zany humour of his Irish breeding or something had startled him into a panic-stricken bolt. Whatever he gave no signs of responding to his schooling.

At three hundred paces from the trees Timothy feared a catastrophe was imminent. The thought of being killed or maimed did not alarm him as much as having the quality of his horsemanship brought into question by father. That would never do. In the nick of time father's words from the distant past, when teaching him to ride, came to mind advising him how to control a rioting mount.

"Use rein and opposite foot to start the turn, and continue to tighten the turn to such an extent the mount will follow an ever-tightening circle until it will have no other choice but to come to a halt."

Paddy deviated slowly as directed, missing the trees by about ten paces, with Timothy continuing to rein and heel him to tighten the circle. At last the mount turned in its own length and stopped. The boy slid from the saddle infinitely pleased to feel solid ground beneath his feet! It was short-lived; father arrived soon after, "Get mounted my boy. We have much to do." He said, gripping the rear of Timothy's collar, and promptly hoisted him back in to the saddle.

They moved at a more leisurely pace, stopping periodically for father to dismount and inspect sections of the estate's fencing brought down by decay or the vandalism of intruders: each of which he noted on a map he carried. Timothy could not resist a smile each time father got down on his hands and knees to examine the traces of a footprint. Then he would stand and sniff the air, in the hope, Timothy presumed, he would be able to detect by the scent the origins of an animal or a human. Fox or badger? Timothy grinned thoughtfully. A local or a gypsy?

From open country they moved into the shelter of woodland whose floor was carpeted with a mixture of bluebells, the bright yellow and orange of daffodils and jonquils and clusters of primrose and forget-me-nots. Their scents filled the woodland like a huge perfumery. A whirling of red and green plumage marked the flight of a passing woodpecker. The stuttering call of a jay sounded further down the wood. A deer leapt from a nearby thicket and charged away in retreat.

At noon they arrived at the widest reaches of Hadley River which was teeming with fish and, according to father, would please the squire no end. The estate enjoyed a steady income from the fish sold at market. Pike glided from the depths and snapped with gin-trap ruthlessness at insects, large and small, hovering above the water line. At a safe height a dragonfly patrolled the river, its long sloping body held skillfully aloft by large transparent wings that were capable of making rearward flight as easy and accessible as forward flight.

Father laid out their lunch packs on a spot close to where the river flowed around a steady curvature of the riverbank. He was regarded as a loyal and conscientious employee of the estate. But it soon evolved that the subject of flight was never very far from his thoughts. He stood close to the edge of the riverbank, holding a sandwich, and said, "Do you notice any difference in the flow of the water around the bank at this point to that out in midstream?"

Timothy looked, not really aware of what father was referring to. "Not really, father." he said doubtfully.

"Look more closely. Do you not notice any difference at all?"

Timothy took a gamble, "The water here appears to be running more swiftly than that in mid stream."

"Well done my boy. But do you know why?"

"It runs downhill slightly." Timothy ventured.

"Begat Paddy! What have you done to the brain of this young man?"

Timothy took a hefty bite at a ham sandwich; he felt slighted by father's scorn. An arm came around a shoulder and father said, "Imagine the curve of the river bank is the curved top surface we have on the wing of the kite."

Timothy nodded.

Father said: "The flow of water around the bank is how I suspect air flows around a wing in flight. If you look closely the pace of the water around the curve is much swifter than that further out in the river. Therefore it would be reasonable to assume the pressure of the water would decrease. Now," he led Timothy along the riverbank to a point where it ran parallel. "If you observe the water you will note the flow is much slower and would suggest the pressure would be greater. Therefore the greater pressure on the bottom surface and the lesser pressure on the top surface would invite the wing to lift and that, in my opinion, is how flight will be accomplished."

Timothy gazed across the river, puzzled and unconvinced. Grandfather Willy's notes claimed a wing moved through an invisible sea of air, but it had not prevented him from losing his life. Furthermore if father's theory was so simple why did he not perch himself on a curved surface and rise to the heights with the agility of a bird.

Father removed two wooden shapes from his pouch, one rectangular, the other in the shape of the wing fitted to the kite. Taking them in turn he spiked them with a dagger and held them in the streaming water and further demonstrated his observations concerning the variations in speed and pressure affecting the respective profiles of the wood.

"How did you come by all these ideas, father?"

"After a careful study of a dead bird I was left in no doubt that there is a distinct curvature of the feathers on the top surface of the wing. This, then, led me, in conjunction with Grandfather Willy's theory of relating the air to the sea, to use the river for my experiments." He altered the inclination of the curved wood section, he was holding in the streaming water, "There – do you see – the flow has slackened at the rear edge of the top surface."

Timothy peered closely, "And is not smooth, father."

"Correct, my boy. Now if I increase the inclination further – you see the water at the rear edge becomes more turbulent and spreads."

Timothy looked on, fascinated. "What would it do to a wing in flight."

"Methinks it would return to earth somewhat briskly."

Timothy was suspicious. In one breath father said inclination was necessary to create lift. At the same time he had proved it could equally deposit a craft abruptly back to earth. It was a contradiction in clear terms.

He put it to father who demonstrated, "Observe as I set the inclination at a neutral point, then, very slowly increase it. Look closely – the flow of water increases swiftly up to a certain point. When I take it beyond that point the flow breaks down into turbulence."

"What knowledge is gained from that, father?"

"It indicates to me that there is a limitation to the amount of inclination we can use in flight. A weight will be fitted to help with the balance of the wing and we will use the horizontal tail to control the inclination." He took the wooden shape from the water, separated it from the dagger and stored them in their respective sheath and pouch.

Timothy said, "From your demonstrations in the water the difference in inclination between that which gives lift, and that which destroys it is so small. How can you possibly gauge or measure it."

Father grinned and patted his head. "I must experiment with that when I get aloft, such is the fate of all pioneering work."

Presently they mounted and continued with the inspection of the estate. They looked in on little spinneys at gatherings of colourful, proud, strutting pheasants. They paid a visit to the trout streams and father made more notes. They had barely broken the cover of a copse when a hare appeared from nowhere and leapt away from them describing a zigzag line of retreat.

In a gully they disturbed a colony of rabbits lazing in the sunlight outside their warren. The mass of furry, speckled bodies melted so quickly as they swarmed for cover that Timothy wondered if they had existed at all.

They stopped several times for father to examine more stretches of boundary fencing, and make written reports, and mark the areas on his map.

Just before nightfall they reached the eastern boundary of the estate, an area of land reserved for sheep to graze. The squire employed Ottie Patterson and his two collies to shepherd the substantial flock. What a great team they were.

The dogs were driving the flock up to the pens for the night when he and father arrived, sloping, crouching black and white figures whose stealth and cunning was a sight to behold. At times they were motionless. Then they were up bursting with speed, to race out and around to hasten an erring stray back into the fold. Sniffy attempted to join in, possibly considering there was some fun to be had in harassing the sheep and what came naturally to him. Father thought otherwise; he thought Sniffy's intervention would be a distraction to Ottie's dogs. He admonished Sniffy and called him to heel.

"Yer jest in time." Ottie closed the gate of the last pen. "I's about to cook some sup. Will 'ee 'av a bite?"

The customary greetings were made with a handshake and Ottie commented on how much Timothy had grown since he has last set eyes on him. He told them to fetch their packs from the mounts, insisting they keep him company for the night; he had not seen another living soul for weeks and wanted father to bring him up to date with the events down on the estate.

Within minutes, under a darkening sky, red, yellow and blue flames from the fire, Ottie had lit, were lapping at the curtain of the night, sending up intermittent showers of white and orange sparks. Ottie hung four skinned rabbits from a metal gallows over the flickering flames and they sat and watched the long lean shapes with outstretched legs grill brown in the firelight. The savoury smell of the cooked meat furthered Timothy's appetite, as too the dogs who mounted guard on the spectacle with a restless tongue and drooling jowls. Ottie produced a kettle of water, which he put amongst the flames of the fire, and later they had mugs of herb tea. Father brought food from his saddle pack and hacked off large slices of bread and smeared them with butter. They ate this with a cooked rabbit apiece, the fourth rabbit being cut up and shared among the dogs.

Timothy experienced an immense freedom sat before the open fire, unrestricted by the walls and roof of a dwelling. The roof of a nomad figured as a large spacious dome inset with a multitude of exquisite diamonds. Jewels purposely kept out of the reach of mankind to avoid arguments over their ownership, according to a fable read to him by mother. Other books claimed the stars aided mariners to steer a steady course across vast tracts of sea, and helped Bedouin tribesman find their way across endless miles of featureless desert.

By the time they had satisfied their thirst and appetite and he helped the men wash and stow the utensils waves of fatigue were rolling over him. He settled for the night wrapped in a single blanket and used his saddle for a pillow. Jeppy and Sniffy stretched out on either side to complete his comfort, noses between their front paws, an ear cocked as a precaution against undesirable or hostile company. On the other side of the fire father and Ottie conversed in low tones over a bowlful of burning tobacco. He felt to drowsy to concern himself with the content of their conversation. He drifted into sleep, facing the fire, no longer able to fight the drooping heaviness of his eyelids.

They took their leave the following morning after an adequate breakfast of mushrooms cooked in butter, and poached Plover eggs. They thanked Ottie for his hospitality. He, in return, requested they did not make him wait so long for their next visit. Timothy recalled his first introduction to the shepherd some ten years past, and noticed rather oddly his appearance had changed little, if at all, since then. The same long, crinkly hair fell about his bearded face, the same warm brown eyes surveyed the world with nothing but kindness. He attired himself in the same long smock over his breeches and, like the biblical figure, illustrated in scripture books at school, Ottie was never without his tall, hooked shepherd's crook.

Not long after they bid Ottie farewell they flushed out a gathering of trespassers on the estate. The culprits made an immediate dash for the boundary, knowing they would be safe once they reached the common land beyond. Timothy followed in hot pursuit.

"Head them off!" father shouted as he and Paddy galloped by, trailed by the furious barking of the dogs. One of the intruders stumbled. Timothy heeled and called Paddy for more speed and rode out and around to cut off the retreat of his other two companions who barely needed two hundred strides to secure their freedom. Once facing them he urged Paddy to charge at them. His pounding hooves and heavy snorting forced them to halt and run back in the opposite direction for them to be confronted by father. The dogs positioned themselves on each side making the capture of the intruders complete.

The most elderly of the group, wearing a small gold ear ring approached father on his knees, hands clasped in prayer, "Sorry guv', he said breathlessly. "But we got a missus and kids to feed. And more on the way."

Father glowered down at him, his blue eyes blazing, his moustache bristling, "Empty those sacks!" he demanded.

Warily the intruders did so and out tumbled a handsome cache of trout, pheasant, pike and the unsightly butchered remains of a lamb. A sadness crept into father's eyes though he was careful not relax the strict, stern line of his moustache.

"I have always turned a blind eye to the pike, and the pheasant for that matter. But I insisted you leave the trout and sheep alone. Now, since you cannot keep to your side of the bargain, I shall arrest you the next time you set foot on this land and make certain you stand before the magistrate. Is that clear?"

Timothy shuddered; he had never seen him so enraged before.

"They ain't the biggest, guvnor." one of them offered in mitigation.

Father pointed his riding crop at him. "Not so! You have willfully regarded my wishes when you know full well I have gone out of my way, and put my employment in jeopardy, to help you and your families. Now refill those sacks and get out before I set the dogs on you."

Another of the three made to speak to be halted by father's raised hand; "The damage is done. Go!"

As they reached the other side of the fence he added, "Make no mistake. I mean what I say."

"We's know guv'. That's what fear us." were the parting words of the oldest gypsy before they disappeared amongst the undergrowth and trees of the adjoining woodland.

Father made makeshift repairs to the disrupted boundary fencing and went very quiet. Timothy thought of questions that he would like to put to him. For instance why were the boundary fences not made higher and stronger? Secondly, why father, after his reprimand and final warning to the intruders had allowed them to retreat with their spoils. He decided that father was not quite in the right frame of mind to answer after his brush with the intruders and Timothy followed his lead when he, wordlessly, clambered back in the saddle and goaded Yorkie on with a clicking of his tongue.

Timothy spotted it as they jogged the horses along the northern boundary of the estate, a red-eyed kestrel hovering up before them, the beat of its wings periodically halting for a fleeting instant. Not once did it sink or waver from its point over the earth. Timothy thought the kestrel's mode of flight totally contradicted all that he had been taught at school concerning the laws of universal gravitation. He drew breath in anticipation of the inevitable. And when it happened his heart raced to his mouth. For a moment longer it hung, fluttering, against the azure sky. In an instant it was plummeting earthwards at breathtaking velocity to swoop upon its prey in the brief time it took to flutter an eyelid.

They left it to its voracious pursuits and in an attempt to lift father's dark mood Timothy questioned him on the bird's unique display of flight. It worked.

Father expounded on how he thought the feathers at the wing tips rotated at speed and, in so doing, caused a flow of air over the inner part of the wing thereby giving sufficient lift for the bird to sustain hovering flight. In normal forward flight the wing worked like a ships paddle, dipping downwards and forwards simultaneously, then changing the inclination at the commencement of each rearward, upward stroke: a cycle carried out with such rapid repetition it could be seen by the human eye as a dizzy whirl of movement.

Timothy was continuing to try to digest what father had said when they broke out on Pritchard's Hill and looked down upon an area of land, painted gold by the sunlight, and which played host to a sprinkling of small figures working busily amongst horse-drawn carts and harvesting machinery. Crops had flourished early that year on account of a long, unbroken spell of sunshine.

"Come," father called. "Let us join the harvesters and seek refreshment."

Paddy trotted evenly down the hill. On level ground he lunged into a gallop, pulling strongly at the reins, flexing his withers and stretching his hind and fore legs to the limit. He raced ahead of Yorkie and father, leaping over fences, hedges and ditches till they were bearing down on the harvesters at an incredible pace with Timothy, yet again, summoning all of his physical strength to goad the over-zealous Paddy into an ever-tightening circle to force him to a halt. It was the second time in two days he had tasted fear and felt threatened by his mount's reckless behaviour. He dismounted as steadily as he could, trying to disguise his trembling arms and legs. His kept his back turned to any witnesses and took longer than normal to loosen Paddy's girth leathers, so as to take time to regain his composure.

Most of the harvesting folk came from Hadley village and were assisted by a number of gipsies: all of who worked under the supervision of the foreman of the farm owned by the Hadley estate. The scene seethed with movement and noise. A panting, throbbing steam engine drove a tall, ungainly threshing machine through a long revolving leather belt. Teams of muscled drays hauled carts piled high with sheaths of wheat. Scantily dressed men and women pitch-forked the bundles to the labouring thresher and, as if influenced by the wand of a magician, the bundles were transformed by the time they reached the chucker at the rear of the machine into orderly divisions of ear, husk and hay.

Timothy left father in conversation with the overseer of the steam traction engine and moved to a wooden table where Mollie Langdon, two years his senior, served pots of cider to thirsty workers during short breaks in their labour. In recent years whenever he met Mollie he found his eyes straying to the division of her cleavage made visible by the low neckline of her dresses. He was perplexed by the manner, in which her swollen breasts seemed to reach out for him and cause a swelling and stiffness at a certain part of his anatomy, making him feel self-conscious and embarrassed. He acknowledged her coyly in greeting. She smiled that devastating smile with her mischievous eyes in return and said, "I take it yee would like a drink for yee and yer father."

He nodded, aware he was looking at her bare sun-tanned arms, her long slender neck, and the fullness of her rose-red lips. A strong urge welled up in him, compelling him to want to embrace and caress her. Then, intentionally or otherwise, she further enflamed his passion when she stooped to ladle the cider from a wooden cask and the neck of her dress fell forward providing him with a view of her ample naked breasts. She ladled the cider into pint pots on the table and made a point of leaning forward again so as to honour him with a second inspection. He badly wanted to respond to her evident invitation. At the same time he felt a need to escape.

He hurried away, clumsily spilling some of the cider in his bid to rejoin father who he found still in conversation with the overseer of the traction engine. From what he could make out, above the noise of the engine, the overseer was explaining to father the workings of the steam engine. Timothy listened as best he could but found his thoughts drifting back to Mollie. He saw her a couple of times looking at him through the stream of visitors to her table. He had a vague idea what she wanted from him. But he couldn't bring himself to believe it.

Father downed his pint of cider and announced they were leaving. He touched his hat and thanked their hosts for the refreshment, and led the way out of the field. Timothy noticed Mollie was still watching him and actually waved to him as they moved through the gate. He stood in the stirrups finding it necessary to make an adjustment to the crotch of his breeches. Being removed from her immediate presence, he noticed had the effect of cooling and taming the tormenting passion she had inflicted upon him.

TWO

Within days of returning from the inspection of the estate they resumed work on the kite with refreshed and renewed vigour and enthusiasm. Timothy was assigned to sawing and planing various lengths of spruce, and shaping sections with a spoke shave. At measured distances he made holes with a brace and bit. And spent hours chiselling a taper on wooden pegs and eventually saw all his bits and pieces come together, under father's supervision, as the supporting uprights and cross members of the toed-up skids. These were intended to support the kite on the ground and provide a protecting cushion when it returned to earth. A brass strip was fitted the full length of the undersides of the skids for the purpose of helping the kite slide more easily over the ground and to reduce the wear and tear on same.

Timothy's next job consisted of making a number of round pulley wheels and gouging a channel around the circumference of each one with a half round chisel. Father fixed the pulley wheels to certain points on the wing struts and ran twine around the pulleys connecting the control surfaces on the wings with a control lever on the centre section. Another control lever operated the horizontal tail surface through the same arrangement of twine and pulley wheels.

Timothy regarded it all as rather clever and somewhat magical in the way the control surfaces rose and fell at the remote commands of the control levers. Though he was not so impressed by the creaks and groans which accompanied each of the movements. He sat his end of term examinations at school, around this time, and fell to third position in his class. Father complimented him for making such an effort saying he had done well considering family life had been disrupted by mother's departure. But Timothy knew full well that if mother had been there that she would have chastised him for the result, insisting, as she always had, that second best was not good enough.

He spent the first week of the school holiday applying a thin film of wax to the calico of the wings to protect it from the elements of the weather with father guiding him and insisting he did not interfere with the drum-tight surfaces and cause sagging.

The more the boy spent working on the kite, the more he pondered on the feasibility of flight. He found himself challenging father's theories, and the merits of some of the information amongst his collection of papers. At the same time he began to formulate ideas of his own. The link between Grandfather Willy's comparison of the air to an invisible sea, and Mr. Lilienthal's use of a vertical steering surface on his craft of the air, prompted him to think that the kite should be so adapted.

"Have you ever witnessed a bird with such a vertical tail surface?" father said when he raised the matter.

"No, father."

"Why, then, should we fit the kite with this unsightly appendage?"

" On the premise you concur with Grandfather Willy's vision of the air as a vast invisible sea. That being so, would it not suggest a craft of the air must have some means of steerage as do ships upon the sea."

After a pause father said: "A credible supposition my boy. However your grandfather and Mr. Lilienthal are no longer with us. But the birds are and continue to proliferate and excel at the mastery of flight." He put a lighted match to his pipe, "You would do well, also, to remember the number of times we watched the gulls, through the telescope, perform rising spiralling flight over the downs. A feat accomplished with a fully-stretched and motionless wing, and without any other visible means of steerage."

Timothy pondered. It was quite true he had seen the gulls soar effortlessly over the hills, as father said. Might it be the comparison of the air to an ocean of water was erroneous? Had the vertical steering surface on Mr. Lilienthal's craft contributed to his premature demise?

In the days leading up to the first flight father fussed around the kite. He worked late into the night inspecting every detail of its construction, double checking the inclination of the wings, making adjustments to compensate for stretch in the numerous runs of rigging, and ensuring the control system of levers and twine and pulley wheels functioned as they should. Timothy arose, of a morning, to find him sat at the kitchen table working on a sheet of paper with pencil. Columns of figures and calculations littered the paper, which, he explained, were used to determine the precise spot on the centre section he should anchor his wicker seat to obtain the correct balance for the kite in flight.

Timothy did not fully understand what it all meant. Nevertheless he told himself not to underestimate father's ability because he was proving more than ever that his skills and talents went far beyond his humble position on the estate, and his past reputation as a soldiering man. It prompted him to remember an unpleasant scene between mother and father when father made known his intentions to go on his quest for flight. Mother scorned his lack of scientific learning and brutally reminded him of Grandfather Willy's fatal end in his stupid endeavour to mimic the birds.

Timothy found his thoughts pondering on the perils likely to confront father on his first flight. How, for instance, would he cope with a sudden surge of wind: a force capable of reaching merciless proportions which uprooted trees, snatched the roof top from a dwelling and, for centuries, had hastened sailing ships across the oceans of the world and, frequently, to disaster on a rock-strewn coastline. He had seen cloud formations scatter before its seething anger. He could recall it massing against the cottage, rattling doors and windowpanes and forcing the dogs to retreat beneath bed or table to escape its eerie menace.

On the evening prior to the first flight they gave the kite its first share of daylight when they drew it from the stable, using wooden rollers beneath the skids to aid its mobility, and positioned it thirty paces from the brow of Hadley hill. The crimson sunset tinged the white calico with a pink sheen. Particles of the remaining sunlight glittered on the varnished struts and formed like dewdrops on the rigging. The overall box shape of the kite differed sharply from the clean, curving profile of a bird, suggesting the air might put up some resistance to its efforts to get on the wing. But nobody could deny the artistry and perfection of father's workmanship. The first impression was one of sturdiness given by the struts and intricate diagonal runs of rigging. Whilst by comparison the delicate membranes of the ribs beneath the taut calico brought to it a strange kind of dignity.

As an insurance against wind and rain, during the unguarded hours of the night, they staked the kite down and threw a rick cover over it. Then he and father sat on the brow of the hill, father smoking his pipe, and they went over father's plans for the flight once more.

He intended to alight the kite in the paddock behind Hadley manor, an area of land no larger than a pocket-handkerchief down there before them in the awesome depths of eight hundred feet. Timothy's part in the plan involved taking the horses down to the paddock to retrieve the kite and return it to the cottage, He was to rendezvous with the Squire and lady Hadley who had expressed a wish to witness history being made – the first ever manned flight. Once they were assembled Timothy would wave a white flag up to father as a signal for him to launch the kite into the air.

For much of the night Timothy drifted in and out of sleep. He relished the idea of father proving to mother and the villagers that he was more than a humble employee of the Hadley estate. But equally he was concerned with the massive eight hundred feet drop from the summit of Hadley hill to the paddock at the manor, and the desperate consequences should father mishandle the kite, or, the hidden strengths of the air caused the kite to fall apart. For certain father would not survive such a fall and Timothy did not welcome the possibility of becoming an orphan.

At last the yellow and white fusion of the daybreak, glimmering on the windowpanes, signalled the night had ended. He vacated his bed and discovered father was already up and about. The dogs had been let out, porridge simmered in a pot on the hob. A kettle of water on an adjacent plate was coming to the boil. He spotted the horses through a window with father fitting them with a nosebag of oats.

He came in presently looking rather dapper in his soft leather riding boots, cord breeches, a white scarf tied at the throat of his olive green blouse over which he wore tan suede tunic. They exchanged greetings and sat in for a breakfast of porridge and toasted bread smeared with butter and damson jam and mugs of herb tea.

"What ails you?" father grinned at him.

Timothy looked at him in surprise.

"Come, my boy. Your expression tells me that all it not well with you."

"The drop you face with the kite from Hadley hill concerns me father. Having lost mother it would sadden me deeply if I were to lose you to a peril of the flight. Do you not think it more prudent to conduct the flight from the north face of the hill where the face is less sheer and only sinks to a depth of two hundred feet."

Father lighted his pipe and held it with both hands. "I have chosen the deeper drop so that if I lose control I will have more time and space to fathom out the reason and correct it."

Timothy did not attempt to argue; father was renowned for giving a lot of thought to anything he tackled; once his mind was made up, he was not a man to go back on his word.

They moved outside the cottage to be greeted by the top rim of the sun inching above the horizon, its distant furnace tempering the sky overhead to blue steel in colour. Layers of mist hung around the peaks of neighbouring hills. In silence they removed the Rick cover and tethers from the kite and pushed it closer to the brow of the hill. Evidently father would get it under way by pushing on it from the rear. Then once it gained momentum he would scramble over the centre section to get at the seat, and take the control levers to hand. He wandered around the kite once more inspecting various parts of its construction. Following which he stood on the brow of the hill for some time looking, thoughtfully, into space.

Suddenly, he turned and strode back to the kite. "Right, my boy. Make your way to the manor, if you will."

Timothy wished him luck and went for the horses. Paddy was not in the best of moods; he detected the restraining shafts of cart or carriage and, equally, kicked up quite a fuss when fitted with a towing bridle. He lunged and backed, stamped his hooves, and fretted in the manner of an unbroken stallion. Timothy looked him straight in the eye and wagged a finger at him as a warning he was in danger of getting a hefty swipe across the muzzle if he chose not to moderate his behaviour.

It worked and they made their way down to the manor, Timothy noticing down to their right the small figures of the village men folk congregating at the carts which transported them to the tin mines. Down to their left the meandering course of Hadley River came to view as the rising sunlight evaporated its nightdress of white mist. Paddy made an attempt to throw a tantrum. But Yorkie, conscious of his seniority and his close bond to father, brought the erring Paddy to order by showing his teeth, snorting angrily and charging his head at Paddy much as a pugilist would throw a punch.

Timothy was greeted enthusiastically by the Squire and Lady Hadley in the stable yard of the manor. They enquired as to whether he and father had taken breakfast, and had all the preparations for the flight gone to plan. At first the boy hesitated with his reply; he had never seen the squire and his lady so casually attired. The squire, never to be seen without a tie or cravat, wore an open-neck blouse under a worn faded waistcoat. Lady Hadley, always seen in public with her hair raised clear of her long, slender neck had released it to fall about her narrow shoulders like a golden waterfall. Timothy answered their questions, and led the way across the yard, through an orchard of rose-red apple, yellow pear, and deep red plum, to the open grassland of the paddock. He left the couple with the horses in a corner and walked to the middle of the paddock and stood looking up at the summit of Hadley hill, waving a plain white flag.

After a long pause the squire shouted: "There it hails!" in response to a white shape emerging from the shadows of the hilltop and floating into space. For a time the kite hung against the blue of the sky. Then it drifted earthwards, gradually disclosing the spars and skeletal rows of ribs through the taut white calico and father's small figure sat between the wings.

It may have been less of a challenge to the intellect had it been a kite riding the air at the end of a tether. This large kite negotiated its passage under the guidance of its passenger; it was nothing short of a miracle. And whilst it did not totally defy the laws of gravitation it descended with great aplomb and dignity.

For centuries a succession of expert minds claimed that manned flight was impossible. And a number of pioneers who had perished in their quest for flight appeared to support this view. Yet here was father, of humble means and modest disposition, proving that the impossible could be made possible.

"Incredible! Absolutely incredible!" the squire exclaimed. "And to think, Timothy, it is none other than your courageous father making it possible for us to witness this spectacular moment in history. For history-making it certainly is."

All went well until father attempted to swing the kite toward the village. The tilt of the wings increased dramatically and headed the kite on a collision course with the shoulder facings of the hill. Only at the last very breath-taking moment did the wings make a hasty reversal of tilt and steer it away from the menacing contours.

Neither did the turn over the village, to make the approach to the paddock, proceed without its difficulties. It compared not at all with the smooth balanced turn of a bird in flight. The dipping wings appeared to fight against the direction of the turn and it wavered and lurched for a considerable time before it headed for the paddock wandering aimlessly from side to side. Father was either not fully accustomed to the use of the control levers or something had been overlooked in the design of the construction. Over the orchard it paused momentarily on a cushion of air, before sweeping down and heralding its arrival with the sound of air gushing over the wings and whistling through the rigging. It glanced across a boundary hedgerow – reared up – almost came to a stop in mid air – then plummeted and drove solidly back to earth, booming out rolls of thunder through the drum-tight calico in protest at the violence of the impact.

Timothy led the field when they raced to greet the landed kite with Lady Hadley coming up in the rear, clutching her dress to stop it dragging on the ground. When they arrived on the scene father had vacated his seat on the centre section and was stood putting a lighted match to his pipe with trembling fingers.

"Well done, Samuel! Well done indeed! The squire congratulated him with a hearty shake of the hand. Father thanked him for the compliment. His pale expression told something of the strain he had encountered during his journey in the heights. But a distinct gleam in his eyes indicated he had been well and truly rewarded by a sense of having ventured, having discovered, and having succeeded.

The squire went off to inspect the kite. And what happened next, came as a shock to Timothy. Lady Hadley stepped forward, stood on tiptoe, and sealed a kiss on father's face. "A magnificent feat, Samuel." she said warmly. "I am so very proud of you."

Timothy cringed; it was considered courteous of a man to kiss a lady's hand in greeting; the intimacy exhibited by Lady Hadley was the special preserve for persons of conjugal status. He dreaded to think what mother would have made of the spectacle.

"Timothy," the squire called. "Come, young sir, and enlighten me on the workings of the control levers."

Timothy spent several minutes with him up on the centre section demonstrating the movements of the control levers and the associated responses of the moveable surfaces on the wings and tail, and how the combinations deflected the kite athwartships, and fore and aft, in flight.

"I say, Samuel." the squire announced. "It must command great skill to control a craft of the air."

Father drew up to the kite in the company of the serenely happy Lady Hadley. "I can scarcely comment on that, squire, until I acquire more experience of getting aloft."

The squire slid down from the centre section, "More difficult than riding a horse, would you say?"

"Perhaps similar in some respects."

The squire ran a hand along the smooth, gentle undulations of the calico of a wing; "Incredible is it not. Here it now stands. And yet back in a brief period of time it was up there in space negotiating with the air to allow it safe passage." He turned, "Very well, my dear. Let us repair to the manor and have me pen a letter to the editor of the Brunton News, to break the news of Samuel's momentous flight." He patted Timothy on the head, "Thank you again, young Timothy, for your instruction on the controlling facets of the craft of the air."

Lady Hadley edged closer to father, touched his arm briefly, and Timothy detected an expression in her eyes that conveyed something more than a relationship between employer and employee. "Take care, Samuel." she said quietly. She looked askance at the boy, smiling, "And you too, Timothy."

Father made a further three flights on that memorable day, successively adding to his knowledge and experience. His quick reasoning soon taught him that to hold a lever too far away from the neutral position not only tilted the wings or tail, but further increased the tilt. He also discovered that by listening to the sound of the air streams washing over the wings, he could adjust the kite's rate of descent and prolong its time spent in the air. He did not, however, resolve the problem of the wing slipping forward during turning flight.

If anything marred the successes of the flights that day, particularly for Timothy, it was hauling the kite back up the hill to the cottage, running back and forth throwing wooden rollers beneath the skids to give the kite smooth mobility and to aid the struggling mounts.

Back on the brow of the hill father set upon a detailed inspection to ensure the kite had not suffered from its passage through the air: a task involving many painstaking adjustments to the wing rigging and which taxed Timothy's patience to the extreme.

The sun had set by the time they arrived back at the cottage for the final time. They stabled the kite. Unharnessed, fed, and turned the horses out. And doused themselves under the garden water pump before taking a change of fresh apparel. Timothy offered to get a supper of thick slices of cold mutton, buttered bread and brewed nettle tea. Father lit the lamps and brought the journal to the table.

This 22nd Day of June 1898

At six of the clock this morning the kite and I made our very first acquaintance with the world of flight, witnessed, as it was, by my son, Timothy, and the Squire and Lady Hadley.

Launching into the air was made by a sliding run from the summit of Hadley Hill that is said to stand eight hundred feet above the level of the sea. The kite behaved reasonably well in full flight and in consideration of my unaccustomed hands on the control levers. The air was motionless and my time aloft was possibly in the order of four minutes.

Three further descents, of marginally increased duration, were accomplished, the final being conducted in the presence of a light breeze which made it difficult to steer the kite and which adversely affected my ability to set down in the exact location of the paddock.

Perhaps the addition of a vertical steering surface, as previously suggested by Timothy, could prove to overcome this shortcoming in the kite's behaviour.

Thus this day ends well. Thanks be to God.

Timothy read it after supper, feeling immensely proud of his mention. He made to thank father for the compliment only to find he had fallen asleep in his rocker chair. His discarded boots lay before his feet and his cap had slipped forward, covering his eyes, the peak resting on the bridge of his nose.

Not wishing to interrupt his slumber Timothy draped a blanket over him, put the boots away, fed the dogs and went to his bed. He lay awake for some time recalling the magical sights of the kite in flight and father's enormous courage to partner it into the unknown, unseen sea of air. So too there must have been a large measure of skill, on father's behalf, to get it into the air and safely back to earth. Timothy drifted into sleep hoping mother would come by news of father's triumphant feats of flight and be enticed to return to the family circle.

Father avoided taking to the air for several weeks. He designed and fitted a rudder to their model kite and he and Timothy spent many a happy hour out on the downs launching the model and noting its responses to various settings. So impressed was father by the results he immediately set to work arranging the fitting of a rudder to the full-scale kite. It involved alterations to the four booms holding the horizontal tail surface and the location of a swivel to pivot the rudder. Plus the provision of another series of pulley wheels, runs of twine and a rudder bar. For Timothy the fitting of the rudder was a feather in his cap.

Having fitted the rudder he thought father would be keen to get back in the air and test its effectiveness. Instead father chose to embark upon adding another refinement to the kite. He enlisted the help of Mr. Cutler, the village Smithy, and between them they bolted a long steel shaft to the skids, to the ends of which they fitted spoke wheels with solid tyres. Thus ended the prospect of those labouring, erratic journeys up the steep winding hill at the termination of each flight.

Again, father did not hurry into the air. But then, Timothy recalled, father never rushed into anything: a trait in his character that had caused mother many a moment of irritation. He spent many evening, after returning from his duties on the estate, sifting through his collection of papers on flight, pondering for long periods of time and poring over the original figures he had used to calculate the balance of the kite. He admitted to feeling uneasy about the extra weight of the rudder and the metal axle and wheels and how they might also add to the resistance of the kite to the air.

At last he decided to take to the air to prove or disprove the merits of the new appendages. On the first flight he barely made it down to the paddock and when he did get it down the kite seemed to cling to the ground in desperation. He was left in some doubt as to the application of the rudder. It puzzled him as to why when he used the rudder, instead of turning the kite like a ship it also caused the wings to tilt. On the more comforting side he found he could use the rudder to stop a wing, slipping forward during a turn. He also noted the additions to the kite had not affected the balance; the extra weight had merely made him descend a little faster.

They made their way back up the hill following the stalwart Yorkie who made light work of towing the kite on its new wheels and axle. His breed, for many generations, had powered the mobility of many a heavily laden cart or carriage. The kite weighed in at about a third of a coach carrying eight persons.

If anything really concerned Timothy at this stage in father's flights, it was the manner in which the kite alighted. He had always envisaged the kite would fall to earth, as did a bird, a controlled vertical descent and halt on impact with the ground.

"We have yet to solve the technique used by the birds for alighting." father said when Timothy broached the matter. "The movements are beyond the capture of the human eye so rapid do they occur and, I suspect there are more than we can imagine. Therefore I am left with nothing but the observations of the model kite and the manner in which it strikes ground after expending its lift."

The second flight went well. The third also until he experimented with different combinations of the athwart ships control and the rudder. The kite, at one stage, suddenly plunged sideways in the air. Only at the last moment did it get back on an even keel, and brush uneasily through the crowns of the orchard trees to reach the open space of the paddock where it sloped to earth and bounced a number of times before coming to a halt.

Gratefully the calico only suffered abrasions from the contact with the trees. Father never gave a chance to be questioned on the kite's behaviour; he backed Yorkie to the kite, called for the traces to be attached to the kite, and led the way up the hill puffing earnestly on his pipe.

The fourth flight was performed with complete mastery from beginning to end. Starting from the hawkish, lingering flight, near the summit and only beginning to give a clue to its diminishing height as father made a gentle turn westwards towards the village, and flew a sloping angle against the rolling faces of the hills. He never went so far as the church this time. He made the final turn for the paddock over the main entrance to the manor. The kite hung, poised, perhaps rocking its wings slightly and moving forward much slower than previous occasions. It sank gently, growing larger, father's polished leather boots reflecting glints of sunshine. He thought, at one point, father had misjudged his intention of alighting in the paddock. The kite's lofty height in comparison to the short distance to reach the point of alighting gave the impression a sharp dive would be necessary. He had visions of father making another thudding return to earth.

It was not to be. The kite floated down almost sedately, glanced over the boundary hedgerows, checked its descent, lost way as father raised the angle of the wings, and pitched to earth with unbelievable gentleness.

By this time the sun was at its midday zenith, pouring down the full force of its light and heat. A voice called out as they reached the exit of the paddock, father guiding Yorkie and Timothy running from side to side to check the clearance at the wing tips as they passed through the gate. A figure dressed in black and white came hurrying through the orchard bearing a tray, "Lady Hadley wishes you to take refreshment." Nancy, a maid from the manor, drew up breathlessly before them. "She says you have been on the go since dawn and deserve some refreshment on this particularly hot day."

The tray contained a pitcher of water spiked with lemon juice, and a platter displaying slices of salted ham and delicately sliced, buttered bread. They thanked Nancy for making the journey, requested she relay their gratitude back to Lady Hadley and said they would return the tray later. Timothy waited for her to disappear and purloined an apple from the nearest tree and fed it to the patient, grateful Yorkie. He and father settled beneath the shade of a tree to partake of the food and drink.

On arriving back at the cottage Yorkie was released from the kite and given a pail of water to tame his thirst. Father gave the kite its customary inspection to check how it had fared from its recent flight, and strode into the cottage and brought a number of his papers to the table and consulted them for several minutes. He unrolled his detailed drawings of the kite and transferred a list of dimensions to a writing tablet and beside these figures he wrote a number representing a weight.

"Right, my boy." he handed the tablet to Timothy. "Here is a chance to put your schooling to good use. Multiply the figures in the first column by those in the second column."

Timothy tackled it with speed and enthusiasm, putting into practice many of mother's quick methods she had taught him. He returned the completed calculations to father.

Father said: "Take Yorkie down to the paddock and leave him there. Get back here on foot and I should be finished with the main calculation by then."

Timothy suspected what was afoot. But was not convinced till he arrived back at the cottage and father said: "Fetch a cushion from my rocker and put it next to my seat on the centre section."

Timothy hesitated.

"What are you waiting for?" father said briskly, grinning broadly. "Do you not want to come aloft with me?"

"Of course, father!"

Father followed him to the kite, carrying four sacks of earth which he lodged on the rear of the centre section and secured with leather thongs attached to a couple of wing struts. Timothy learnt later they were used to compensate for his extra weight and to satisfy father's obsession to give the kite the correct balance. Timothy clambered onto the centre section, got seated, and wrapped an arm around father's wicker seat and held onto a strut with his other arm.

"Are you ready, my boy?"

Timothy looked over his shoulder and nodded sheepishly. The kite edged forward encouraged by a push from the rear by father. As it gathered pace father came scrambling forward to get in the wicker seat and take the control levers to hand. Timothy drew breath and fought a growing sense of insecurity as the kite rumbled and shook, and lurched down to the brow of the hill, echoing a flurry of drum beats from the tight cladding of the calico of the wings. It came to him starkly that there could be no turning back now. He closed his eyes in anticipation of reaching the part of the hill that fell over in a sheer drop; he clung desperately to seat and strut. Visions of the fate to have overtaken Mr. Lilienthal, Mr. Pilcher and Grandfather Willy loomed large in his imagination.

Suddenly the disputing wheels and skids, and the drumming calico ended abruptly. He felt a cool wind upon his face. Everything had gone unbelievably still and quiet. He opened his eyes and blinked in disbelief; they were on the wing, floating away from the shoulder of the hill. He searched all around for the source that was supporting them. There was nothing, only a feeling of magic mixed with mystery, reality blended with unreality. He saw a gathering of white puffy cloud resting on the distant horizon. The earth so far, far below posed as a Toyland with its diminutive features: smooth, verdant pastures girded by the meandering of waterways that mirrored the blue sky and glittering sunlight. Occasionally the kite rose and fell causing a deep, ticklish feeling in his stomach that made him laugh uncontrollably. At times a wing dipped steeply and father brought it level again, using a deft movement of a control lever. All about them the airstreams hushed around the wings and had occasion to pluck at the struts and rigging to the merry overtures of a lute player.

The wings tilted – this time in response to father's commands on a control lever. The kite swung lazily around in a turn. Timothy looked down between the regimented rows of wing struts, noticing the undulations of calico between the intervals of ribs. Beyond the wing tips the earth revolved slowly. Time and time again he had to remind himself that he was not dreaming or had become the victim of a magician's trick.

Presently father made another turn and they headed back toward the paddock, sinking steadily. The earth lost its Toyland complexion; it resembled something more real – more solid.

"Hold firm! And prepare to alight." father shouted. The needle point spire of the church passed beneath the wings. Down to the right the village school slid from sight beneath a wing. Up on the slopes cattle grazed. A line of poplar trees loomed. They sailed over them with barely feet to spare and flew into an eerie silence. Timothy grew concerned; he feared the kite would come to a halt in mid air and fall rearwards. He looked over the centre section and saw a groom leading a mount from the manor stables. The kite regained momentum. Crowns of the orchard trees reached ever faster for the wings, and just as it seemed they would surely strike ground at too stiff a pace father made small, hurried movements on the control levers. The kite levelled out a few feet short of the paddock floor, floated for a short distance, grew very quiet, lost way, and tumbled to earth that it greeted with a boisterous protestation of sound from the thundering calico and juddering wheels and rasping skids.

Father jumped down from the centre section. "What did you make of that, young man?"

Timothy, maintaining his seat on the cushion and whose thoughts had not reached the ground entirely, said: "It was nothing short of a miracle, father."

"Miracle?"

"I could not perceive what source was supporting us. I had the most strange feeling we were dangling on an unseen thread."

Father laughed, "Would you care to sample another trip aloft?"

Timothy slid down from the centre section, "How can I refuse if I am to follow the tradition of the Herby family."

Father patted him on the back, "Well said, my boy. Well said!"

It took over half an hour of the clock for Yorkie to haul the kite back to the summit of the hill. And whilst father looked the kite over Timothy, to save time, tacked Paddy up and rode him down to deposit Yorkie in the paddock and then returned to father thus avoiding the slower journey on foot.

The second flight left a much larger impression; unlike the first he had an inkling of what to expect notwithstanding he suspected it would be some time before he got accustomed to the nerve-taunting, breathtaking journey down the slope of the hill to launch the kite into the air. It made him realise how much courage it demanded of father to pitch off into the gaping chasm of air and keep a cool head and steady nerve since there was no turning back and precious little margin to make an error.

Once they were on the wing Timothy felt more relaxed despite the presence of an evening breeze. The patchwork dress of the lowlands swayed beneath the gently rocking motion of the wings whose struts and rigging creaked and groaned spasmodically to absorb the invisible pressures of the air. Father sat, serious, intent, working continuously at the levers, his cap turned back to front: a habit he had started from his very first flight. They sailed over a small copse of beech trees – a woodsman's cottage. The driver of a farm cart, mending its way along a country lane, looked up as they passed silently overhead. Timothy smiled; could the driver actually comprehend there were two mortals like him sharing the sweeping flight of the kite.

A clue to something being amiss revealed itself shortly after father made the final turn toward the paddock in preparation for alighting. He turned his head from side to side, his facial expression changing dramatically to a mask of consternation. Timothy looked hurriedly around for the possible cause of father's concern. He saw nothing untoward. The wings and all were safely intact. The kite cut the air no different to his first flight. But as they swept over the hedgerows, bordering the paddock, the opposing boundary came racing toward them before the kite got a chance to desert the wing. "Brace yourself!" father shouted and juggled with the control levers. The kite remained on the wing seemingly oblivious to the imminent collision. Father pulled the fore and aft lever fully back – the kite rose steeply – paused – then dropped like a stone. He dived for the nearest strut whilst Timothy gripped his strut with both hands, a fraction of a second before the kite slammed back to earth and crashed into an unruly crop of blackberry bushes.

After freeing the kite from the arresting bushes and ascertaining it had only suffered minor scrapings and lashings to the underside of the bottom wing. And they had removed the thorny foliage that had become entangled in the spokes of the wheels father, indomitable as always, stated he would make a further flight, alone, to confirm what he thought to have been the cause of their recent mishap.

The sun had set by the time the kite broke out from the brow of the hill, and contrary to all previous flights it turned east out over the farmland of the estate. It glided slowly, flying into a position to approach the paddock from the opposite boundary, bucking, shying, slipping and skidding at times to negotiate the antics of the freshening evening breeze. It dipped its wings in turn as it passed over a gathering of hawthorn, collected itself, and alighted in the paddock to the hollow rumblings of the wheels and taut calico. And came to a halt in such a short distance Timothy had to walk half the distance of the paddock to meet it.

"Did you prove your theory, father?"

"Methinks, I have." he said jubilantly as he jumped down from the centre section and put a match to his pipe. "Grandfather Willy makes mention of it in his notes and, I too, have observed it: all birds head upwind to benefit their launchings and alighting. To do otherwise, that is launch or alight downwind, is to add distance to our endeavours. It accounts for why we ended up in the blackberry bushes."

*   *   *

Almost a week later the village made its annual pilgrimage to the seaside, one of the highlights of the Hadley calendar. It came as a great adventure for the village folk and the employees on the estate who never ventured beyond the village and their place of work for the remainder of the year.

It involved a long journey by horse and cart, courtesy of the Squire, but it was rewarded by the luxury of walking barefooted on the golden sands of Bournemouth seafront, inhaling the fresh, salty sea air. And playing in the tidal swirls and crashing foaming breakers as they came ashore. Mr. Sawyer, the estate manager, treated every member of the outing with a twirl of white ice cream resting on a crunchy cone, each year

It was the rare occasion they met persons from the towns and other villages. It was the only time of year their knowledge was extended further than the existence of horses and oil lamps. They learnt of other power sources in the form of gas and electricity. They looked in amazement at two tiered carriages, running on rails in the streets, trailing an arm connected to an overhead cable from which, it was said, the carriages received a supply of electricity to power their movement. Their swaying, clanging, busying importance often caused a skirmish with a horse carriage – a cyclist – a carefree pedestrian.

For the price of a platform ticket it was possible to gain access to a railway station and see a steam locomotive at close quarters. Large monsters made of heavy metal, leaking small pockets of steam with a pall of smoke lingering above the cap of the chimney stack perched upon a large black cylindrical boiler. A figure wearing a soot-flecked uniform and black shiny cap stood on the footplate looking back at the carriages and embarking passengers. Behind him a fireman, noticeable by the sweat rag around his neck, shovelled coal into the red-hot throat of the firebox. Along the platform the guard scrutinised his chained pocket watch and signalled by several shrill blasts on his whistle of the train's imminent departure. He strutted along the platform checking the carriage doors were shut. Then on arriving back at his van, coupled to the last carriage, he waved a green flag at the driver. The seething locomotive lunged forward, its large iron wheels revolving in unison with loud snorts of steam and a growing cloud of smoke from the chimneystack.

Father did not accompany the outing that year for reasons he did not disclose. Timothy paired up with Harry Griggs, a school friend, a joker, and a prankster. Turn your back on Harry and you risked being prey to one of his pranks. He tied bootlaces together when his victims were distracted. He hung messages on the backs of other children that read in capital letters: I AM AN IDIOT. The unsuspecting victim walked into pockets of ridicule and derision from other children. He smuggled frogs, mice and spiders into school and provoked many a shriek from a girl making the discovery of such creatures when opening the lid of her desk. They invariably fled the classroom in terror.

Neither did the teachers escape his reign of pranks. All of them, at one time or another, had suffered a sharp pain in their hindquarters when sitting on an unforeseen tin tack placed by Harry on the seat of their chair.

It was Timothy who caught Harry in the act of plotting a prank that most certainly would have him up before the headmaster with a hefty punishment in prospect, should he be caught. Timothy, out of a brand of boyish loyalty, promised not to expose him, and he and Harry became the best of friends.

Harry came from one of the poorer families in the village. His father never did a full week's work and nobody quite knew whether it was because he did not enjoy full health or that he was merely work-shy. Mrs. Griggs struggled gamely to raise her six children, helped in her struggle by Mrs. Sawyer who had founded the village relief society on behalf of the Squire and his Lady. Harry, for his part and being the eldest child, ensured the family never wanted for food. He made a catapult and snares and, before long, pigeon and rabbit were regularly going to the table. It was also known for him to make nightly excursions up on the estate to poach fish and pilfer fruit from the orchard and eggs from the hen runs. All quite illegal activities which the Squire, Mr. Sawyer, the estate manager, and Timothy's father agreed to turn a blind eye to on account of Harry's intention to join the colours when he came of age. Hadley had a big reputation, in military circles, for producing fierce, hardy soldiering men.

After a full day at the seaside the Hadley party moved on foot, in orderly fashion, up through the town to return to the carts left at a roadside in the suburbs. Mr. Sawyer led the way with Harry striding briskly at his side. The younger children, exhausted by the relaxing sea air and never-ending adventures upon the sand building castles, inspecting seaweed, hunting for crabs and other marine life, succumbed willingly to their bed rolls on arriving at the carts. The older children helped the adults to light fires and cook supper and brew nettle tea. In the fading daylight they sat recalling the events of the day, deeply happy and content with the new faces and scenery they had met in their explorations outside of the boundaries of Hadley village.

The fires died, the stars came out, and the air carried the saltiness of the sea. The groups dispersed and individuals went in search of a spot to put their head down for the night. Timothy found a space in the lee of a cart and slid into his bedroll. Harry Griggs settled down beside him, wrapped in a single blanket. They chatted for a time about the sailing ships they had seen out to sea that day, fleeing before the wind. They exchanged ideas on how they thought the steam locomotives converted the steam pressures, built up in the massive boiler, to moving the heavy iron wheels. And the huge amounts of power needed to haul six or seven carriages.

As for the carriages running on rails in the streets, both of them admitted they were mystified by the electrical source of power. According to Mr. Sawyer it ran through specially sheathed cables because it could give a nasty shock and if the voltage ranged high enough it was lethal. It could kill a mortal.

Disgruntled voices from the cart floor above their heads complained the boys' conversation was denying them their sleep and silenced reigned.

Timothy could not tell how long he slept before he awoke to shouting voices and girlish screams. After collecting his senses he noticed the rear flap of the next cart had been drawn aside and a group of anxious faces, caught in the flickering light of a lantern, were peering over the tailboard. "There it is!" a voice screamed and an arm pointed to a ghostly white figure hurrying from the scene and making a floating disappearance over a hedgerow lining the roadside.

Some time passed before the commotion died down and the adults were able to pacify and reassure the girls they had come to no harm. Timothy lay looking up at the starlit sky, in the ensuing silence, unaware of Harry's absence till he came crawling on his hands and knees to his blanket, a small white bundle tucked beneath an arm.

"Did you see what it was, Harry?"

"See, what?"

"It was rather like a ghost."

Harry chuckled, "That was no ghost. That was me."

"You joker, Harry. You nigh frightened the girls to death." and he buried his face inside his bedroll to muffle his unrestrained laughter.

THREE

Samuel rode Yorkie down the long winding path from the cottage in the cool, tranquil evening, attired in his best sandy coloured breeches and tunic. A white cravat sported the collar of his shirt and he wore the cap he used for the flights in the kite. A blissful silence filled the air. The deserted manor and village reached up for him, the inhabitants having left at daybreak for the annual outing to the seaside. He had seen the horse and carts off from the Village Square and provided Timothy with a supply of food, a bedroll and a small amount of money.

He normally accompanied and helped to supervise the outing. But on this occasion, due to an arrangement with Squire Hadley, he had been excused. An arrangement that continued to give him cause for concern and make him feel most uneasy and which had its origins in a meeting with the squire three weeks past.

He had returned from a routine inspection of the estate. His dismounted in the stable yard, finding it necessary to lift his hat to wipe the sweat from his brow with an arm; the sun bore down mercilessly and the odd butterfly making the short journey across the yard laboured awkwardly in flight against the oppressive heat. He led Yorkie to a water trough and loosened his girth leathers, and in his mind he prepared what he should report to the squire.

The meetings, on average, lasted for an hour of the clock. Then he was free to go home. However, on this occasion, when they had concluded all the matters arising from the estate the squire requested he tally a little longer to discuss a matter of a personal nature. By his sombre tone Samuel suspected it to be a rather serious matter.

The squire sat staring at his clasped hands, caught in a ray of sunlight slanting through a nearby bay window. "To begin with, Samuel," he said humbly. "The matter I am about to discuss with you must be treated in the strictest confidence." He paused. "Should you not agree with my proposal, I must have your personal assurance that you will depart from this room and forget the meeting ever took place. More importantly you must make a solemn oath never to mention it to another living soul."

Samuel said: "Have I ever given you any reason to doubt my allegiance to your family, squire?"

"Never Samuel. However, this matter is quite, quite different. In essence my family are asking a huge favour of you which, if overtaken by the ears of the public, would place the Hadley name in an uncompromising situation." He hesitated. "The truth is: it would please me if you would agree to father a child for Lady Hadley."

Samuel shrank back, shocked and unable to believe his ears.

"Have you never considered it odd why Claire and I are without children." the squire continued. "It is not by choice I assure you. We have consulted numerous physicians over the years, all of which have failed to come up with a solution to our problem. Now they are lamenting that time is running out; Claire is approaching her one and a half score years and I am told she is already at risk to her well-being at giving birth to a child."

Samuel paused uneasily. It appeared his consultants who, Samuel thought, were doing so to cover their inadequacy at finding a real cause for the problem had panicked the squire into a race against time.

"From what you say, squire, you are assuming I can succeed where you have failed. Have you or your advisers considered that Lady Hadley could be the weak link in your attempts to conceive a child? If this should be so my services would prove to be a worthless and unwarranted intrusion."

The squire raised his clenched fists, and restrained them at the last moment from thumping down on his desktop, so acute had his frustration and desperation become. "All I know at this moment, Samuel, is that Claire is brooding for a child and I am in need of an heir."

Samuel was conscious of the eyes of previous Hadley generations looking down at him from portraits scattered around the walls of the study. "Is Lady Hadley aware of your proposal?" he said gently.

The squire nodded, "She is only concerned this matter be confined to the three of us. At all costs we must take every precaution to prevent it reaching the ears and eyes of the public. Not only would our families lose face in the village, we would also be banned from the Royal court."

Samuel rose from his chair, "With your permission, squire, I would welcome a few days to ponder on the matter."

Particles of dust flew slowly up a ray of sunlight. From outside a window on the opposite side of the study came the sound of hooves on the cobbled surface of the stable yard. The squire stood, "But of course, Samuel." they crossed the room together and halted at the door. "If you should consent, might I suggest we make the necessary arrangements to coincide with the annual outing to the seaside so that Claire and you will feel free do as you will."

Yorkie turned into the main entrance of the manor without prompting and jogged him along between scented shrubbery that lined the drive. In shady parts midges swarmed. Overhead he spotted swifts and martins demonstrating speed and agility as they took supper on the wing. He grinned thoughtfully; it was far superior to the mode of flight he was pursuing. The tall white façade of the manor came to view, its imposing tall pillars standing like sentinels over the stone steps. In places the walls wore a mask of ivy, in others rambling roses. His decision to agree to the squire's proposal had not come easy. He enjoyed a special relationship with a family that treated him as one of their own, it having been started by the late Walter Hadley who took him and his mother in shortly after father Willy's tragic flying accident.

Not one to live off charity mother had insisted she go into domestic service at the manor. Samuel, being of similar age to Walter Hadley's son, meant the two boys grew up together until the young Hadley went off to public school and Samuel stayed on at the manor to receive his education from a private tutor.

Following a tradition of the Hadley family both boys joined the colours and Samuel was offered the same privilege of purchasing a commission. He refused on the grounds he felt he would benefit more by joining the ranks and working his way up through the chain of command. It disappointed the fatherly Walter Hadley of course. But his breeding as a gentleman did not allow him to hold it against the boy.

The two young men served eight years in the colours, in the same regiment, and spent much of their time on foreign soil. Samuel earned his commission during this time and both young men ended up with a couple of medals and mention in dispatches, the latter of which neither of them attached much importance.

On their return to Hadley, Walter Hadley set up a Squiredom for his son, Richard and had Samuel in mind to work alongside his son to manage the estate. Samuel declined saying that his services would be more usefully employed protecting the areas of land owned by the estate. It raised a few eyebrows at first then his critics eventually accepted it was the right decision.

Amongst the plans for his son Walter Hadley proposed selling off or renting parts of the land to tenant farmers so that continuing generations of the family were assured of an income. His son quickly saw the flaws in such ideas and argued with his father that if he pursued selling off the land the estate would surely end up with nothing to its name. What was more he wanted to chance his arm at farming. Walter Hadley suddenly realised his son was no longer a youth but a grown man with a mind of his own.

Aided by Samuel they embarked upon cultivating the land and waterways and gave much-needed employment to the inhabitants of the neighbouring village. Within five years the produce from the land and the fish from the waterways was regularly finding its way to market, and providing the estate with a steady income of revenue. Most of the financial excesses were put to increasing the beef and dairy herd and increasing the flock of sheep. Cheese, cream and butter help to further the income.

When Walter Hadley died he died a happy man; he had seen Richard paired up in marriage to a beautiful elegant young woman, and he had seen his estate transformed into a quiet, busy hive of industry.

Samuel guided Yorkie to the stable yard at the rear of the manor and dismounted. He had been driven to accept the squire's proposed indiscretion by a sense of loyalty to a family that had raised him at their expense and as if he were one of their own. And neither had he fallen from favour when he spurned their wishes on a number of occasions. It was not a question of right or wrong, he decided; it was a matter of going to the aid of this outstanding family in its hour of need. He turned to find Claire's smiling figure sweeping elegantly across the yard to meet him, her golden hair glittering in the evening sunlight and which was drawn back from her face whose colour and texture reminded him of a peach.

She had her origins in the Goddard family tree. A family which had a reputation for mixing the blood of the aristocracy with that of the commoner and producing a brand of offspring, much like Claire, who were talented both academically and practically. She was as much at home galloping a mount at full tilt during a hunt as she was with the etiquette of an official social occasion, both locally or at court. Equally, she was just as much at ease conversing with Royal personages as she was with the estate employees and the villagers.

He lifted her hand and kissed it in greeting. She thanked him and said: "Shall we partake of a goblet of wine?" She slipped an arm through his and steered him into the manor where their footsteps and voices echoed in the vast emptiness, caused by the mass desertion of the servants who were included in the annual outing to the seaside, each year. Two Irish wolfhounds stirred as the couple entered. But on recognising Samuel they resumed a dignified pose before the unlit hearth.

She poured the wine and they stood by a window, talking. She questioned him eagerly on his progress with the experiments of flight, an interest that went back to the time he started experimenting with the tethered kites. He told her that in the early days he thought more of what he would find on reaching the freedom of the air, rather than how he would desert the earth to secure that freedom: a somewhat erroneous approach to the challenge. Claire made light of it by claiming that sciences were fraught with ponderables, and that only patience, perseverance and dedication would get at the truth and solve the problems. And because he was blessed with all these qualities and a boundless store of courage she was confident he would succeed.

Rebecca, on the other hand, had accused him of following a vain hope, a lost cause. As far as she was concerned the paper kites he played with were just that – a toy. She fuelled her scorn by adding that his education had not prepared him adequately for the science of flight, and he would be prudent to remember the fatality that overtook his father, Willy Herby.

By comparison Claire's encouragement never faltered and had come to be very special to him when Rebecca deserted the family home at short notice. He managed to hide his most personal feelings at the time so intent was he to maintain a stable home for Timothy. Claire it was who came to him in private to inquire how he was coping with the situation. Her closeness, her warmth, her gentle words, her smiling face shone out like a beam of sunshine in the cold, loneliness of the world he was forced to endure.

"Come, Samuel." she broke into his reflections. "I have something to show you."

He followed her into the hall and up numerous flights of stairs to an attic room. She unlocked a door and they moved into a scene lit by two large skylights. Paint canvasses set on easels littered the room, her studio as she called it. Palettes scalloped with every colour of a rainbow, pots of paint, tubes of paint and brushes of various lengths and density lay scattered around the studio. She led him through the disarray to a canvas shrouded by a dust cover. She paused before she lifted the cover to disclose a portrait of himself, painted in oils, standing before the kite, dressed in his light brown tunic and breeches, white muffler, riding boots and his flat cap.

"Do you approve?" she said quietly.

"Approve!" he exclaimed, moved closer to her and draped an arm around her narrow shoulders. "I am astounded." His eyes wandered over the painting; she had captured so much detail – the exact number of wing struts and runs of rigging, the runs of twine and pulleys connecting the control levers to the wing and tail moveable surfaces, the shallow scallops of the calico between the wing ribs. It was all there including his choice of turning his cap back to front before a flight so as not to restrict his vision.

She slid an arm through his and leant her head against his arm; "I would like you to accept it as a gift, Samuel. Not only as a token of our friendship but also in commemoration of your courage in challenging the mysteries of the air."

He squeezed her arm in acknowledgement of her compliment. "Others say I am a fool like my late father, Willy. And did not the Brunton News tell the squire my glides are no more spectacular than tossing a model from a hill top, and therefore do not warrant a mention in the columns of their newspaper."

She turned to face and look up at him, "I care not what they say dear Samuel. I have every confidence you will succeed."

He drew immense warmth and inspiration from her words, and her sparkling blue eyes; for too long the intimate comfort of a woman had evaded him. "Nonetheless you must understand my recent flights were, as the Brunton News rightly described, no more than accomplished by Messrs. Lilienthal and Pilcher. The ultimate goal must be to achieve sustained, manned flight. And that, I warn you, is the most formidable challenge, Claire."

She cupped his face in her hands; "You differ from the others you mention, Samuel, in that you have survived your flights. You also tackle your experiments with great gallantry; you deserve to win."

He removed her hands and held them, "Attire yourself in a riding skirt and boots, and take a light cloak."

She frowned heavily, "Are we to leave the manor?"

He nodded; he did not want to perform the act, to which they were committed, in the manor, because he felt it would blemish the name of the family. "We are to take supper under the stars." he told her.

"But, Samuel," she said frantically. "It was agreed with the squire that we would keep the arrangement very private. It would distress me greatly were he to hurt by any foolhardiness on our part."

"You must trust me, Claire. I am taking you beyond the boundaries of the estate where, I alone am known to these people. Come now – we have a long ride ahead of us."

She checked him, "Do we risk meeting personages from Brunton or Compton who are acquainted with the squire and myself."

He pulled lightly on her hands, "No. Our destination is elsewhere. And we shall be protected by the cover of darkness."

*   *   *

With her sitting before him on Yorkie they journeyed deep into the countryside. Daylight faded to dusk. The dusk fell slowly as a victim of the shroud of night. For a time their surroundings disappeared in the black void. Then the moon came up painting the features of the landscape as black silhouettes against the skyline. The warm night air breathed the mustiness and fragrance of the meadows and wild flower and, as always, the drift of wood smoke.

He reined Yorkie to a halt on the brow of a hill. Down before them they saw a cluster of caravans and figures squatting around the flickering flames of a crackling campfire.

"When did you last dine under the stars?" he laughed.

"Perhaps once or twice as an unwedded maiden. But never did I feel so enchanted as I do for the scene that confronts us now."

He heeled Yorkie to move on, "You may find these folk unusual in their behaviour. Treat them as you find them; they have hearts of gold."

A pack of dogs growled and barked ferociously, as they descended upon the scene, dark, scrawny shapes, long nosed and quick of fang.

"Whoi! It is Mr. Herby and his lady-wife to be sure." Patrick O'Boyle, the leader of the Tinkers, emerged from the darkness and, using a heavy hand and foot, dispersed the threatening dogs. Greetings were made with a handshake. To Claire the jovial Irishman said: "What a pretty little ting you are, to be sure. Oi always be tinking how you look." He turned to Samuel. "You make a good choice Mr. Herby." He rubbed his hands. "Now would you be caring to join us for a few goblets of wine, a bite to eat and a little music and dance."

Samuel nodded, and Claire smiled, in agreement to which Patrick ordered a place to be found for the couple in the throng around the fire. Many a voice called out to Samuel, in greeting, who, in the eyes of the Tinkers, was something of a Samaritan. They travelled this way quite regularly in the course of their nomadic wanderings and but for his benevolence they would have suffered great hardship during the long, cold winters. He came to their aid by bringing joints of sheep, a handsome supply of rabbit and pheasant to fill their hungry bellies. At Yuletide he brought vegetables, fruit and fish from the conserving larders of the estate. In return the Tinkers made a solemn promise not to trespass on the estate.

Claire held a goblet of wine up against the firelight and inspected it doubtfully. An unexpected dig in her rib cage from a neighbouring elbow prompted her to face the culprit whose eyes smiled out from beneath a mop of black, curly hair and whose comical expression was advanced by the absence of a front tooth.

"You can be sure, m'darlin, it will warm the cockles of your heart." the Irishman winked at her and set up an invitation for other figures sitting nearby to join in with his bout of raucous laughter.

Samuel looked on, amused and proud of the way she took it all with gracious humour, without taking offence. In the more difficult moments when the culture and traditions of the travelling folk threatened to expose her ignorance and unease she rallied with the poise and confidence of the Goddards and the Hadleys by imposing on her hosts a measure of feminine charm they could not ignore, or resist.

For certain the choice of what to eat could not have been more alien to her taste. An old lady ladled the contents of a large pot, hanging amongst the flames, to a huge serving dish. "Rabbit stewed in sorrel leaves." Samuel whispered.

Then he diverted Claire's attention to two men using crutches of beech to draw a lump of clay from near the heart of the fire. The point of a dagger was used to scribe a line around the clay. "What is it, Samuel?" she whispered in his ear. "It poses rather unsightly."

"Be patient and observe."

She clung to him, watching intently as the dagger scribed progressively deeper into the clay. Until it split in half to reveal a light brown, muddy-coloured flesh that gave off an earthy savoury smell.

"That m'lady," he murmured. "Is hedgehog baked in clay, a considered delicacy in these circles."

Claire turned her face away and hurriedly sipped at her wine.

"For preference I will partake of the rabbit stew." she said presently.

It came to her in a wooden bowl with a side platter bearing potatoes baked in their jackets dressed with a portion of whipped, sour cream and sprinkled with a variety of wild herbs.

Uncertain of how the food should be taken she discreetly looked around at their hosts for guidance. Some, she noticed, peeled the potatoes, dabbed them in the cream and herbs, took a mouthful and followed it with the stew. Others dumped the potatoes in the stew, added the cream and herbs, and gave the whole concoction a good stir.

She followed the latter and after a number of tentative tastings she devoured the contents of the bowl, declaring it to be both a savoury and nourishing recipe. She similarly complimented the wild berries and thick cream that followed. And the small flat cakes and the nettle tea that concluded the eating.

More wood was added to the fire. The chatter and laughter increased. Here and there a briar or clay pipe glowed with burning tobacco. On the other side of the fire Claire noticed a figure throwing scraps of food to the dogs. She saw a woman sitting on the doorsteps of her home with two children at her side. The leaping flames of the fire lit up a sea of happy, smiling faces. She looked up at the stars swimming in the dark blue sea of the night sky in which the moon hung as a large gold medallion. Never in her life before had she realised how rich life could be in such simple surroundings. Here she was confronted by a simplicity that was nothing less than enchanting. It promoted a zest for living wooed, as it was, by the homely smell of wood smoke, the intoxicating wine, the warmth and hospitality of the travelling folk.

The air grew alive to the strains of a fiddle and accordion. Couples roused themselves and danced to the music, stepping to the lively tempo of a jig or reel, or, at intervals, shuffling, swaying to a nostalgic melody that dated far back in the history of the tinkers.

Tactfully arranged by Samuel, Claire slipped away with Patrick's wife to attend a personal need. She returned suitably refreshed and she and Samuel joined in with the merry-making. The evening passed in a maze of music, laughter and song, punctuated by pauses to nibble at sweet meats brought around on a silver tray by a young girl who followed up by refilling the goblets of wine.

"What potion is this?" Claire peered unsteadily at her fifth goblet of wine. "A trifle coarse to the palate and considerably more potent than the wine taken at the manner."

Samuel grinned; gone was the grooming demanded by her position on the estate. She had let her long fair hair fall loose about her shoulders. And spots of wood soot dotted the contours of her glowing face. An old lady suddenly confronted her and proclaimed: "It is in the stars that this will be a night to remember, my dear. A cherished wish will bear wings of reality." She paused to delve into a basket hung over an arm. She turned to Samuel, "Here, sir – take this rose and plant it in the lady's hair, as a celebration of this occasion."

Samuel dutifully complied. A crowd gathered, cheering and clapping hands. The old lady disappeared as quickly as she had materialised. The music grew louder and faster. He and Claire were pushed into a circle and made to dance a sprightly jig. He pranced around in time with the music; not really knowing what he should be about and letting Claire take all the adulation of the crowd. She spun and stepped gracefully, twirling her skirt, whilst her beautiful long hair flowed and tumbled about her face to the twists and turns of her head. For a long time the crowd cheered her on, singing, and clapping their hands in harmony with the enthusiastic concert of the musicians.

The night wore on, the stars changing position as every hour passed. The pace of the festivities slackened. The crowd gradually melted away as the tinkers retired to their wheeled homes until he and Claire were left alone sitting by the smouldering remains of the fire. A log, already consumed by the heat, crumpled into a heap of grey ash. A squat, winged shaped flew erratically and blindly across the lingering firelight. Somewhere distantly a vixen coughed her familiar call. A dog belonging to the Tinkers answered by trying to mimic the call of a dog fox. The vixen did not call again.

Low in the east a chink of pale, yellowish light heralded the birth of a new day. The couple rose and took their leave unable, in the absence of the sleeping tinkers, to pay their thanks for the hospitality lavished on them. They rode before the growing daylight, rocking to Yorkie's nonchalant step. Hilltops came to view against the skyline. Meadows, pastures, woodland and a winding river rose up from milky vapours of mist. The air breathed the warmth and freshness of the birth. He kissed her on the bareness of her neck. She leant heavily against him, placed his hand on her swollen breasts and turned her head to look at him with desiring eyes, "Make it soon, dear Samuel. Make it soon.

He chose a secluded spot on the banks of the trout streams. She slid down from the saddle into his arms, and sank to the ground urging him to follow her. They lost count of time in the process of removing their garments. Senses went berserk with desire and tempestuous passion. They wrestled amorously on the grass, their movements growing frenzied – desperate. And as their bodies fused into one they both drowned in the delirious confusion of the act.

*   *   *

Following his return from the outing to the seaside Timothy curiously noted how much father had changed in the short time they had been apart. Gone were the lines upon his brow, as were the creases about his eyes and the grave expression, which had haunted him since mother left. There was a new tone of enthusiasm in his voice, a definite spring in his step. Before Timothy had a chance to determine what was responsible father got him involved in making the preparations for the forthcoming annual fete that proved to be a rather grand occasion each year

Amusement stalls littered the grounds of the manor. A fancy dress parade assembled in the village and made its way to the manor where a panel of judges declared the best entries and awarded prizes. A host of competitions featured in the programme: running races, sack races, pillow fights on greasy poles, tilting the bucket from a running charge made on horseback. And bandsmen from the squire's old regiment provided musical entertainment.

The entire village came as guests of the Squire and Lady Hadley. And were party to a minor feast on the back lawn consisting of salad vegetables and a variety of cooked cold meats, lamb, beef, ham and legs and breasts of fowl which was followed by a large bowl of strawberries and cream.

Timothy's only regret was that mother would not be in attendance that year. If anything, in the past, had sparked her into life and put a rare smile on her lips it had been the annual fete. Father treated her to a new dress and bonnet for the occasion. And she proudly paraded herself before the large gathering of people, exhibiting her fashionable high neck, lace-trimmed apparel, with the wide brim of her bonnet casting an intriguing shadow across her dark brown eyes, her finely sculptured, Grecian nose and the unpredictable expression of her lips.

He dared himself to hope she might put in an appearance at the fete; in the long absence of any news from her he doubted if she would. His thoughts drifted off to what the squire may have planned as a special event for the fate. Without fail he always kept it up his sleeve and produced it at the last moment, causing a great river of excitement amongst the spectators.

Last year had seen three teams of horse-drawn gun carriages charging noisily from the manor drive into the paddock. Whereupon the gunners released the mounts from the shafts with strict military precision, prepared the cannons for action and startled the crowd of onlookers with the thunderous retorts of the dummy charges they fired. It was quite something!

Two years past a complement of Calvary staged a charge, with half their number posing as the enemy. The British were camped in the paddock when they were descended upon and forced to take up arms at short notice. Scarlet tunics jostled in combat under the glaring sunlight, tunic buttons and spurs glinted amongst the foot and horse contingents. Swords wielded flashing curves. Here and there the discharge of pistol and musket added to the ferocity of the scene.

For some time confusion raged as equal numbers on each side fell to earth feigning death as a victim of a fatal blow from a musket ball or the lethal thrust of a sword. Then, much to the spectators' delight, just when it seemed the British would be overwhelmed they rallied and staged a counter charge. The display ended with the enemy being routed back along the long drive of the manor, pursued by the determined beat of hooves, poised swords, a cry of revenge and the harrying notes of the bugler boy.

It evolved that the squire had chosen father and the kite as the extraordinary feature of the fete for the current year. At three of the clock the master of ceremonies, using a loud hailer, sought to catch the attention of the crowd.

"As you know, ladies and gentlemen, Squire Hadley endeavours to add a little extra to our fete each year. Today you will be both privileged and honoured to witness a remarkable feat of manned flight." He paused. "Cast your eyes to the summit of Hadley hill, ladies and gentlemen, where, presently, you will have positive evidence of this courageous adventure." He paused again, searching.

"There it hails!" he shouted excitedly. The white calico form of the kite edged into view from the peak of the hill, floating effortlessly, noiselessly. "Forget not this sight, ladies and gentlemen, because you are witnessing history in the making. And being made by none other than Samuel Herby who will allow you to view his craft of the air at close quarters following his return to earth in the paddock beyond the trees to your right."

Father performed admirably, flying the kite in long, graceful, sweeping curves, balancing his turns with precision. But Timothy noticed the flight was only having a small impact on the spectators. He suspected the silence of the flight had something to do with it whilst others could not comprehend what they were seeing because they were firmly convinced it was a dimension of life reserved exclusively for the skills and natural instincts of the birds.

A few more heads turned when the kite got lower and approached the paddock with father's capped and booted figure plainly visible between the wings. Nevertheless only a handful of people chose to follow when it came back to earth in the paddock. Some stood at a distance from it, uncertain what to do. A couple of figures walked around the kite touching it with a nervous reverence. Father lingered by the kite looking decidedly handsome in his brown breeches and polished boots, his white muffler and a new flat cap he had bought for the occasion. Lady Hadley, who had waited on the fringes of the paddock, approached him, wearing a pastel lemon, low neck, sleeveless dress, short lace gloves and carrying an open parasol as a shade from the hot, glaring sunlight. She touched father briefly with a hand and the manner in which she held him with her eyes spoke of pride, admiration and warmth, and caused Timothy to feel a trifle hurt. If only, he thought. If only it was mother paying tribute to him, in the manner that lady Hadley was.

Eventually, apart from two odd looking characters the kite was deserted. The first kept very much to himself, regarding the kite from various angles and scribbling notes in a small book. Timothy learnt later this fellow was a reporter from the Brunton News. The other individual, a short, stocky man, peered inquisitively into every crook and cranny of the kite, paying particular attention to the moveable surfaces on the wings and tail. A suspicious type, he beat a hasty retreat from the paddock when Timothy tried to approach and question him, on his interest in the kite.

Father performed another spectacular feat that day. He took to the air at night, aided as he was by a full moon and using the traditional bonfire to get his bearings. The kite appeared as a gliding nocturnal. A large shadowy moth with pale white gossamer stretched over tenuous ribs and framing. It swung in and out of view until its expended height forced it to swoop back to the paddock where the squire and Mr. Sawyer had laid out a line of oil lamps to help father select his place for alighting.

But despite all his magnificent achievements that day none of them registered of any significance in the minds of those who witnessed the flights. In the corner of its centre pages the Brunton News reported father's flight at the fete as nothing more than a controlled descent notwithstanding the report acknowledged that, 'Mr. Samuel Herby maintained expert control of his kite at all times, and accomplished a safe return to earth'

Timothy reacted angrily to what he considered to be a shabby, scornful report. "Reading between the lines, father, the report is mocking you."

"Not at all, my son. It accurately describes what the reporter perceived with his own eyes."

"He writes not at all about your knowledge, experience and courage."

"How can he? When he has never tasted a journey in the heights." They were walking back to the cottage after taking the dogs for a run down to Four – Mile Cross. In the still summer evening a lark was up singing nervously, possibly worried by the dogs straying too close to the nest and the vulnerable chicks.

"If the reporter had any measure of integrity, father, might he have interviewed you after the flight?"

"He obviously did not think it worthwhile."

They reached the cottage and father led the way to the stable. He looked in on the kite every evening and Timothy amused himself by thinking the ritual was an excuse for father to say, 'Good night.' to his creation. The kite rested on its wheels and skids, peering at them like a wise old owl in the fading light of the stable. Father stood looking at it pensively for some time. Suddenly he stirred and turned to face the boy. "I think the time has come for you to take the kite aloft, my boy."

"Do you think I am capable, father?"

" If you have inherited any of the Herby seeds you should cope."

Thus began a series of daily rehearsals, after father came home from work, in the stable, sitting on the centre section of the kite at the control levers with father beside him instructing in detail the usage and responses of the control surfaces. Time after time they went through the motions of breaking out from the hill. Settling the kite in gliding flight, moving the levers to simulate a gentle turn, estimating the diminishing height, choosing a feature on the ground over which to make the final turn and practising the control movements to get the kite back to earth.

From the rehearsals in the stable father got him at the levers in real flight. They made five descents on a Saturday. Early on the Sunday morning after one descent with father he was sent off alone. Father removed the balance bags of earth and said, "Now is your chance to show Grandfather Willy what you are made of, my boy." And with that gave a hefty push on the rear of the kite to get it under way.

Timothy gripped the levers as the kite accelerated down the slope, jolting and bumping on its stiff undercarriage. There was something desperately insane about the manner in which the slope fell away to a sheer drop, posing the stark reality that there could be no turning back. It demanded great courage and coolness of thought. He now had very good reason to bless Paddy and his frightening bolts of speed. It had prepared him well for the great challenge he was now facing. For a moment the earth appeared to look up at them vertically. He eased the fore and aft lever back and the kite fell into the void, ridding itself of the rumbling wheels and drumming calico. He listened to the invisible airstreams, as father had taught him, gushing around the wings and whistling softy through the rigging, knowing the kite would desert the wing if the flow of air fell silent. Alternatively, should the flow be excessively noisy it was an indication the kite was losing height unreasonably. The art of controlling the kite hinged on striking a balance between the two levels of sound. Equally important was the need to keep the wings level if the kite was to glide efficiently. Father had told him to relate the level of the wings to the contours of the surrounding hills.

In theory it was easy to understand. In practise it called for constant corrections on the control levers and rudder bar to make it effective. There was much to assess and co-ordinate. Flying the kite commanded an undivided attention to the task in hand and allowed him none of the casual sightseeing he had enjoyed as a passenger. He searched eagerly for the manor entrance amongst the bewildering scatter of the landscape – found it – and sank the kite apace before attempting the final turn. The white architecture of the manor rose up slowly to drift out of sight beneath the wings to the rear. Then came the orchard reaching ever closer to the kite. Over the paddock boundary hedgerows at rather a stiff pace, he juggled the fore and aft lever to discover the kite had not lost enough way. It hung on the wing ignoring the growing presence of the bushes lining the opposite boundary. He drew the fore and aft lever slowly back to its aft limit; the kite made a feeble attempt to climb – failed – and collapsed on the paddock floor with a solitary loud thud and ran on like a lame horse. The bushes raced toward it posing the hazard of a collision. Timothy debated on whether he should abandon the kite to spare himself from injury. But, gratefully, fate made the decision for him by bringing the kite to a halt with six paces separating him from the threatening bushes.

Father overlooked his trembling limbs when he arrived on the scene. Furthermore he did not question him as to how the flight had gone; he merely beamed his admiration, gave him a hefty slap on the back and voiced his congratulations. Then he attached the kite to the traces and gave Yorkie the order to move on.

Timothy made three more descents that day with the final flight ending in calamity. He alighted in a crabbing attitude – failed to correct it – a wing tip struck ground – two of the wheels detached themselves from the axle, and only a solid grip on a the nearest wing strut prevented him from making an undignified departure from the centre section when the limping kite veered sharply and came to an abrupt halt.

Father made light of the damage. He made makeshift repairs to get the kite back to the cottage, where Timothy helped him raise the kite onto trestles and the bent axle was removed. Father took the axle to Mr. Cutler, the village Smithy, who straightened the axle in his forge. Back at the cottage they worked late to refit the axle and the errant wheels and Timothy was quite ready by this time to go to his bed; it had been a long, exhausting day of excitement and high adventure. Father had him feed and turn Yorkie out, write up the journal over supper, and then listen to his plans to equip the kite with what he referred to as an oil engine. The boy had a job to keep his eyes open and his mind focused. He vaguely heard father say the engine would drive two large canvas paddles through an arrangement of chains and sprockets. And when the paddles were rotated at speed they would impart motion to the kite and launch it into the air.

In the dark sanctuary of his bed later he concluded that father had bitten off more than he could chew and, for certain, sustained, powered flight would never be accomplished without the assistance of more learned and experienced engineers.

Weeks later it transpired that father was always a step ahead in his thinking and the boy told himself he should have known better. It began with father enlisting his help to tidy up the cottage with a bout of sweeping, dusting and polishing and selecting a food and drink menu. Next they gave the kite a detailed inspection. Six lengths of frayed rigging were replaced. They meticulously checked and readjusted the inclination of the wings. The control runs were looked at to ensure the pulleys ran free and that the slack was taken up in the runs of twine. A whole lot of activities, father told him, in preparation for welcoming seven guests to the cottage.

They came of a Saturday afternoon, Mr. and Mrs. Sawyer and their daughter, Marie, came on foot to be followed shortly after by a clattering, lurching motorised carriage transporting the Squire and Lady Hadley and two strangers.

What a day it turned out to be. Father took the squire and lady Hadley to the air in the kite, in turn, and delegated Timothy to treating Mr. Sawyer and Marie to a sample of flight. Mrs. Sawyer and the two strangers expressed a preference to stand and watch the proceedings.

Timothy took Marie on the last flight of the day, a quiet, intelligent, active girl who not only handled a horse with great aplomb but also understood the language of music and played the piano with a delightful touch and skill. At the village school she was often enlisted by the teachers to help the less gifted children, so advanced was her knowledge. Timothy was drawn to her by her elegance of speech and deportment, and the manner in which she coiled her fair hair on the back of her head. Her nut – brown eyes twinkled at the world and a permanent smile danced upon her lips. He felt a combination of pride, happiness and jubilation as he broke the kite out from the hill. He banked the wings gently to head for the village and as he looked down he caught a glimpse of her red velvet dress and laced boots sitting on the cushion beside him. He turned his head further to note she was holding on to a strut with one hand and gripping the back of his seat with the other, whilst she smiled at him in admiration. Occasionally the kite lurched and bucked in the wake of an irritable patch of air but she remained unperturbed and gaily pointed down to her home at the manor entrance, and the village church, and the school. In so short a time she displayed a cool, steady nerve and all the makings of a natural navigator.

Timothy's ordeal on any flight was getting the kite safely back to earth. More often than not he had incurred a damage of some description. Father never complained; he simply got on with repairing the damage and merely said, 'Practice makes perfect, my boy'.

The previous flight with Marie's father had amazingly ended without incident. Timothy was not certain what he had done differently to accomplish it. He could reasonably judge the kite's height from the ground. His trouble lay in judging the kite's speed by listening to the sound of the air streams over the wings; his assessment was inconsistent and never the same over several flights. His problem seemed to mock him severely in those perilous moments prior to taking the kite back to earth.

He swung the kite over the entrance to the manor, the scenery drifted leisurely beneath the wings accompanied by the swishing of the air. His speed sounded about right and he reckoned his height was acceptable. The manor slid from sight to the rear, the orchard floated up, drifting from side to side as he made small corrections on the control levers to align the kite with the paddock. He eased the fore and aft lever back to check the speed, as father had taught him. Not too far or the air streams would fade into silence and he would drop from the sky like a stone. Equally he must watch his height or risk coming to ground before the paddock.

It was his lack of confidence and ability to strike a balance between controlling the speed and rationing his height that gave rise to his dilemma. And so it was on the flight with Marie. The slow drifting scenery suddenly rushed by as they swept low over the paddock boundary. He eased back on a lever to stop the kite from dashing into the ground. The kite bottomed out – paused – lifted temporarily – then fell at great speed, jolting heavily to earth, the undercarriage and wings grinding and shaking vigorously at his unintended punishment. For a tense moment he thought the pitching, rumbling kite would tilt them on their noses. But for reasons better known to the kite it limped to a halt, falling backwards onto the tailskid.

Obviously unaware of the dangers he had exposed her to; Marie slid down from the centre section her face glowing with elation from the adventures of her first flight. "A truly magical experience, Timothy! You are to be congratulated for your superb steersmanship."

He grinned his thanks at her for her compliments and quickly made his way beneath the bottom wing to inspect the undercarriage for signs of damage caused by the severity of the alighting. And to hide from her his trembling hands and legs.

Much to his profound relief the kite had not suffered any apparent damage. For certain father would need to give a second opinion and undoubtedly insist on carrying out an examination to ensure the rigging and inclination of the wings had not been disturbed by the heavy impact.

Before the flight Marie had brought Yorkie down to the paddock using Paddy to transport her back to the cottage, a system they had used to retrieve father's flights. The errant Paddy behaved impeccably with Marie in the saddle. Following their previous practices Marie backed Yorkie up and secured the traces to the kite. She checked the wing tip clearances at the paddock gate exit then went in the lead, encouraging the mount with a pat and talking to him in quiet tones.

Timothy walked beside her up the long winding hill to discover that there was very little that escaped her attention. She had noticed that Lady Hadley had enjoyed her flight on a par with her own. The squire evidently had returned from his flight looking pale and pinched and was overheard to confess to the two strangers that the oscillations of the kite in flight had invited him to feel more than a trifle queasy. Marie's breeding also included diplomacy; she requested Timothy not to mention the Squire's discomfort since she did not want to be accused of causing him unnecessary scorn and ridicule should it get into the ears, or on the tongues, of the villagers.

At the cottage she helped unhitch the traces and stable the kite. Then she attended to Yorkie; she watered and fed him, gave him a good rub down and put a comb through his mane and forelock. Yorkie nudged her with a long, hard cheekbone and snorted twice in a manner of saying, 'Thank you'.

She and Timothy watched with a smile when they turned him out in the cottage paddock and the mount, after a vigorous kick with his hind legs, charged away to meet Paddy who came out of the shadows of the twin oaks on the distant boundary.

Timothy turned to Marie in the fading daylight, "I am much obliged for your help today, Marie."

She stood on tiptoe and kissed him. "Think nothing of it, Timothy. I enjoyed every moment of it."

The touch and brief taste of her lips remained deep in his memory: his first intimacy, it brought a new and novel complexion to his life. Marie added to it by taking his hands and looking fondly in his eyes. "I am also aware of the great unhappiness you have endured since your mother took her untimely leave," she said quietly, considerately. "Therefore, as one young person to another, please feel free to talk to me on the matter, if you feel the need to do so."

He embraced her in appreciation. Likewise she put her arms around him and he enjoyed a joyous warmth long denied him. In celebration he kissed her and enjoyed the sweet succulent taste of her lips. And in return she responded with equal fervour.

"We must go, Timothy." she laughed breathlessly and eased away from him. "Our absence will not go overlooked for much longer." She hurriedly straightened her dress and patted her hair into place.

They walked into a small riot of conversation and good cheer in the cottage. The lamps flickered in the growing darkness and logs burned in the hearth. The squire and Lady Hadley occupied rocking chairs on each side of the hearth and they were laughing and chatting with one of the strangers. Mr. Sawyer was conversing with another. And Mrs. Sawyer was helping father distribute pots of ale and goblets of wine. The dogs lay beneath a table opening an eye or cocking an ear to a sudden raised voice or eruption of laughter.

On noticing him and Marie enter, father called the room to order and said, "Ladies and gentleman, could I suggest we propose a toast to Marie on the occasion of her baptism of flight. And to Timothy on the completion of his tenth solo flight which, I think you would agree, is a fitting tribute to the late Willy Herby who died so gallantly in his quest for flight."

"To Marie and Timothy!" the gathering chorused, raising their pots and goblets to the couple. "And to grandfather Willy!" the squire added, his voice coming over as boisterous and slurred.

Timothy cringed; he had never been the focus of attention, by so many people, before in his life; it embarrassed him. Marie, he noticed, bred by gifted parents, smiled and curtsied in response. Father came over and handed him a pot of ale and a goblet of wine to Marie; a privilege denied them in the past.

Marie raised her goblet, "On behalf of Timothy and myself, may I thank you all for the toast. I can truthfully say it has been one of the most thrilling days of my life and I am indebted to Timothy for making it possible. His skilful airmanship dispatched us safely to the air and allowed me, for brief moments, to view the earth as might a monarch view his kingdom. And with equal dexterity floated us gently back to earth."

A rousing cheer followed. The squire waved his pot in the air, sloshing ale over the rim. But nobody took any notice.

Timothy quietly blessed Marie for her compliments and her cover up of his appalling return to earth. 'Floated us gently back to earth, indeed!"

He seated himself at the table and the ladies distributed bowls of broth to the gathering. Father knew how to concoct a good broth, adding generous quantities of barley, lentils, carrots and onions into a pot of boiling water which had previously removed the meat from a leg of mutton. He threw in a handful of rosemary, gave it a good stir, and let it simmer for two hours on the hob. The very smell of it created hunger.

After the events of the day, the cooler air of early autumn, and the consumption of the wine and ale, the broth came as a luxury aided by thick slices of crusty bread smeared heavily with butter.

Timothy and Marie were surprised and amused to notice that much of the dining etiquette, they had been taught by their parents and school, had been willfully abandoned by certain individuals. The squire tore off chunks of bread, dipped it in his broth, and popped it into his mouth. One of the strangers broke his bread and dumped it in the broth and spooned it to his mouth therefrom. His companion made slurping sounds as he sucked the broth from his spoon. From the scullery came the sounds of mutton bones cracking between the teeth of the dogs, father having led them there to take their food.

Later Mrs. Sawyer went round with offers of seed cake, much of which was refused so filling and nourishing was the broth. The conversation and laughter resumed over refills of wine and ale. The more ale the squire consumed the more his countenance glowed and the more he amused everyone by bursting into fits of laughter for no apparent reason. Father passed a bowl of tobacco around. Before long the smell of burning briar and honey hung in small clouds against the lamps. The two strangers, now sitting before the hearth, launched into a cabaret act of mimicking the pipe-of-peace ceremony said to have originated from the culture of the North American Indians. They exchanged conversation in a foreign jargon, beat their chest, made whooping sounds by patting their mouth, attempted to blow smoke rings and exploded into fits of coughing and choking: a performance that won rapturous applause from their small audience and a request for it to be repeated.

To Timothy's knowledge the cottage had never been the scene of such unrestrained laughter and merriment. Neither had he or Marie seen their elders behave with such gay abandon. The squire put a hand to his mouth but did not succeed in stifling a loud belch. He followed it with a roar of infectious laughter that spread quickly to the other guests.

Father told a string of Irish jokes whose zany contents made Mrs. Sawyer and Lady Hadley cry tears of laughter. Timothy saw a little more of father he had not seen before.

During a lull in the activities to open window and door to ventilate the smoke-filled confines of the room, and for pot and goblet to be replenished, father introduced Timothy to the two strangers as Mr. Charles and Mr. Robert Carlton. Who, evidently, were engineers and were working on the construction of motorised carriages powered by an engine of their design. They had a medium size workshop over at Barton, ten miles north of Hadley. Father had made their acquaintance after an introduction by the squire who was very interested in their latest invention.

It needed little effort on Timothy's behalf to deduct why father had invited the two engineers to the gathering. It was linked with his ambition to fit the kite with a source of power. Timothy took to them immediately, having been impressed by their depth of humour during the Indian cabaret act. They spoke to him as an adult and highly complimented him on his zest and courage to take to the air, like his father. And like all men of invention they were curious to know how the control surfaces deflected the kite in flight.

He explained as best he could, well aware the invisibility of the air would create a barrier for them to reach a measure of understanding, much as it still did for him and father. They listened patiently, frequently frowning or raising an eyebrow and eventually displayed great honesty by admitting it was beyond their comprehension. Their mechanical practices, they said, were based on tangible metal objects and were not associated with the corridors of pure science that thrived on mysterious and magical theorems.

In appearance the brothers were very much alike. Both had balding pates, long sideburns, dark eyes and bushy moustaches. They attired in identical pinstriped suits and a waistcoat that accommodated a pocket watch and chain. They spoke in rich, deep baritone voices.

Timothy felt a genuine regret when they took their leave with the other guests shortly before midnight and they assembled before the motorised carriage outside the cottage gate. Father held an oil lamp up to the proceedings. Mr. Robert lighted a twig from the lamp to light the headlamps of the carriage. The staggering squire, attempting to be courteous, assisted his wife and Mrs. Sawyer to mount the running board and take a seat in the rear of the carriage.

"Marie!" he called. "Come now and occupy the front seat with Mr. Robert. Your father and I will ride the running boards." his voice slurred against the dark serenity of the night and, quite oblivious to his audience, he broke wind with the volume and power of a stallion. His attempts to blame it on the creaking of the carriage brought a muttered response from Mr. Charles who suggested he might like to try lubricating his hindquarters with an oil can. His brother chuckled in agreement, Mr. Sawyer nudged father and there were faint sounds of giggling from the occupants of the rear seat.

"Perhaps you would do better to share the front seat with Marie." father said. "And allow Mr. Robert to ride the board."

"Not so, Samuel!" the squire retorted. "I am quite capable." But as he lifted a foot to prove his point, he missed his step and collapsed in a heap on the running board.

Mr. Robert rushed to his aid, "I think Samuel has a point, squire. The seat will be much more to your liking."

The Squire drew himself up, swaying uneasily, and found it necessary to cling to Mr. Robert, "I have chosen to ride the boards!" he shouted aggressively. "And upon the boards will I ride."

Lady Hadley intervened at this point to bring order to the growing ugliness of the situation. "You do our friends a great injustice, Richard, after what has been a truly entertaining day. Come now, kind sir, the hour is late and time we all retired."

Without further dissent the squire let rip another crackling bout of wind and struggled onto the running board, helped by Mr. Robert, and fell heavily on the front passenger seat and shouted for Marie to join him.

Timothy squeezed her hand in farewell. She, in return, using the shroud of night, reached up and kissed him before making her way to the carriage.

"Give the...give the ...give the air...airman another drink." the squire slurred and stammered.

Mr. Robert walked to the front of the carriage and shouted to his brother poised on the driving seat, and began to crank the engine: a motion that transmitted itself to pitching and rolling the carriage upon its squeaking suspension. A loud report smote the air and brought a chattering life to the complete machinery. The engine gasped, faded and, as quickly, coughed back into life again, chugging hesitantly. Another loud report startled all those not accustomed to the stunning noise. The carriage jerked forward and came to an immediate halt after covering six paces, reminiscent of a mount refusing at a fence. Mr. Charles requested his brother and Mr. Sawyer step down from the boards and encourage the carriage with a push from the rear.

Their assistance worked. Their energies gave the carriage momentum and as it crept past the brow of the hill and started its descent back to the manor the two men jumped back on the running boards. Timothy and his father watched the diminishing taillights, and listened to the periodic reports of the engine, until both sight and sound were swallowed by the intensity of the night.

Four

Under the waning sunlight and dulling sky of autumn, and in view of the barren fields and falling leaves of woodland, the estate and village alike began provisioning for the forthcoming winter. Trees were felled and sawn and chopped into logs to fuel the home fires. Cattle sheep and pig were butchered and salted, some of the meat being lowered to the depths of Hadley River in special netted wooden crate to preserve it in prime condition. Deer, rabbit and pheasant were put through a process to dry the meat hard. Thereafter it hung in store or pantry until required for a meal. When it would be boiled in water to resurrect its succulence and taste.

Remnants of the apple crop went to the cider presses. Stocks of fruit, vegetables, hay and straw were meticulously counted and recorded, and Mr. Sawyer, the estate manager, had the unenviable task of deciding what quantities should remain to meet the needs of the estate and village. And what was available to go to market to generate funds to finance the expenses of the estate, and hopefully end up with a little in reserve.

After completing the preparations the work tailed off for many, whereas father toiled on with his duties, patrolling the estate to discourage the incursions by elements who thrived on stealing rather than paying for their wares. Timothy frequently accompanied him, to be reminded it needed a stout heart, a boundless store of patience and the cunning of a fox to crouch for long periods in plunging temperatures in order to outwit and dispatch the offenders from the land.

Father had every right to shoot the intruders on sight. He never did. He confronted the less hostile elements by delivering a sharp rebuke. To the villainous fellows he shouted a warning from a distance. And if they chose to be defiant he discharged a musket ball from a catapult he carried. The missile was not enough to be lethal when aimed at limb or hindquarters. It did, however, serve to hasten the poacher's retreat from the land of the estate.

For those who came by night, using the cloak of night to mask their illegal activities, he left to Snippy and Jeppy to bring to justice. Sniffy's strong sense of smell could pick up a scent at four or five hundred paces. He, in turn, would yelp a signal to Jeppy who raced ahead and brought the culprit down by running between his scampering legs. A capture made complete by fastening his jaws on a limb, without spilling blood, much as he did when retrieving game. He remained thus until father and Timothy arrived on the scene.

Timothy came to regard it all as nothing more than a game, and proof that father's bark was bigger than his bite. He always issued a train of warnings and threats, but made no attempt to confiscate the ill-gotten gains of the trespassers.

After a long, cold night on patrol there was nothing quite like the welcoming view of the cottage windows glowing red from the reflection of the hearth fire. They threw off their heavy garments, fed the dogs, and ladled broth from a huge pot left simmering in their absence. By the time they finished eating the dogs had devoured their food and collapsed before the hearth.

Father's habit of taking to his pipe after a meal, following the late night excursions on the estate, usually ended up with him falling asleep in his rocking chair, an arm hanging lifelessly, his pipe falling from the grip of his fingers. Timothy made a point of putting the pipe back in its rack on the mantelpiece covering him with a rug and leaving him for the remainder of the night in the company of the dogs sprawled before his feet. He, himself, also heavy with fatigue, did not bother to change into his nightshirt. He fell upon his bed, vaguely conscious of the pillow touching his head before a giant hand drew him down into the captivity of sleep.

It was late November before they obtained a chance to take the kite aloft. In their haste to do so they overlooked the boisterous nature of the wind. Immediately they launched from the hilltop the wind lifted the kite bodily, taking them for the first time, and for some glorious, breathtaking moments, above the summit of the hill in full view of the cottages and the hill ranges to the north. But as father steered the usual route against the shadowing hills the kite suddenly abandoned its ascent and plunged below the brow of the hills into a boiling cauldron of vortices that were so severe the wings shook violently. Three lengths of rigging snapped under the strain of the attack and trailed in the air, followed shortly after by the twine connecting the rudder and rudder bar; father had the rudder hard over at the time to stop the kite being blown southwards away from the manor. By the time he managed to head back for the manor using the athwartships control and tilting the wings at an acute angle another three lengths of rigging broke free. Timothy cringed; in his imagination it was only a matter of time before the wings collapsed entirely and plummeted them headlong to earth – to their death.

Father showed such courage. He sat wrestling with what little control he had, fighting to keep the crippled kite descending with a measure of poise, and helping it negotiate the insane wind which had lost all sense of direction and speed. They normally alighted in an easterly or westerly direction. Not so on this occasion. They were forced to approach the paddock from the south, slipping, skidding, rising and falling with alarming repetition.

"Hold tight, my boy!" father shouted as the earth loomed. Timothy closed his eyes and increased his grip on the strut and the back of father's chair. The newspaper report of Grandfather Willy's death flashed across his mind. Was he and father destined to share a similar fate? And was the fear and desperation seizing him now, the same that consumed Grandfather Willy in those closing moments of his life. A violent movement jerked him to the right, followed by another to the left almost wrenching his arms from the seat and strut. He lurched forward in company with a heavy rasping sound from the rear of the kite, suggesting they had snagged a tree or hedgerow. He sat wide-eyed and gasping at the sudden up -rush of the earth. He closed his eyes again; this must surely be the end. The kite crashed to ground with a resounding booming sound, to be punched back into the air – a temporary silence. He opened his eyes just as the kite fled back to ground with the solid heaviness of a mount failing at a jump. The impact made him leave his seat and his head narrowly missed colliding with the under surface of the top wing. He slammed back down dazed and breathless.

Very slowly his surroundings came back into focus. The winding path leading up to the cottage, overlooked by the blue sky had never looked so serenely attractive and secure. He felt infinitely relieved to find he was still alive because in those moments past, when his thoughts scattered into confusion and fear, he was convinced his days on earth were over.

The pale face and hunched figure of father stirred beside him and slid down from the centre section. He struggled for some time to hold a lighted match to his pipe with fingers that visibly trembled. He drew heavily on the burning tobacco and exhaled long streams of smoke in relief from his most recent dilemma.

They spent the remainder of the day making good all the necessary repairs on the kite, working alone with their respective thoughts on how they had measured up to the trials and tribulations of the flight that morning.

Days later they were out on the downs flying the model kite in an equally ferocious wind hoping to glean a clue as to what had caused the rigging lines to sever on their recent flight. In fact they learnt precious little. The model kite remained aloft for a whole hour of the clock, dancing a lively jig at the end of the captive line, constantly buffeted by the rushing and roaring of the wind. But on hauling it back to earth they were amazed to discover it had suffered none the worse for its time aloft.

The arrival of Christmastide and a heavy fall of snow halted further experiments. Timothy always looked upon such festivities with great joy; he was not so inclined this year. He missed mother at the best of times; the prospect of her not sharing it with them this year saddened him deeply. Father never gave him a chance to mope; he involved him in dressing a tree, hanging paper chains, baking bread and making a plum pudding.

On Christmas Eve' father took him along with Mr. Sawyer and a couple of estate hands on the annual charity errand of goodwill. Harry Hawker, a local haulier, provided a horse and cart free of charge. And, under the cover of darkness, they delivered a hamper of food and two sacks of logs to the most deprived families in the village. A tradition carried on by successive generations of the Hadley family in conjunction with the church, which advised the squire of the families in most need. Timothy felt particularly pleased when father told him quietly to set down a hamper and logs at the door of Harry Griggs and Molly Langdon. It was not intended for the families to know whom the gifts were from.

The deliveries took about two hours to complete. Then he and father were invited to the Sawyer's home to take supper of grilled trout dressed in breadcrumbs, sided by cobs of bread. Marie and her mother served goblets of red wine.

They made their way to church in time for the midnight mass and Timothy noticed the wine had made him light-headed and rather unsteady on his legs. The compassionate Marie came wordlessly to his aid, putting an arm through his and leaning against him to stop him toppling. Ahead of them her mother walked between father and Mr. Sawyer, her arms linked to theirs, a trio that had occasion to lurch and stumble on account of the snowy conditions underfoot.

They filed into the small church and huddled together in the pews to keep warm. Tiny islands of flickering candle light dimly illuminated the faces of the congregation, and clouds of condensation caused by breathing warm air against the chilled air of the building. Here and there an occasional sniff or cough broke the silence.

At last the church roused itself to the entrance of the Reverend Peach who quickly had them standing and singing through a succession of Christmas carols. In consideration of the bitter cold he kept his sermon short. Timothy heard little of it; he dozed off enticed by the muzzy, relaxing effects of the wine.

The service ended with Holy Communion. Marie had been confirmed; he had not. He sat listlessly in the pew, leaning his head against the stone wall of the church, vaguely watching the pews empty and refill as the congregation went up to take their bread and wine. He could not remember having felt so strange and carefree. The world floated about him in a series of disorientated images. Mother's desertion no longer disturbed him and when the church emptied at the end of the service he floated out with the tide of bodies to be greeted by a cold, crisp air that served to heighten his complacency. Shaking hands with Marie and her parents in farewell had all the makings of a comedy. They just could not stop still and he began to laugh uncontrollably. He did not know the origins of his mirth and did not greatly care. Suddenly they were gone and he was trudging through the snow with a steadying hand from father. Overhead the twinkling stars swam uneasily across the ocean of the sky, and each time he inhaled the cold night air the more he staggered and lurched. It reached a point where all he wanted to do was lie down and sleep.

He awoke the following morning to a blissful silence. He rested comfortably amongst the bedclothes, totally at ease with the world, but was conscious of the fact the previous evening had taken him through a new and untried experience precipitated as it had been by the excessive consumption of the red wine.

"Happy Christmas to you, my son." father entered the room. "I trust you are in fine fettle."

"I have never felt better, father."

"Good! I am heading across country to take food for the sheep and collect Ottie to spend some time with his family. On account of the perilous conditions underfoot I would appreciate your assistance."

"Certainly father." He was aware the entire livestock were being denied grazing because of the deep snow. He also thought there was something noble about giving up his Christmas day to collect Ottie so that he could spend Christmas with his family.

The journey, using Yorkie to haul a cart piled high with bales of hay, did not go smoothly as they anticipated. They met drifts of snow at almost every twist and turn. Time after time they were forced to clamber down from the cart to lighten its load, and put a shoulder to a wheel to aid its traction. They came upon a trail of arrowhead footprints marking the recent transit of a fox. They came across a deer foraging in the snow around the roots of an oak. The dislodging of snow from another tree drew their attention to a pigeon searching for food. They heard the scream of a rabbit fall victim to the small powerful jaws of a stoat or weasel.

At long last they reached sheep country, a great white expanse rising slowly to a blue sky. Near the summit they could just make out the fencing of the pens and Ottie's small croft which issue a steady plume of smoke from its chimney.

It took as long to reach the summit as it had to cover the journey thus far, it being necessary to run back and forth throwing clumps of hay beneath the wheels of the cart to help them get a grip on the snow covered slope. Whilst the loyal, stalwart Yorkie made his strong, heaving contribution.

"I's be glad to see ye, Samuel." Ottie came shuffling out of his croft. "Another day and theys be eating each other."

Father pulled the first bale from the kite, "It be just as well they had not started feasting on you personally, Ottie." He laughed. "Otherwise it would have been a wasted journey."

Timothy helped them unload, and unbale, the hay and distribute it amongst the pens and famished sheep, hastened in their endeavours by father's plans to make the journey back to the village before nightfall because of the hazardous conditions.

They set out under a heavy sky, father and Ottie sat up front puffing on their pipes and chatting merrily. Timothy sat with his back to them in the cradle of the cart snuggled up to the four dogs. He was amazed to overhear, that in spite of Ottie's remote and lonely isolation with the sheep, he knew a great deal of what was going on down in the village and on the estate. He knew about their flying experiments. He heard tell that Lady Hadley was carrying a child. Of all things he was in the knowledge the squire was considering the purchase of a motorised carriage. A crow winged lazily overhead, croaking harshly to the world. At a distance a rabbit bobbed in and out of the snow pursued by a young, clumsy dog fox whose coat and undeveloped limbs suggested it had yet to reach the first year in its life. Each time the fox pounced the rabbit was one leap ahead and eventually reached the sanctuary of a hedgerow.

By the time they reached the village and were dispatching Ottie to his delighted wife and excited daughters, Petal and Rose the stars were out and flurries of wind sucked the powdery snow upwards in miniature whirling eddies. Timothy took to the reins whilst father had some last words with the shepherd. Behind them a window displayed the reflections of flickering firelight and the etchings of a small firtree outlined by lit candles and glittering trails of tinsel. Petal and Rose, prompted by their mother, came to the cart, shyly wished him a happy Christmas and thanked him for helping to bring their father home for the festive season. He returned the compliments of the season and requested his part in bringing their father home as being a Christmas gift to them. They said they surely would.

The steep winding hill to the cottage in the snow proved too much for Yorkie. He and father left the cart, father going to the rear to put his weight against the tailboard and telling him to go and talk encouragement to the mount. It took a good hour of the clock to get up to the cottage and Timothy assumed the duty of taking Yorkie from the shafts, rubbing him down, giving him a well-earned bag of oats, fitting his rug and turning him out. Father meanwhile organised hot water from pots left simmering on the hobs and ladled it into a wooden tub bath set before the hearth.

After he had bathed and he watched father take his turn in the tub his thoughts began to dwell again on mother's absence. How might she be spending Christmas? And with who?

Father always treated her courteously and had never raised his voice in anger. And God knew there were many times when men of lesser patience and self-control would have reacted severely to her demanding and patronising tone. What was more nobody could deny that father was of handsome appearance, a solid, compact figure of medium height, he kept his dark hair short and regularly trimmed his moustache. Evidence of his manly virility was produced when he stood naked in the tub and doused himself with a pail of cold water. It begged the question: Why did mother disapprove of him when Lady Hadley openly admired him? Women in the village and on the estate always greeted him warmly. What did they see and mother did not?

Not once since her desertion had anyone, including father, mentioned her name. Could it be she had been branded an outcast and banished from Hadley or society in general?

"Do you think we will ever see mother again, father?" he posed the question as they took supper later, and expected it to meet a resistance of some kind.

Father said awkwardly, "It would be unwise of me to raise your hopes. Who knows she might find it in the goodness of her heart to put in appearance for your sake? That would please me no end."

Timothy said: "What if she were to come back, beg forgiveness, and request to return to the family circle. What say you then?"

Father stirred uneasily, "I would need to cross that bridge when I came to it." He moved to their small, decorated tree. "Come, my boy. Time you opened your gifts."

Timothy sensed father's change of tack in the conversation was to get off the subject of mother. He willingly obliged and knelt beside the tree and delved into his collection of presents.

He received a speckled brown suit of jacket trousers and waistcoat, complimented by a cream coloured shirt and brown silk necktie from the Hadleys. He got a green, white polka dot muffler from father. And a fixing stud embossed with the figure of a bird in flight which, father said, had belonged to grandfather Willy and whose origins had been traced in grandmother Rosemary's diaries.

From Marie Sawyer he got a long woolen scarf, she had knitted herself, and in her presentation note suggested he wear it aloft to keep him warm. Her parents gifts consisted of a bridle and badly needed stirrup leathers for Paddy

His final gift, wrapped in brown paper, he handled cautiously; it was from Harry Griggs. He carefully removed the paper and on opening the lid of a cardboard box inside he quite expected to fall victim of a hoax, such was Harry's reputation. He discovered however a cone shape piece of wood equipped with a circular formation of feathers. A spiralling groove carved in the circumference of the cone accommodated a wound length of cord. By pulling the cord sharply the cone spun up to speed and under the influence of the whirling feathers the cone lifted into the air, gyrating for several paces before dropping back to earth. After playing and examining it for a time he and father concluded that Harry had something of the designer about him. Perhaps a touch of genius, father smiled.

There was nothing, however, from mother. Not even a greetings card. It puzzled him as to why she could be so thoughtless and uncaring. He knew of many mothers in the village who endured more hardship than she ever had. None of them packed a trunk and deserted their children and men folk to escape the burdens in their life.

He saw the strain in their expressions down at the manor the following day when they arrived with their families for the annual Boxing day party hosted by the Squire and Lady Hadley. Premature lines upon the brow and heads of hair turning grey before their time, they put a brave face on the many difficulties in their lives and smiled defiantly at any suggestion of sympathy for their plight.

The Hadleys greeted them one by one at the manor entrance and later, following a tradition of the family carried over from several generations, they waited on them at the meal table serving platters of ox meat roasted on a spit, accompanied by a variety of boiled vegetables. There followed a massive Christmas pudding, decorated with sprigs of holly, whose interior secreted a wealth of silver three-penny pieces. Before long the large hall filled quickly with cries of laughter and delight as each child made the discovery of a coin in a portion of the pudding.

Later they formed an orderly queue at the large Christmas tree in the outer hall to individually receive a small gift from the Squire and his wife. It might only be a bag of fruit or sweets. But it was significant because the gentry performed the kindly deed out of the goodness of their hearts when they could have quite easily have chosen to remain aloof and remote as did many on neighbouring estates and villages.

Timothy and Marie worked in the kitchen to help wash and dry the pots and pans and a mountain of crockery and cutlery: chores shared by the squire, father and Mr. Sawyer. The kitchen maids were given the day work free. Lady Hadley, Mrs. Sawyer, Doctor Markham's wife and the wife of the Reverend Peach organised party games for the children.

Amongst the clatter of industry in the kitchen doctor Markham sat in the shadows of a corner smoking a cigar, looking rather pleased after consuming several measures of port wine. Periodically the Reverend Peach crept in from the hall to join him and partake of a swift draught before returning to the growing noisy chatter and laughter of the celebrating children in the hall. As his number of visits to the kitchen increased so his face glowed like a hot ember, and he grew unsteady on his legs.

Mr. Sawyer dried his hands, thanked all those present for their help, and took a cigar from a box the squire put out each year for the kitchen workers. During the short time he and Mrs. Sawyer had been in the employ of the manor they had done much to improve the welfare of the village folk, Timothy recalled.

For many years the village men walked ten miles to their place of work in the tin mines at Craig's Ridge and after a long laborious day, were faced with the long, tiresome trek back home to snatch a few hours sleep before getting back on the road again. Mr. Sawyer went to their aid by persuading the squire to supply horse and carts to transport the men to and from their place of work, thus reducing their hardship and allowing them more time with their families. As it was they worked six days a week.

Mrs. Sawyer complemented him by seeing to the needs and welfare of the womenfolk in the village. She taught many how to knit and sew and listened patiently to their fears and anxieties. Within a short time her warm smile, gentle voice and sound advice inspired a great number to work that much better to improve their circumstances by taking a pride in managing a clean and comfortable home and instilling in their children the importance of good manners and mode of speech.

They were a unique couple, having arrived suddenly and mysteriously, under the cover of darkness, four years past, without any warning to the estate employees, including father. Timothy recalled father telling mother about it at the time, mentioning something about Mr. Sawyer having resigned his post at the Colonial Office following a disagreement with his superiors. From what father could gather Mr. Sawyer had been used as a scapegoat to cover a gross error made by a senior member of government. Timothy never really understood what this implied; he only knew that fate had dealt the village and estate a timely and kindly hand by bringing him and Mrs. Sawyer into their lives.

With the list of party games exhausted, in the hall, and for everyone to take a pause for breath, Lady Hadley announced that Harry Griggs would take the floor to entertain them with his pet spider. They gathered around Harry who crouched in the middle of the floor beside a cardboard box that caused a great deal of speculation on what size the spider must be to come from such a large box.

He lifted a flap of the box – flicked a finger against a thumb – and two cranked hairy legs emerged, followed by six more supporting a sinister black body that had two big, menacing eyes. Gasps of astonishment and nervous giggles rippled through the throng of spectators as the spider commenced to amble across the wooden floor and advance on the fringes of the crowd. A small girl put her hands up to her face. A young boy attempted to trample on it to be pushed roughly aside by Harry. Some figures, including adults, froze in terror at the unsightly creature. Others departed the scene entirely. Many laughed nervously when Harry, using a jargon of his own making, and using a long thin cane, made the spider change direction away from the edge of the crowd and head back for the box.

Timothy lost count of the number of times Harry went through the amusing routine of rummaging in the box before releasing the spider to go to another point on the perimeter of spectators. More jeers and cheers, Harry strutted after his pet tapping the floor with his cane, serious and agile as a lion tamer. Eventually he left the floor, carrying the box, to a rousing chorus of cheering and boisterous applause from the adults in recognition of his talents as an entertainer.

Timothy learnt from him later that his mother had made the spider from black cloth, using buttons for its eyes and binding tree twigs with wool to give the effect of the spidery legs. The credit for its mobility went to Harry who used a cotton reel, a portion of candle wax and an elastic rubber band, which was attached to the wax and threaded through the eye of the reel. A small length of wood passed through the ring at the other end and was employed to wind the rubber band through a great number of turns. Then when placed on a flat surface and released, the rubber band unwound against the length of wood and the cotton reel rotated and conveyed the spider across the floor. Many of the adults thought it very realistic

Following Harry, Molly Langdon sang several songs accompanied by Miss Featherbed, on piano, a mistress of Hadley school. Few people paid attention to Molly's flat and often out-of-tune voice. They stood admiring her stunning white silk gown, given to her by Lady Hadley for the occasion. She swayed before the audience gesturing with her hands in the continuance of her repertoire, displaying the fullness and division of her ample bosom made visible by the low-neck line of the gown. A soft glow lighted her face and her hair, drawn up on the back of her head, gave a view of her slender neck and pearl shaped ears. She drew the whole world to her with her delightful come-hither eyes and rose-red lips.

Many were drawn to her in sympathy for her wretched family circumstances: a father who found work infrequently because of a recurring illness, a mother who struggled against all the odds to raise a brood of six children, of which Mollie was the eldest. The audience, young and old alike, shared her moments of glory as she swayed before them in the spotlight of their attention. And added to her pleasure by awarding her a rapturous applause at the end of her renderings.

She was honoured to be taken home in Lady Hadley's carriage at the end of the party. Before she left lady Hadley said she could keep the gown on a promise she would take good care of it. Molly threw her arms around her and tearfully confided it was the best present she had ever had.

Following the departure of all the children and their parents a silence fell upon the manor. The servants were brought back into play and went off to lay up the tables in the drawing room. Lady Hadley, Mrs. Sawyer and the wife of Doctor Markham and the Reverend Peach moved around the hall picking up litter and putting chairs straight. The doctor made an entrance, thought the chore beneath him and retreated. His Reverence rose unsteadily from a chair and followed him.

At eight of the clock a string of carriages began to arrive at the manor carrying friends and business acquaintances of the Hadleys. Timothy volunteered his help to the grooms to receive the carriages, feed and water the horses and to direct the drivers of the carriages to the back door of the kitchen to receive their customary ale and plate of cold meats. They remained there in isolation from the guests for the rest of the evening, indulging in some 'slap and tickle' with the kitchen maids, so a number of tongues claimed. Although what it implied Timothy had yet to discover.

The Carlton brothers were included in the guest list. They abandoned their motorised carriage outside the main gates of the manor as a precaution against its mechanical clattering and periodic minor explosions startling any of the horses in attendance and making it bolt for its life. Timothy met up with them in the bubbling conversation and merry laughter of the crowded drawing room. They made inquiries about his and father's progress with the mysteries of flight. He told them of their recent experience with the savagery of the wind and how they fared precariously at its hands. He admitted father and he were at a loss as to why the wing rigging had come adrift under the strain when they had seen birds master flight in similar conditions without coming to harm. So, too, their model kite had returned to earth unscathed after battling with the raging elements for a whole hour of the clock.

"Timothy, young sir." Mr. Charles grinned down at him. "That is the very cut and thrust of pioneering the sciences. It is nothing less than a relentless challenge to pierce the walls of ignorance in order to get at the truth beyond. But rarely do we find behind the walls what our theories have led us to believe. And often, as my brother will tell you, you may find a solution to a problem only to come up against another obstacle as a result of the solution." He paused to light a cigar and his brother Mr. Robert took up the conversation. "That is what makes pioneering work so interesting and absorbing, Timothy. It constantly poses a challenge to the intellect and imagination." He went on to explain the numerous problems they had encountered in their attempts to fit their motorised carriages with a form of gearing. After discovering their journeys down hill were a risky frantic dash, steering round obstacles at great speed and which quickly wore through the blocks used for braking the wheels. They fared even worse when attempting journeys uphill; the carriage barely covered any distance before it laboured to a halt and the engine gave up the ghost.

After a succession of failures, using leather strops to affect a ratio of gearing, they had moved on to the use of metal cogs, based on the meshing principle of a timepiece, which worked reasonably well for a time. Then in recent weeks the gearing seized up, through what they thought to be a lack of lubrication. They were currently putting their brains to a system to overcome the problem,

Father interrupted at this point to explain that there were many other guests, at the gathering, eagerly waiting to speak to the brothers, and he led Timothy away. He further mentioned the brothers had invested personal sums of money in the development of the carriage and their only hope of recouping their losses was by selling a number of the vehicles. There were a number of personages at the manor that evening only too ready to improve their image and standing in local society by purchasing the most recent of inventions. Father led him down the room to the end to come across a figure standing alone, a glass of sherry in one hand, a smoking cigar trapped between two fingers of the other hand. Timothy frowned; he was certain he had seen the obese stature, the balding pate, and the narrow-set eyes on a previous occasion.

Father introduced the man as a Mr. Fanshaw who, it transpired, was also pursuing the mysteries of flight. It came to Timothy in a flash! Mr. Fanshaw was the man he spotted snooping around the kite after father's spectacular flight on the day of the annual fete at the manor and who had beat a hasty retreat when Timothy had approached him.

During the ensuing conversation Timothy's suspicions about Mr. Fanshaw were aroused still more. Not once did he admit to taking to the air, and evaded every question on whether he had a craft to do so. He put up a feasible idea of twisting a wing to achieve turning flight. But failed to explain what device he used to actuate the flexing. Timothy noticed he spent most of the time questioning father on what materials he used for constructing the kite, and by what means he used to operate the moveable surfaces on the wings and tail. He also failed to understand how the kite was deflected in flight. In fact father had to repeat his explanation on the matter, three times, before the little fat man gave a glimmer of understanding.

Timothy came to the conclusion that Mr. Fanshaw was more than a little devious in the manner he bluffed his way through most of the conversation and the subtle tack he used to poach father's ideas. To crown his impertinence he declined an offer to go aloft with father, claiming more important matters on his time.

Timothy made known his reservations when he and father trudged home through the snowdrifts.

Father, renowned for never talking unkindly of another human being, said rationally, "You would do well to remember, my son, you may possess skills and talents that are denied to Mr. Fanshaw. Likewise he may have skills denied to you. Additionally you might like to consider that his shortcomings could be turned to our advantage if fate so decides."

"How so, father?"

"I know not exactly. The fact Mr. Fanshaw has been brought into our lives must have some connection with our destiny, I feel sure. But what part he will actually play is something that must be left in the laps of the Gods."

Timothy did not attempt to pursue the matter; Father's outlook on life, at times, puzzled him deeply. Especially when he began theorising on the purlieus of fate, destiny, and what he termed as laps of the Gods.

Out of the darkness of the night and through the cloudiness of his thoughts a large bright, twinkling star arrested his attention. It seemed to hang only a few feet above the chimney pot of the cottage. On an impulse he took a deep breath – looked intently at the sparkling light – and made a wish for mother to come home.

FIVE

Timothy reached his fifteenth birthday in January. And as a gift father turned him loose with the kite before setting off for work, giving him full responsibility for inspecting the kite and taking it to the air. He helped fetch the kite from the stable, judged the air to be smooth enough for the flight and rode away on Yorkie wishing him every success and taking Paddy with him to deposit in the paddock in preparation for the mount to haul the kite back to the cottage.

Timothy moved around the kite checking its condition, as father had taught him, the security of the struts and wing attachment, the tension of the rigging lines, the freedom of the control lines around the guide pulleys. Everything about the kite came cold and brittle to the touch. He secretly wished father had been there to help him. The awesome drop over the brow of the hill to launch the kite into the air, and getting it back to earth with a measure of dignity, remained uppermost in his train of anxieties when a flight was in prospect. By choice he would have preferred to remain earthbound but he was well aware that if he refused to take to the air it would be a betrayal of father's trust in his capabilities. And also be construed as an act of cowardice, which, if Grandfather Willy's courageous flights were anything to go by, was not a streak of character, associated with the family name.

He pushed on the rear of the kite and as soon as it gathered momentum he scrambled over the centre section into the wicker seat and took the control levers to hand and clamped his feet on the rudder bar. He careered down the hill, the rumbling wheels and the drumming of the calico growing louder as the pace increased. Twenty paces ahead the hill fell away to a sheer drop. If he lost his nerve now all would be lost. He held the levers, grim-faced and tense. The air smote his face with an icy hand. Suddenly the commotion of rumbling and drumming stopped abruptly, the hill was behind him. He listened intently to the sound of the air streams and adjusted the position of the fore and aft lever. He descended gently flying a little further out from the hill face before making the first turn. He grinned and expelled a great sigh of relief; he had overcome the first obstacle of the flight; getting into the air safely. Within seconds he was confronted with another dilemma: the snow covered landscape beneath him was featureless and devoid of all the familiar land marks he and father used in the navigation of their flights. He thought he saw a thin trace of Hadley River worming its way through the white blankness of the countryside. He was not certain. Occasionally the black blob and smoking chimney marked the presence of a dwelling, none of which were enough to tell him of his exact whereabouts. To compound his problem the earth appeared to blend in with the sky creating an impression of travelling in a sphere of infinite boundaries: a fish swimming in an endless circle.

A mariner could clearly see the wash streaming back from the bows of his ship and foam white at the stern. A man of the air had no such indications of his progress; it was a matter of cultivating an instinct to listen to the music of the air in response to the kite's passage and learning that every note had a message to tell of the kite's plight. How often father had reminded him to avoid allowing the air streams to fade into silence. It was a dire warning that if they did so the kite would relinquish all desire to fly and plunge uncontrollably to earth.

He kept his nerve and continued descending, looking urgently all around in an attempt to get his bearings. Quite by chance, and somewhat ironically, the village church came to his rescue. He spotted its needle point spire piercing the white blandness. This in turn gave him a clue to the location of the manor made visible by its large chimneystack issuing plumes of smoke. He banked the kite gently, his eyes smarting and watering from the icy air. On coming out of the turn he saw the swept surface of the manor stable yard, and two tethered mounts, ahead of him. Soon they slipped beneath the wings and the orchard presented itself beneath him as dark blotches down between the gaps of the snow-capped trees. The hedgerows on the paddock boundary came up as a solid white wall. He eased a control lever back a little more, holding his breath and fighting a temptation to close his eyes; the white wall passed close beneath him without snagging the wheels. He drew the lever back a fraction more; the sinking kite paused for a moment or two. Then fell to earth with astonishing gentleness.

He did not venture again into the air that day. The perils of his blind navigation, his frozen fingers and the incredible time it took to get the kite back to the cottage made him seek the warm refuge of the cottage to thaw out after seeing to the needs of Paddy, rugging him up and turning him out.

He was sprinkling drying powder on wet ink after writing up his observations of the flight, in the journal, when the dogs stirred and went through to the front door to be met by the rapping of the doorknocker.

"Master Timothy Herby?" a youth attired in the uniform of the Post Haste Service greeted him. "I have been instructed to hand this letter and two parcels to you, personally, young sir."

Have you travelled far?" Timothy grinned.

"From Brunton sir."

"Then you and your mount must be in need of refreshment."

" I only have little time, sir. But it would be most appreciated."

Timothy organised a rug drape and a bag of feed for his mount and led the lad indoors to ply him with heated onion soup, cobs of bread and a mug of tea. He was a cheerful sort who prided himself on working for the postal service. He had ambitions to get on the long distance deliveries as a driver of a coach and six. Timothy reckoned they were much the same age and Yarpy, as he called himself, featured many of the traits of Harry Griggs: the same impish smile, a similar accent in his speech and the lost possession of a front tooth. Evidently he was not a stranger to the district having, he said, delivered mail to the manor on a number of occasions.

"Nothing snooty about that lot down there," he declared. "A real good hack they are. Not like some I know. Come rain or shine I never leave the manor without a drink, a bite to eat and a florin in the palm." He paused to consult a pocket timepiece. "I must be getting on, master Timothy. My guvnor will be asking questions like, why I took so long."

"What! In the conditions you encountered today?"

"Whatever the perils the mail must get through on time, he says. And I do my best to keep in his good books 'cos I want to get on the coach and six."

Timothy accompanied him outside and removed the rug from Yarpy's mount which rose to sixteen hands and whose long slim legs suggested it hailed from the hunter and steeplechase breed. Typical of its highly-strung nature it constantly tapped its hooves and nodded its head in its impatience to get on the move.

So high did it tower above Yarpy he was forced to put it alongside the front gate, and climb up the gate to get astride the saddle? He touched his cap in farewell and departed. Timothy watched him ride to the eastern brink of Hadley hill where he stopped and gave a wave of the hand before sinking from view on the other side. Timothy returned to the cottage, smiling and refreshed by his acquaintance with Yarpy; he rather hoped he would pass this way again.

His amusement took on a more serious dimension when he read the letter Yarpy had delivered:

My dear Timothy,

I hope the book I have presented you with will help you with your education since you know how important it is to me for you to be a top scholar at school.

Please accept my apologies for failing to write to you at an earlier date. Suffice to say that times have been extremely difficult for me.

However my fortunes have taken a turn for the better and it should be possible for us to meet in the months ahead. An event I look forward to with eager anticipation.

In closing I hope the letter and gifts make up, in some way, for my absence which was brought about not by choice but more so by the circumstances forced upon me...

He threw the letter down on the table in a fit of exasperation. His first reaction was to condemn his mother for her continual obsession in his education. And he saw no reason why she should lament her present difficulties when she had made the decision to leave a secure and happy home. Then his thoughts clashed; another part of him argued that, after all said and done, he was part of her flesh and blood. A distance may part them at this moment in time but there remained a spiritual bond that had retained its connection at the severing of the umbilical cord – a loyalty between mother and son. A great surge of emotional identification brought a trembling to his hands, a choking lump in his throat and a welling of tears in eyes.

He shed a few tears and felt the better for it. He unwrapped the first parcel to find it was a late Christmas gift from mother, a book entitled, Advanced Mathematics. He put it on a bookshelf next to his bed.

The second parcel, also from mother, for his birthday, contained a greetings card and a pair of pigskin gloves which he decided there and then would be used exclusively for handling the control levers of the kite. He proudly stored the gloves in a small trunk, he kept under his bed, and in which he kept the attire he used for the journeys into the air. Deerskin boots, long stockings, thick, corded breeches, moleskin waistcoat, tweed tunic, woollen muffler, flat cap and, recently acquired by father to protect them from the ravages of the winter weather, a knitted helmet.

He had barely got over the shock of the letter and parcels when the dogs were up and racing to the door again in advance of the knocker being used. Timothy answered the subsequent rapping by opening the door to a group of youthful smiling faces muffled against the cold, greeting him with a vociferous chorus of 'Happy Birthday, Timothy!"

Marie Sawyer led them into the kitchen and placed a cardboard box on the table and acted as a host by relieving all the visitors of their hats and coats. Each of them came in turn and shook Timothy by the hand and voiced their special wishes of the day. There was Spindle Baker so named because of his lean anatomy. 'Tubby' Cracknel, a short, rotund boy, 'Cryer' Popham who's constantly weeping eyes would not respond to medical treatment. Benjamin Hampton whose enthusiasm for the sea, motivated by the annual visit to the seaside, had earmarked him for a place at a seafarers training establishment when he came of age and would be sponsored by Squire Hadley. Last of all came Harry Griggs carrying a wooden box that exuded suspicion by the very nature of his mischievous reputation.

Marie's quiet, polite persuasion got them all seated around the table and left them chatting amongst themselves whilst she made nettle tea. In the absence of parental authority they talked about their families and about incidents at school and in the village, most of a serious nature but which Spindle had a knack of turning into a highly amusing tale. Guffaws of laughter rippled through the small room.

Silence reigned when Marie opened the box on the table and removed a cake decorated with pink and white icing. She cut portions and served them on small white plates, setting many an eye and tongue dancing with delight. Most of the recipients had tasted bread and cake, never icing. Tubby Cracknell asked for a second helping to which all the others followed suit. Marie just managed to give them all a second helping, which they washed down with nettle tea, in silence.

When Marie removed the plates and mugs Benjamin Hampton said: "When do you intend to let us into the secret of your box, Harry?"

"Nothing secret about it." Harry chuckled. "It's my pet frog."

"What happened to your pet spider?" Spindle scoffed.

"Gone to sleep for the winter."

"Sleep!" Cryer teased him.

"Spiders do not hibernate, you fool, Harry." Benjamin backed him.

"Whoever told you that, Harry?" Cryer said.

Harry viewed them seriously. "Spiders eat flies. But because the flies are killed off by the cold in winter the spider has nothing to eat. So they curl up in a ball and go to sleep to forget they are hungry."

Timothy looked on in amusement as Cryer looked to Spindle for confirmation of Harry's claim. Spindle shrugged. Benjamin Hampton was bewildered into silence. Marie said kindly, "Come now, Harry. May we see your pet frog."

He lifted the carton and placed it on the table, lifted a flap, slid a hand inside and teased them by rummaging inside for a considerable time.

The rapidity of the movement took them all by surprise. The top flaps of the box flew open releasing a strange slimy green shape with piercing eyes, large cranked legs with widely spaced toes. It shot vertically and collided with the ceiling of the room. And descended, at great speed, to the table where it hopped about without any sense of direction, frightening all and sundry. Spindle fell off his chair. Cryer put his hands over his face in fear. Finally the frog, spent of its energy, came to rest on Tubby's head and he frantically swiped at it as if to ward off a marauding bee. Shrieks of nervous, youthful laughter filled the kitchen.

Harry comforted Tubby by returning the frog to the box. Only to release it again moments later causing another spate of panic. Its unpredictable antics and its slimy feel to the touch had figures reeling in fits of diffident mirth.

On Marie's advice they took their leave before nightfall to avoid falling into one of the many snowdrifts. They congregated by a sledge constructed by Spindle and his father, laughing and joking and continuing to tease Harry about his theory of spiders and hibernation and the wickedness of his pet frog. They placed Marie in the centre of the sledge. Squatted to her front and rear to protect her, and Spindle gave it a push with a foot to get it under way. He jumped on the remaining space once it got moving and held on to two supporting vertical rails. It went dashing away down the winding hill trailing a verbal orchestra of farewells till it disappeared from view in the shadows of the lower reaches of the hill. Timothy stood, smiling, grateful for such good friends and Marie, in particular, for she had obviously arranged the cake and organised the visit. Sniffy nudged his hand with a cool, velvety nose and led him back inside the cottage. All in all it had been a good day. A very good day indeed!

Father arrived home later than usual that day, having spent much of the day up sheep country delivering another cart load of hay and, with the help of two estate hands had managed to clear an area of snow to allow the sheep access to a small quantity of grass. On their way back to the estate they stopped to axe some openings in the frozen river and trout streams. Back at the farm they loaded the cart with more hay and delivered it to the beleaguered cattle wandering aimlessly on the southern slopes of the estate.

He trudged heavily into the cottage, his eyes sorely enflamed by the excesses of his work. Timothy sent him off to refresh himself and attended the needs of the weary Yorkie. On returning indoors he found father sat in his rocker, a bowl of stew and dumplings to hand abetted by thick slices of bread. A sheath of papers on the kitchen table, father later explained as plans for equipping the kite with power.

Even more significant it evolved that father, despite the heavy demands on his time, had set the plans in motion. Mr. Cutler, the village smithy had consented to build a steam traction engine to suit the size of the kite. Mr. Pook, the local carpenter, was in the throes of completing shafts and leather strops and two paddles constructed of canvas stitched to spruce framing. The paddles would be rotated by power from the steam engine, through the shafts and strops. And once up to speed the force of air thrown back by the paddles would impart motion to the kite particularly when it broke free from the restraints of the earth and reached the freedom of the air. At least, this was father's theory.

The conversion to power necessitated alterations to the kite in the form of reinforcing the centre section of the bottom wing to take the weight of the engine, and adding stiffeners to the top wing to support the shafts and paddles. Father engrossed himself in weighing all the new appendages and carefully recording their location. His demands for the kite to be correctly balanced never deserted him.

By the end of February the transformation was complete. But March came in with strong blustery winds and deterred father from taking the kite aloft with its controversial partner. April too put him off with its continual flurry of spring showers; he felt the calico would get wet and lose its all-important tautness.

It was shortly after daybreak on a quiet, calm morning in the middle of May when they drew the powered kite from the stable and perched it on the brow of the hill. Father carried out a final inspection whilst Timothy took a small cart, drawn by the irritated Paddy, down to the village to collect Mr. Cutler who had been in attendance at all times during the fitting of the engine and had instructed father extensively on how he should operate it. Nevertheless father insisted he be on hand for the day of the first flight in case he should encounter unforeseen problems.

On his arrival he checked the small boiler was filled with water and brought flames to the guarded furnace beneath it. The design was not of the best; if left unchecked the flames could reach the combustible areas of wood and calico. Timothy noticed father looking on cautiously, possibly going over in his mind, for the umpteenth time, of what he could expect from the kite's behaviour once it reached the freedom of the air with its untried partner.

A long, shrill scream and a jet of vapour prompted Mr. Cutler to finger a small lever with a piece of rag. A nearby flywheel jerked into action, spun madly for a time, almost coming to a halt, before it engaged with the leather strops, which lost their slack as they strained to rotate the paddles. A further adjustment to the engine had it chugging evenly as a mount at the trot. The paddles revolved, thrashing the air hesitantly. Mr. Cutler left father alone in his seat on the centre section and walked to the wing tip opposite to where Timothy was waiting. The trotting tempo of the engine broke into the brisk rhythm of a canter, urging the paddles to swat the air in a surge of revolutions that transformed the kite into a mass of shuddering wood and calico. Father signalled he was ready by thrusting an arm forward, much as Timothy thought he would have done when charging into battle as a soldier. Timothy and Mr. Cutler heaved on the wing tips to get the kite under way, and moved aside when it moved down the slope of its own accord. They watched it gather pace and listened to the fading rumbling wheels, the snorting steam engine and swishing paddles till it slipped from view over the brow of the hill.

They quite expected it to reappear moments later and sail effortlessly to the heights with the agility of a bird. When it did not they moved carefully to look over the lip of the hill to discover it continuing earthwards, trailing a stream of vapour and noticeably lacking the grace and artistry of previous flights. It appeared to plummet like a stone, the wings rocking violently, as it made the final turn toward the manor, a strong sense of urgency and desperation consuming its dire need to reach the paddock.

Timothy did not wait for it to reach ground. He leapt onto Paddy, already tacked up for the proceedings, and rode at full pelt down to the manor, gravely concerned at what he might find. He narrowly missed colliding with a carriage making an exit from the main gates of the manor. He thundered along the drive through the cobbled stable yard and orchard and jumped Paddy over the hedgerows into the paddock where, to his immense relief and great joy, the kite stood in one piece, its paddles stilled, a miniature cloud of steam lingering above the wings. Father stood nearby drawing heavily on his pipe, looking pale and strained.

"What happened father?" He slid hurriedly down from Paddy, grateful that he was otherwise unharmed.

Father removed the pipe from his mouth with trembling fingers. "It would seem the kite objected to the company of the engine and paddles." he said. "It was as much as I could do to bring it safely back to earth. And I am much puzzled as to how I did it."

Just how close he had come face to face with a fatal disaster was revealed when Timothy followed father's habit of inspecting the kite to check how it had fared from its ordeal. He found leaves and broken branches in the spokes of the wheels and lashed and ripped calico on the bottom surface of the lower wing. It did not require a lot of imagination to realise father's dilemma, traversing close to the earth, fighting to control the overburdened kite and prevent it falling victim of the fatal 'drop' and wrestling at the same time to clear the crowns of the trees to get into the paddock. A lesser mortal might very well have panicked and succumbed to the inevitable. Gratefully father had not despite the fact he stood at this moment in time, shoulders hunched a haggard look about his face, drawing thoughtfully on his pipe, attempting to rationalise his thoughts and feelings.

Two weeks later, after making good all the repairs and further consultation with Mr. Cutler and Mr. Pook on the operation of the steam engine and the paddles, father took to the air again with the powered kite. A flight spared once more from a disaster by his reserve of courage and his ability to act decisively in a moment of crisis. The boiler of the steam engine exploded about mid point in the descent, mercifully having its scalding contents carried rearwards by the air streams, thus saving father from injury. The resulting loss of power, however, ground the paddles to a halt. He later described the drag they created as a mighty hand battling to wrench him and the kite from the air. Only descending at great speed was he able to stop the stricken craft bolting out of control. He crashed through the boundary hedgerows and struck ground at such high velocity the impact swiped two wheels from the axle, a wing tip collapsed to earth and the lame kite spun violently, coming to an abrupt halt and ejecting father over the control levers.

By the time Timothy arrived on the scene he was on his feet brushing himself down and plucking small blades of grass from his moustache. In his hurry to retrieve his cap he set it askew on his head and in the circumstances it struck Timothy as very comical.

"Please forgive me, father." he roared with laughter. "I am so relieved to find you in one piece."

The grim expression, facing him, dissolved into a grin. Father raised a fist to the invisible agents of the air. "Methinks you have not defeated me yet!" he declared.

SIX

If the Reverend Peach hesitated once, he did so a dozen times during his Sunday morning sermon, and shot a look of disdain toward the high-reaching arches of the church roof from which a mixture of strange noises appeared to bear down on him. They impinged on his eardrums as a distant roar interspersed with spates of buzzing and droning and all quite unfamiliar to him. The sounds were not exactly loud but they were enough to be annoying and distracting.

He looked up again at an increase in its volume inviting the curious congregation to do likewise. Could it be a hoard of hornets had taken up residence up there out of sight in the shadows of the arches, or, had war broken out among the bats in the belfry? Without warning it lapsed into silence. He breathed a welcome sigh of relief. The tranquillity of the church, the sunlight through the stain-glassed windows, the chirping of the birds and the expectant expressions on the sea of faces looking up at him were the traditional features of Sunday morning worship. He referred to his notes, rested his hands firmly on the pulpit, grinned, and was about to continue his oration when the infuriating noise renewed itself with a vengeance.

He threw his hands up in despair and in blustery tones ordered the congregation to stand and sing hymn 409.

Timothy stood plugging his ears with a finger as a defence against the tumultuous roaring sound of the Carltons oil engine that had replaced the steam engine on the kite. By comparison the oil engine was a much bigger and noisier monstrosity. The kite stood before him consumed by a deluge of shuddering and shakings, squealing driving chains and the air thrashing revolutions of the paddles. A cacophony of noise interrupted by the intermittent decisions of the engine to miss a beat and strike the air with the violence of an explosive detonation. Father sat on the centre section, surrounded by the chaotic din, tinkering with the engine: a heavy metal contraption limbering up and down on its rubber mountings. An amalgam of iron and steel polished brass fittings and a long copper pipe, jutting out to the rear of the kite, that disposed of the burnt gases of the engine and was responsible for causing the deafening crescendo of sound. A large brass cylindrical tank, perched on top of the engine, contained a volatile liquid spirit. A small push/pull valve gravity fed the spirit to a complex device which mixed it with air and metered it to the engine cylinders. Whereupon another magical component generated electrical pulses across the points of the sparking plugs which ignited the mixture in the cylinders and brought life to the engine.

A cranked starting handle inserted in the front of the engine initiated the mixing and ignition by turning it over several times. The Carltons had warned him and father to treat it with the utmost care and respect because, if not gripped correctly with the hand, it had a ferocious habit of kicking back and resulting in a serious injury to wrist and fingers.

The addition of the oil engine had changed the docile image of the kite into something more aggressive, more powerful. Timothy was not impressed by the profusion of oil that liberally deserted the engine and attacked areas of the wings with small black spots, much like the clusters of black fly on the stem of a flower.

Father beckoned to him and shouted: "Be patient a little longer my boy. I think I have, at last, learnt the secrets of this powerful beast."

Timothy had barely acknowledged and retreated a few paces when an unusually loud report rent the air asunder, wedging the kite hard against the wheel traps, making it shudder like an alarmed mare, and for father to abandon the centre section in a state of shock.

Only when they recovered their senses did they realise the brutish engine had lapsed into silence. The dogs, which had been cowering under the kitchen table in retreat from the roaring monstrosity, came racing from the cottage and stood barking at the kite, daring it to repeat its offensive uttering. Father stood, hand on hip, scratching his head, looking perplexed and puzzled. Timothy started to laugh uncontrollably when he recalled father's famous last words of, having learnt the secrets of this powerful beast.

Father turned on him with glaring eyes and bristling moustache.

"Father!" Timothy checked him. "Did you not tell me on an occasion that laughter is an important ingredient of life?"

The fierce expression melted into a broad, knowing smile. He drew closer put an arm around the boy's shoulder and said, "Indeed I did my son. Yes, indeed."

He did not attempt to tamper with the engine again until the Carlton brothers arrived early the following Saturday morning to check on his progress. They arrived in their gleaming, chattering motorised carriage, dressed in leather coats flat caps and goggles, and listened patiently to father's explanation of the difficulties he had encountered with the engine. They sat around the kitchen table in discussion and Timothy served them refreshments.

Their decision to supply father with an engine had come at short notice and shortly after father had told them about his failures with the Mr. Cutler's steam engine. He was confident he would have no such trouble with their oil engine, he told them, and which Timothy saw as a subtle form of flattery that enticed the brothers to oblige.

They removed their leather coats, wrapped themselves in long aprons, fetched a chest of tools from the carriage and had father lead them to the kite in the paddock behind the cottage. Father had abandoned the flights from the brow of Hadley hill. At least until he grew more conversant with the oil engine. The flights with the steam engine had nearly cost him his life on both occasions; he had grown more cautious. He continued to plan everything down to the last detail like removing the horses from the paddock and tethering them to rings on the back of the cottage and out of sight of the kite and its noisy, unpredictable appendage. He also got the dogs to stay in their company as an assurance that the distant roaring, spasmodically exploding engine was more of a nuisance than a danger to their welfare.

The kite rocked upon its creaking undercarriage to a murmur of wind and which stirred more so when father and Mr. Robert clambered up on the centre section. Mr. Charles went behind the wings to inspect the paddles chains and sprockets, which had replaced the leather strops used for the steam engine.

Timothy lost count of the number of times the engine was started and stopped that day interspersed, as it was, by numerous discussions and adjustments. The morning wore on, witness to the engine struggling to keep alive to a train of misfiring, gasping for the right quantity of air, and roaring and belching to excesses of the liquid spirit, running evenly for brief moments, but more often than not vibrating madly on its rubber mountings.

Just before midday they began to get the engine under some form of control. It ran evenly for longer periods and father gave the impression he was getting the hang of operating the engine controls. He called a halt for his guests to take refreshments at noon and Timothy was delegated to serving steaming hot broth with bread and cheese and mugs of ale, and he overheard the brothers claim the engine would be tamed and tuned before the day was out.

A claim that only began to gain some credibility late that afternoon when the October daylight started to fade and Timothy, chilled by the long wait and lack of progress, rubbed his hands and stamped his feet to keep warm. Mr. Charles cranked the engine yet again into life and it settled down to a constant roar, thundering through the kite like a regiment of drums and shrouding the rigging in a blur of vibration. He patted father on the back, jumped down from the centre section, and signalled to his brother and Timothy to take up their position by the wing tips. He removed the wheel traps and waved to father whereupon the engine roared dramatically accompanied by a frantic thrashing of the air by the paddles. The kite inched forward but only got up to a walking pace which it refused to improve upon. And when they exerted more push at the wing tips to encourage it to do better it only ever reached the tempo of a trot. Very occasionally, very briefly it departed the earth – a fleeting moment of daylight beneath the wheels – it fell back to earth grumbling, and frustrated, by the reluctance of the air to accept it onto the wing.

The last shreds of daylight found Timothy catching his breath after the countless runs back and forth across the paddock pushing on a wing tip in an endeavour to give the kite more speed. Mr. Robert joined father on the centre section to help coax the engine to produce more power. The noise from the long copper exhaust pipe pitched so high it shook the ground beneath the feet. The kite moved off and Mr. Robert signaled for renewed effort at the wing tips.

Timothy dutifully conformed but was convinced they were flogging a dead horse now that the kite was carrying extra weight and the power had only marginally improved. The kite lurched along and they sweated and stumbled as frequently as previous attempts to hopefully help it into the air. In the swooping darkness the engine note suddenly went berserk followed by large fragments of wood flying away from the kite. Timothy tripped over a tuft of grass, shocked by the spectacle, and as he lay on the ground a paddle deserted its shaft to spin over his head and land several paces distant. Smoke squirting from the other paddle shaft spurred him onto his feet in time to witness the shaft break free and fall amongst the runs of rigging and rent a huge gash in the wing calico. The unleashed driving chains lashed and severed a wing strut, ripping the surrounding calico to shreds. Second by breathless second it continued its merciless destruction of the kite, gradually hacking it to death.

Timothy raced around to the front of the kite where father and the Carlton brothers were huddled over the crazed engine on the centre section, shouting and gesturing wildly. He desperately wanted to help but they were fully engrossed in their frantic attempts to harness the insanity of sound and devastation. They appeared quite oblivious to the whipping and snaking chain, to the rear of them, as it writhed in circular motions stalking like a Viper preparing to attack its next victim. And soon enough it did so, choosing the cylindrical tank containing the liquid spirit. The chain, driven by the unstoppable engine, lashed and grated the tank at first. Then progressively tore into the brass casing and sparks flew. Father and the Carltons leapt from the centre section, grabbed Timothy in their retreat and propelled him to safety a second before a horrendous explosion blasted the air apart and rocked the ground beneath them, causing a temporary deafness, and stagnation of thought.

In the ensuing silence they gradually surfaced from their state of shock to hear wood crackling and splitting in the wrath of a fire. They stood to investigate to be confronted by the sight of the kite being consumed by a raging inferno. The calico melted into obscurity leaving the skeleton of the wing framing and ribs to char in the intense heat. Piece by piece the beloved kite crumbled and collapsed amongst the flames until all that remained was the scorched, black lump of the engine and the bare-rimmed wheels surrounded by a heap of grey smouldering ash.

How long they stood there viewing the aftermath of the ghastly episode, Timothy was not sure. For certain he would never forget father's pitiful figure as he led them slowly back to the cottage, numb and grief-stricken as mourners leaving a funeral.

Equally disturbing father led him back to the grisly remains, the following day, to salvage a number of items. They found the metal paddle shafts, the drive chains and sprockets buried beneath a layer of wood ash. The wheels were too distorted to be of further use. They retrieved the paddle that had broken free at the start of the fiasco; it landed a hundred paces from the kite. Amongst the scant remains the engine remained intact. Although it was obvious it would need extensive refurbishment to get it to function again.

The Carlton brothers kindly offered to do it, but father said he badly needed something to fill the gulf in his life, created by the demise of the kite, and requested they provide him with the necessary tools and advice.

Timothy felt quite sure that father had it in mind to use the overhauled engine on the completion of constructing another kite. It turned out that he did not have adequate funds to buy the materials. And the Squire who had put up monies for the original kite had turned his attention and resources to the purchase of a motorised carriage from the brothers and for which he was waiting for delivery.

If father grieved the loss of the kite he did well to disguise it. He dedicated his spare time to stripping the engine down to its shell with Timothy lending a hand. The workbench in the stable became a display of valves, rockers, collets and springs, pistons and connecting rods, journals and the crankcase. There was an assortment of gear wheels and a gadget called a magneto that supplied electricity to the sparking plugs. They took apart and cleaned the sophisticated fuel/air mixture control, and marvelled at its tapered throat and precisely made jets whose purpose was to supply exact quantities of the liquid spirit in the chain of fuelling the engine.

Timothy would have enjoyed the messy work on the engine had there been some prospect of fitting it to another kite. He rather hoped father's initiative and ingenuity would come to the fore. But as the days and weeks drifted by it looked as if their future attempts at flight were doomed. He often saw the ghost of the old kite as he worked alongside father on the engine in the empty stable. The delicate wings and the ribs showing through the taut calico, the specks of dust clinging to the rows of wing struts, the diagonal runs of rigging that issued a deep bass note when plucked by a finger. Father's empty wicker seat and the tall wooden control levers and, beneath the wing, the long varnished skids accommodating the axles with twin wheels at each end.

At times work on assembling the engine had to stop and wait the advice of the Carlton brothers who had got into a habit of visiting the cottage every Saturday afternoon. Father had built up quite a rapport with them, and Timothy suspected they came as much for social reasons as for the more obvious of checking father's progress with the rebuild of the engine. After an hour of serious discourse about the engine father invited them indoors to partake of a couple of jugs of ale. Informal conversation normally followed, and bouts of laughter grew more frequent as the men exchanged jokes, which he did not quite understand. The brothers invariably took their leave, glowing in the face and talking louder than normal.

To spare them the embarrassment of his presence, when they were on the ale, Timothy took to going out on the downs with the dogs and the model kite. Father fitted the model kite with additional lead weights and had instructed him to observe its behaviour, and to also adjust the position of the weights and note any improvements in its conduct of flight.

During one such flight, after he altered the position of the weights, the model flew from his hand and rose up in a long gentle curve. Then just as it almost came to a halt in mid flight it tilted forward and picked up speed. And just when he thought it would strike ground it collected itself and rose back to the heights. A succession of dives and climbs it was to repeat until it came to rest at the base of the hill.

He carried out three more launches with the model, noting the exact position of the weights, growing more excited as it dawned on him the kite had led him to an important discovery. Father had continually reiterated the presence of the undesirable 'drop' that plucked a craft from the air, and out of the control of the aerial steersman. It was something to be avoided like the plague. But Timothy was now convinced that it was possible to recover from the 'drop' providing there was remaining height to do so.

Father congratulated him heartily for his observations but confounded the issue by stating the 'drop' had advantages as well as disadvantages. He claimed it could be used to bring the kite back to earth with more decorum if instigated a couple of feet above the ground.

Another week passed without father making any apparent mention or making any effort to find funds to construct another kite. He appeared more concerned with completing the assembly of the engine and mounting it on a stand brought over by the brothers. Much to the surprise of everyone concerned the engine started at the first flurry of turns on the starting handle. And many congratulations were exchanged when it performed better than of late. For father it made up in a big way for the loss of the kite; the old smile lurked about his mouth and there was a twinkle in his eyes. He proudly announced to the brothers that the experience he had gained on assembling the engine had done much to improve his knowledge.

Timothy thought it all well and good to be talking about the engine when, above all else, they had no kite to accommodate it. He wished he could have measured up to father's calm cheerfulness but inwardly, he seethed with an impatience and restlessness that had been inherited from mother. It reached a point where he seriously considered approaching the Squire, Mr. Sawyer and the Carlton brothers and asking them to make a financial contribution to building another kite. He rehearsed over a number of days what he should say to them because he had a feeling that father would not approve. Rather more he would regard it as begging: something he and mother had always been loath to do.

On the eve' of making his approaches to the three parties, suitably prepared after several practices of his speeches, in the cottage, father arrived home from the estate one evening, his work bag slung over his shoulders, and a roll of papers tucked under an arm. He came in, smiling, to the usual excited greetings of the dogs. "Our patience has been rewarded, my boy." he announced jubilantly. He hurried around disposing of his bag and topcoat, and washing his hand under the kitchen tap. Timothy served him a bowl of stew he'd prepared for his homecoming. But he pushed it aside and unrolled the papers and weighted them down with an assortment of table accoutrements.

The skeleton of a craft of the air, drawn in three dimensions, looked up at them. A closer inspection revealed that it copied the outlines of their original kite but contained enough subtle difference to cover up the poaching intentions of the draughtsman. Timothy eyed it suspiciously. "This is not your design father!"

"Quite so, my boy. In fact Mr. Fanshaw has invited me to construct it for him."

"Mr. Fanshaw!" Timothy exclaimed. The name brought to mind the image of a short fat man with predator-set eyes who had sneaked around the kite on the day of the annual fete and who, during their introduction at the manor, last Christmas had failed to account for his knowledge and experience of manned flight.

"The man is a cheat, a fraudster father. He would go to any lengths to poach other persons' ideas and invention and claim credit for himself."

Father mused awhile, his eyes wandering over the drawings. "Whatever he may be, my son. I regret we have little choice. Beggars cannot be choosers, is the position in which we find ourselves."

The drawings were expertly presented with each part described in neat printed letters. "And did these also come from Fanshaw's hand?"

"No. He gave the details to the Carlton brothers to draw for him."

Timothy laughed sarcastically. "Father, do you not see he is manipulating each and everyone of you!"

"My son, you may argue till you are blue in the face. The truth is – we either accept this opportunity or possibly lose our last and only chance to take to the air again."

"Father, the kite, as portrayed on the drawings, will not take to the air and it will give him the satisfaction of proving you are anything but a pioneer of flight. He is envious of your successes to date and would gladly put you down."

Father eyed him sympathetically. "Your imagination is running away with you." he said. "I have signed a legal document in which I have agreed to construct the powered kite for him, and to hand it over directly we have proved that it can fly. In return he will pay me a certain of money plus all expenses for any extra tools we may require. And to show his good intentions he has provided me with a substantial monetary deposit."

"And should the venture fail, I suspect you will have to return all the monies."

Father sighed heavily, "We will make certain it will not fail. Unless of course you are not going to back me and choose to be argumentative like your mother."

Timothy smiled; it was the first direct reference to her since she left the family home. "Is it such a bad thing, father. After all I am only trying to protect your reputation."

Father drew himself erect and looked him straight in the eye, "Are you? Or are you not? Prepared to help me construct another kite." he said bluntly, in much the same way he addressed mother when she pushed him into a corner.

"I think that goes without saying, father. Though I must urge you to consider altering the flaws in the design."

"Come then clever Dick. Show me the faults."

Timothy pointed to the drawings, "The wings are curved on both the top and bottom surfaces. Your demonstrations in the river that day suggested the curvature need only be on the top surface to encourage the wing to lift. If therefore the bottom surface is curved would it not suggest the lift will be in the opposite direction and in so doing equal the lift on the top surface. The wing would remain neutral and not lift. Am I correct?"

"A valid consideration. What else concerns you?"

Timothy ran a finger over a drawing, "Compared to the original kite the tail and rudder are too close behind the wing."

"So?"

"Is there not a possibility the air streams trailing from the wings would disrupt the air streams over the tail and render it ineffective?"

" It could be argued that the solitary paddle fitted to the engine will provide sufficient backwash to the tail and smooth out the irregularities you mention."

"Possibly so, father. But might it also affect the balance?"

"The balance!"

"You have always maintained there is a difference between balance and control, and you also said that it was the ignorance of this fact that led to grandfather Willy's and Mr. Lilienthal's premature demise. If the engine failed in flight I would wager the kite would suffer a great imbalance."

Father looked at him proudly, "Your knowledge has come a long way, my boy. What else do you wish to dispute."

"I seriously ponder on whether the single paddle will produce enough force to impart motion to the kite knowing, as we do, the old kite would not depart the earth using two paddles."

Father looked down at the drawings, "It could be argued the single paddle, connected direct to the engine shaft, will rotate at a greater number of revolutions creating a force of two paddles. Of a further benefit the absence of the shafts chains and sprockets would mean we would have less weight to take aloft." He broke off to reheat the bowl of stew; it had gone cold in their discussion. He turned back to the boy. "You are entitled to your opinion of Mr. Fanshaw. But you must realise that if we refuse to build the kite for him there are others who would rise to the challenge."

Timothy regarded it as blackmail. "Father, that may be so. They would not, however, be capable of getting a craft into the air. And should there be gifted engineers, like the Carlton brothers, in your considerations, you would do well to remember their work involves tangible metal, objects. They would fail miserably in tackling the invisible intricacies of the air. And they would admit to it."

Father brought the reheated bowl of stew back to the table, "Then, do I take you are prepared to take on, with me, all the challenges of this new venture and cast aside all of your reservations concerning Mr. Fanshaw?"

Timothy said; "I accept out of my respect for you father and grandfather Willy. And on condition we build the kite to our design."

Father sat before the bowl of stew, spoon poised, "You drive a hard bargain." he grinned and fell upon the stew with a ravenous appetite.

SEVEN

The huge black cauldron stood empty upon the grill of the vacant fire pit. The large bellows, used to pump the fire, hung forlornly on a nearby wall. The top of the work bench, once hidden beneath a layer of wood dust and shavings, stood clear to view, its drawers crammed with plumb bobs, spirit levels, straight edges and inclinometers. Shelves above the bench displayed pots and jars, remnants of nails, screws, glue, wood stain, varnish and needles and thread. A mallet, hammer, a small and large planer, a fine and coarse toothed saw, a pair of pincers, and master shapes to check the accuracy of the workmanship, hung on nails driven into the stable wall. It all provided a neat and tidy background to the new kite that looked resplendent in its lightly-waxed fresh white calico, sturdy tan coloured struts and skids, sparkling spoke wheels and black tyres and the dark shape of the engine lit up by its many brass and copper fittings.

It had taken twelve weeks and, as Timothy predicted, a small army of people to construct the kite, employing the services of Mr. Pook, the village carpenter, Mr. Cutler the village smithy, Mrs. Pettifodder, a seamstress, and the Carlton brothers. A construction that had not been without its share of trials and tribulations since father insisted on carrying out several refinements learnt from their experience with the original kite.

A further five feet had been added to the span of the wings, father claiming it would reduce the overall loading on the wings caused by the burdensome weight of the oil engine. The haberdashery at Compton did not hold enough calico in stock and the kindly Carlton brothers drove to Oxbridge to collect the extra that was required. Father also decided to use piano wire in place of the twine for the wing rigging, and for the linkage between the control levers and rudder bar and the moveable surfaces on the wings and tail. This also proved to be in short supply and the brothers went off on another long jaunt to acquire it.

In another attempt to reduce the weight father came up with the idea of making lightening holes in the wing ribs, a feature he copied from his studies of the hollow bone structure of a bird, and which grandfather also made mention of in his observations. By the same token father was not totally at ease as to whether the holed ribs would stand up to the hidden and unpredictable stresses and strains of flight if weakened by the reduction in rigidity. He consulted Mr. Pook on the matter and between them they evolved a compromise by marginally increasing the thickness of the ribs and ensuring the grain in the wood ran in a certain direction.

Mrs. Pettifodder was considered a seamstress of merit, but her advancing years and ailing sight made her painfully slow in her work. Timothy had to collect her and transport her to the cottage at every convenient opportunity. She mainly stayed all day Saturday and Sunday and always came in the same black dress and fingerless gloves, carrying a small chest containing a vast array of needles, thimbles, thread and small tools. The more she grew familiar with the unusual nature of the work the more she grew adept at stitching the calico to the wing framing and ribs. Father claimed the stitching drew the calico more taut compared to the glue they had used on the old kite. Mrs. Pettifodder overlaid the stitching with narrow bands of glued tape that did much to enhance the finish of her work and smarten the image of the kite.

Before they fitted the engine to the kite father wisely decided to run it again on its stand. He was eager to check if it could sustain power over a longer period of time and without blighting the calico with stains from oil leaks, a shortcoming on the original kite, which Timothy remembered only too well. As it happened the engine performed admirably, much to the astonishment of them all. It ran non-stop for two hours at high revolutions, not misbehaving once throughout or losing power. The Carlton brothers jovially accused father of feeding it with a secret medicine during his overhaul of the engine.

Father's precaution to run the engine on the stand was to spare them, yet again, from a disaster when he fitted the new paddles to the engine, in turn, to check if all was well. Only minutes after running the engine with the first paddle, the stitching that held the canvas to the framing broke loose, followed shortly after by the canvas flying away from the framing. The second paddle fared little better; the hub of the paddle split in two and both parts deserted the engine shaft at great speed. It needed little reasoning to deduct that had the engine been fitted to the kite it was certain the errant paddle would have wrought havoc by puncturing the calico of a wing or possibly two.

They tried the third paddle, a day later, and run it at half engine speed and although it remained intact father said the kite would never get into the air using the reduced power. He made a tentative attempt to increase the revolutions slowly. All was well for time. Then a solitary loud cracking sound, they all cowered as a blade snapped from the hub and spun in the air before coming to earth on the other side of the cottage. The engine went berserk with vibration and Mr. Robert beat father to switching it off.

Father was to spend sleepless night after sleepless night going through his papers on flight in a search for a solution to their problem. And Timothy did not delude himself that it was a very serious problem. Father showed him a paper that reported a Mr. Clement Ader had made a steam engine that powered a propeller. But there was no detailed drawings or written indications as to how it was achieved.

The days slipped by, the crisis unresolved. Father sent the Carlton brothers to Mr. Fanshaw to explain the delivery date of the kite would need to be put back due to a small mechanical problem. Timothy felt deeply concerned and threatened by the delay, for was it not him who had argued with father to make changes in the design – and now this. The boot would be on the other foot now and he had visions of Mr. Fanshaw, in public, posing with a sardonic grin, accusing him and father of being cheats and fraudsters. There was every chance he would report it to the Brunton News and the whole world would mock father. His reputation in the village and on the estate would undergo a drastic change in the eyes and hearts of many.

Trapped and hemmed in by the gloomy and alarming prospects, Timothy took to riding on the downs to escape the doomed atmosphere of the cottage and the frustrating impotence of the kite. He wished earnestly for something to come to father's aid and solve his problem with the engine paddle. And when nothing happened in the following days his despair deepened, particularly when he overheard father talking to the Carltons preparing them with another excuse to convey to Fanshaw concerning the delay in handing over the kite.

Then, of an afternoon, as Paddy jogged him homewards after an energetic gallop across the downs, he was passing through a stretch of woodland when, quite by chance, he spotted an object spiralling gracefully down from a tree, its descent carefully controlled by the screwing motion of its flight. He goaded Paddy to the spot where it came down, and dismounted, to find two tenuous rounded-tip blades from a sycamore tree. He threw the joined blades into the air several times and watched in fascination as they spiralled lazily back to earth each time, balanced and in control of their destiny. Something told him they were a clue to their need for a paddle for the kite. He raced around searching for more sycamore blades and raced for home.

By the time father arrived home that evening he had paired up six sets of the blades, each set having the blades set at a different pitch, ranging from fine to coarse pitch. He stood on the kitchen table and dropped them one by one and noted the characteristics of the differing modes of descent, some mastering the descent more efficiently than others. Timothy explained his theory that the sycamores gave an important clue to the requirements of an effective paddle for the kite and was enough proof that the paddle should be of solid construction, have rounded tips and whose blades must be of a certain pitch. The pitch would have to be worked out by experiment.

Father stroked his chin thoughtfully and took the blades outside the cottage and threw them skywards in turn and observed for himself the various speeds and mannerisms of their descending flight.

Within a matter of hours he drew up detailed drawings and placed an order with Mr. Pook to carve three paddles from solid wood, horizontally opposed blades, slim, and each paddle having a slight variation in the angle of the blades. Timothy did not care that he was left very much out of the negotiations; he was more concerned that they outwit Fanshaw and preserve father's reputation.

They collected the first propeller, as father now decided to refer to it, a week later, from Mr. Pook's small workshop. Father was of the opinion the new name was more in keeping with the fact the component was intended to propel the kite through the air. Hence its name, propeller. Mr. Pook led them to a bench, removed a dust cover and there looking up at them was a master piece of workmanship. Carved from a solid piece of wood, from a central hub the blades on either side flowed out, twisting evenly in opposite directions and tapering slightly toward the rounded tips. Stained and polished on completion the grain of the wood rose up with a pride and dignity that only becomes a work of art. The aging craftsman looked on, proudly, his frame bent by hours spent over his workbench, his eyes requiring spectacles to maintain the perfection of his work. "I 'av checked the dimensions many times, Samuel," he said. "And they tally exactly with yer drawings."

Father ran a hand along the smooth, rising falling curves of the propeller that measured exactly six feet in diameter. "You have done me real proud, Tom. I am much obliged. Is it too much to ask when the other two will be ready?"

"All being well, Saturday next."

Father beamed his gratitude, and Timothy suspected he received the news with a huge sigh of relief; Fanshaw could not be put off forever. Father pressed four florins into the palm of Mr. Cutler's hand, and closed the fingers over the coins. "It is more than we agreed. But you deserve it for the long hours of labour and the expediency you afforded my order."

Mr. Pook made to protest the sum was too much. Father would have none of it and changed the subject and asked for material to wrap the propeller. They departed shortly after with Paddy pulling the trap and the propeller secreted in the folds of hessian sacking.

Their next dilemma was how they should secure the propeller to the engine shaft. The wood and canvas paddle had merely been a push fit on a straight shaft. But having witnessed the paddles break free, father felt something more substantial was needed. He consulted Mr. Cutler, and in conjunction with his resourcefulness, and the engineering expertise of the Carlton brothers, a tapered extension, forged to the engine shaft, was designed with a key and key way. Mr. Pook made a small alteration to the propeller hub and with Mr. Cutler inserted a metal core also having a key way cut in it. The principle was that of lock and key, locking the propeller to the shaft. Father, however, was not totally convinced. He argued that too much was at stake; he could not afford an injury to the kite should the propeller break loose. He insisted there should be a standby device should the key and key way fail.

After a great deal of discussion on the matter, Mr. Cutler and the Carltons cut a thread on the engine shaft extension and fitted a castellated nut through which a hole was drilled to accommodate a pin which stopped the nut undoing.

The static running tests of the propeller on the stand were to prove much beyond their expectations. The smooth finish of the propeller took a lot of strain off of the engine, reducing the vibration, and the increased backwash was powerful enough to knock a man off his feet standing to the rear of it. As it was,

Timothy lost his cap to its powerful blast of air, and the engine would surely have tipped over on the stand, several times, had the engine revolutions not been moderated.

In the past the noise of the engine had been wearisome enough. The solid wooden propeller added to the nuisance with an ear-splitting, high-pitched tone, causing Timothy to spend much of the time plugging his ears with a finger. Father and the Carltons ran the noisy, irksome beast of engineering over a three-hour period, stopping it every hour to check the propeller attachment for fractures and security of the propeller to the shaft.

For some time after the engine had completed the tests they all suffered a temporary deafness. After a prolonged silence the dogs rushed from their hidden sanctuary in the cottage, and drew up before the kite barking furiously, daring the engine to resume its bedlam. The engine's refusal to react calmed them down and they wagged their tails and rubbed their cold noses in Timothy's hands. He tried to draw them closer to the engine to demonstrate it meant no harm. They dug their heels in and pulled at his coat sleeves for him to follow them to the paddock which had the effect of reminding him to check how the horses had fared the three hour offensive noise of the engine and propeller. They came to the gate to receive an apple and a reassuring pat that all was well. Then wandered off to graze quietly in the middle of the paddock in company with a pair of mischievous magpies.

The men laboured right up to nightfall to transfer the engine from the stand to the kite, a task requiring many strong hands and a good helping of planning to prevent an accident, and to position it on the centre section, exactly to father's drawings. He persisted in saying that any error in the location of the engine would seriously affect the balance of the kite. It was as well he had engineers and craftsmen like the Carltons and Messrs. Pook and Cutler to assist him and who shared his meticulous and fastidious method of working. Timothy was instructed to fetch lighted lanterns to aid them in the rapidly fading daylight to make the final bolting down of the engine on the center section.

On completion of the work father invited them all into the cottage. And rewarded them with jars of ale and a supper of thickly-sliced ham, poached eggs and cobs of bread, and butter; the long hard day and the promises of the propeller had whipped up a healthy thirst and appetite. Timothy helped father by acting at their beck and call to carve more ham, poach more eggs, slice bread, and refill their jars of ale. Five red-eyed lined faces sat around the table. Five dedicated menfolk who had lost so much sleep over the weeks to help give birth to the kite. They now sat as a conglomerate of intellect and skill numbed by fatigue, eating to restore their strength and drinking in celebration of their joint success.

Suddenly father rose up out of the gathering hunched around the table. "Gentlemen," he called. "It would please me to propose a toast. The first of which is to you all for your unstinting help in bringing the latest kite into being. I say, in all humbleness, that without your respective skills and advice I would, at this moment of time, be nothing more than a stranded mariner." He raised his mug of ale, "My very grateful thanks to you all."

Their appreciation for his compliment showed distinctly in the faces of the aging smithy and carpenter. Whilst the Carlton brothers dismissed it by saying, that the success they had all enjoyed so far would never have come about, had father not led them in his enthusiastic pursuit to unravel the mysteries of the air and prove that manned flight is possible.

Father acknowledged their modesty with a grin and said, "I would also like to propose a toast to my son, Timothy, whose contribution to the design of the propeller, we must all agree, rescued us from the brink of defeat."

"Here, here!" Mr. Robert shouted.

"Without a doubt!" his brother added.

Timothy felt the colour rise to his face as the expressions of admiration focused on him.

"It goes without saying," father continued. "That I am honoured to have such a gifted boy who has proved beyond all doubt that he has inherited the pioneering spirit of the Herby family. And is fitting tribute to his late grandfather, Willy, who perished so young and prematurely in his attempts to advance the knowledge of manned flight. He raised his jar, "To Timothy!"

"To Timothy." the others chorused, raising their jars.

The boy cringed, grateful for the dim light of the oil lamps that did something to disguise his acute embarrassment. As quickly he was drawn back into the spotlight when, after take a fill of ale, Mr. Robert shouted: "Speech!" he insisted. "Speech!"

At first Timothy faltered. "Gentlemen." he coughed to clear a tickle in his throat. "I...I...I can think of little to add to what father has already conveyed to you. Only, perhaps, to thank you myself for your invaluable assistance and boundless skills in helping us build the latest kite and who I must include Mrs. Pettifodder whose skill with needle and thread has brought a great credit to the finish of the kite. I thank you graciously, each and every one of you. In closing my speech I want all of you to know that if I am all that father claims me to be it is because he has shown me much charity throughout my life. His examples of strength and perseverance in times of overwhelming difficulty, both in connection with the kites, and here in our home, especially when my mother deserted us, has given me much to live up to. I trust I will not disappoint you, father."

The room echoed to cheers and a round of applause. He sat down, trembling, to a hefty slap on the back by Mr. Charles. "Well said, Timothy! Well said."

"What a relief it was when the focus of attention left him and the men resumed conversation amongst themselves, lighting pipe and cigar. Very soon the smoke hung thick against the lamps. Father fetched another flaggon of ale from the cold stone floor of the larder. The men began to drink in earnest.

Timothy found an excuse to escape by taking the dogs for a run; he was conscious of ruining the men's' fun by being in their company and overhearing comments and jokes not meant for his ears. He ran the dogs up to the summit of Pritchards hill in time to hear the distant blaring of a coachman's horn. He squinted into the depths of the darkness and spotted two pinpricks of light creeping past Four Mile cross, heading northwards. He knew by the time of day that it was the night express taking the mail, a prestigious service equipped with the best of drivers, and sure-footed mounts, to cope with the blind navigation of the highways. He watched the lights slow a little as the unseen coach made the long climb to Pilleys Ridge. At the top another swift overture from the horn and the lights slipped from view on the other side of the ridge. And it was gone.

He ambled back to the cottage, enjoying the smell of dry grass, the balmy silence and the view of the scattered stars twinkling overhead. He thought of Yarpy and wondered if he had got his promotion to a coach and six, yet. He thought of Mollie Langdon and Marie Sawyer; he felt lonely and would rather like to spend time alone with them; Mollie's curving anatomy appealed to him, and he had not forgotten the sweet, succulent taste of Marie's compelling lips. This in turn made him think of his parents and their severed relationship. He ached for them to patch up their differences and reunite the family. It was inconceivable that two intelligent, mature persons could not live rationally with one another, and it puzzled him deeply. A loud detonation pursue by a constant train of clattering startled the hollowness of the night air, destroying his train of thought; the Carltons were preparing to depart the cottage in their motorised carriage. He arrived in time to see father helping the staggering carpenter and smithy up on the running board into the back seat. Mr. Charles waved an arm in the air, honked the horn several times and released the brake. The carriage lurched forward accompanied by another detonation. It travelled about fifty paces and fell away over the brow of the hill and headed for the village, way down there in the depths, to take Mr. Cutler and Mr. Pook to their homes before heading northwards to the home of the brothers.

Father put an arm around his shoulders as they watched and waited for the carriage to fade into obscurity. And as it did so father said, "A cheerful ending to a long hard day, my boy. And the annual fete ahead of us tomorrow. Time we got abed."

It was then that Timothy noticed the heavy weight of his arm, his tired speech and a slight stagger to his step as they headed for the cottage; the ale had taken its toll. Timothy helped him into the bedroom where father fell on to the bed fully clothed. The boy quietly took a coverlet from a closet and covered him, and extinguished the lamp.

*　　*　　*

Needless to say certain individuals suffered a sore head next morning and struggled for a time to perform their duties at the annual fete. Timothy was allocated to the task of receiving guests who lived outside the estate and the village and who began to arrive, in a steady stream of carriages, after midday. At about two of the clock his mind seemed to explode with shock. His thoughts and feelings ran amok; he did not know whether to laugh or cry. In fact he felt quite,

quite helpless. It was the burgundy-coloured gown that first caught his eye and the soft leather bag hung over a cuff as the lady lowered her head to exit the carriage. Then as he took her hand to help her descend from the carriage he came face to face with mother. The gown had been a present from father four years past. Surely she must still have feelings for him to be wearing it that day. He stood gaping at her.

"Are you not pleased to see me, my dear son."

He unfroze slowly. "But of course, mother." he drew her away from the carriage, asking her to excuse him a while longer so that he could assist other disembarking passengers and for him to give instructions to the driver where to park his carriage and obtain feed and water for the mounts.

Eventually he turned to her. "You have lost weight, Timothy." she smiled.

He grinned at her, "But I am taller than you."

She continued smiling out from the shadows of her winged bonnet.

He said: "Do you know father has carried out many flights?"

"I did read something about it in the Brunton News."

"I, too, have been aloft on my own, mother."

She smiled ruefully, "But you have not scored so well at school, I am reliably informed."

Her change of subject and the criticism of his schoolwork irked him at first. But suddenly an idea came to him and he said: "What else could you expect, when you were not at home to help me, mother."

His remark struck deep in her feelings and she reeled back, a flash of anger in her eyes that briefly lit up her sharp sculptured nose and the grim expression of her mouth. She said: "I compliment you for your wit, my son," and as was her habit to maintain the upper hand in any conversation or situation she added, "But I must caution you about the sharpness of your tongue when addressing your superiors."

He did not comment. As far as he was concerned he had nipped her criticism of his school reports neatly in the bud. He thought she knew that too.

For so slight a stature she was a formidable woman. Her desertion of him and father, and her absence from the estate, had done little to change her, as he was to discover during the course of her visit. She bribed the young, innocent Bobby Laverty with three pennies to take on the task of receiving the guests and their carriages, and had Timothy accompany her to the back lawn and the paddock where the activities and celebrations were taking place. She walked with an arm through his, head held high, a look of defiance in her nut-brown eyes, her chin thrust forward in determination. And not at all put out by numerous acquaintances who turned away and refused to acknowledge her presence because she had abandoned her young son and her hard-working, popular husband.

There were others who held strong reservations concerning her intentions, her cunning dominance to get her own way, her shrewd moves to get involved where she was not wanted, wreak havoc on a host of emotions, and walk away, claiming it was not of her doing. Such as she did when she and Timothy came across the Squire and Lady Hadley on the back lawn. Compliments of the day were exchanged, with mother congratulating them on the arrival of their long-awaited treasured offspring, a perfectly natural and courteous comment. As was the proud Lady Hadley's offer to take mother to introduce her to the infant: a move she was, later, to deeply regret in the trail of devastation that ensued.

They gathered around the cradle in the nursery and mother peered in closely at the baby Samantha, crowned with fair hair, and who looked out at the world with bright blue eyes and in greeting with a warm, contented smile.

"Do I detect features of the Herby line in this child?" mother said casually but whose comment slashed through the calm atmosphere of the room with the viciousness of a knife thrust, causing a tense, uneasy silence.

The squire's face darkened. Lady Hadley smiled diffidently and said, "How absurd, Rebecca. Whatever gave you such a notion?"

"Ladies!" the squire raised a hand. "I think Timothy should leave the room."

"Why so?" mother responded positively. "He should stay on account of what I have to say about his father."

"I protest!" the squire shouted.

Lady Hadley, on calculating the growing ugliness of the situation, said, "Very well, Rebecca. Say your piece and kindly take your leave."

Mother said haughtily, "Rumour has been circulating in Brunton market for several months. Began, so I am told, by a band of travelling folk." She hesitated.

"Continue, Rebecca." Lady Hadley challenged her.

Mother said, "Gossip has it that Samuel spent an evening of festivities with these folk in the company of a lady whose speech and manners were far removed from that of a commoner. From the description afforded to me I would suggest that lady was you, Lady Hadley."

Timothy expected Lady Hadley to deny it. Therefore it came as a huge shock when she said: "What if I were to admit to it and say the Squire had full knowledge of this social liaison. What say you then, Rebecca?"

Mother's eyes blazed with anger, "And was the Squire also aware that you and Samuel behaved improperly in full view of these simple people, by holding hands and kissing on the mouth?"

Lady Hadley said: "Have I not told you already, Rebecca, the Squire is quite aware of what happened that evening."

Then mother delivered the shattering blow, "Is he also aware that you and Samuel committed an adulterous act on the banks of the trout streams: an act witnessed by Jake Howson, a notorious poacher of these parts. That was when you conceived this child, was it not?"

The squire turned away and stood looking through an adjacent window, hunched, defeated the pained figure of a man. Lady Hadley stood her ground but was unable to hide the colour draining from her face, and her trembling lips

Father arrived at that moment searching for Timothy to help him at the fete. Lady Hadley, trying to cope with tears trickling down her face, said, "You have arrived at an opportune time, Samuel. Rebecca has important news for you. I beg of you to remove her from this room forthwith."

Ruthless to the end, mother said: "I trust in future you will not distract Samuel from his duties on the estate, Lady Hadley. The likes of Jake Howson, as you have leant to your cost, can cause endless damage to one's reputation."

For Timothy it was only the start to what was to be a day of incidents. Father dismissed him when they reached the grounds of the manor, saying he and mother had very serious matters to discuss. They would meet up with him later.

He wandered amongst the array of amusement stalls and sideshows in the bright sunshine, only taking in half of what was going on. Time and time again the scene and conversation in the nursery flashed across his mind. Did it mean, he asked himself, that father, not the squire, was, in fact, the father of the infant Samantha? If so it would indicate father had violated the sacred cloisters of Lady Hadley's body to affect the conception of a child. And that, according to his learning at Sunday school, was a cardinal sin if two persons were not joined together in holy matrimony. He laughed at the absurdity of it all. No, it could not be true. Father and Lady Hadley were too sensible and upright to succumb to such an immoral temptation. A speculation that was to reverse itself drastically later in the day and bring home to him the frailties of both male and female gender when consumed by a confusing blend of lust and passion.

Molly Langdon, on the pretence of wanting to show him something, lured him away from the fete and had him take her in the deserted orchard. And before he had a chance to enquire after the reasons for so private a venue she embraced and kissed him feverishly. She led his hands to her intimate parts and, in turn, displayed parts of her anatomy that he had only ever seen clothed before. Then she explored him, reaching inside his tunic and forcing her hand down below the belt of his breeches...

"Who goes there!" the voice came like a bolt out of the blue. Intended for him or not, he forced himself away from Mollie, and ran like the wind, fighting to secure his bulging breeches.

He wandered around the stable yard to compose himself. It would be a long time before he forgot the adventure with Mollie; just the thought of what he had seen and touched aroused him deeply just as did the manner in which she had groped and fondled him.

The daylight was fading when he made his way back to the fringes of the back lawn where figures had gathered to watch others dancing on the lawn to the lively music of a regimental band, in the light of lanterns hung in overhanging trees and nearby shrubbery.

"What a pity that Samuel and Rebecca are unable to reconcile their differences," the words arrested Timothy as he made to pass to the rear of two ladies in conversation. He recognised the voice of Mrs. Peach, the pastor's wife and, presently, that of Miss. Crossley, a teacher at Hadley school.

"I think Rebecca and Samuel would succeed if they took up residence elsewhere." Miss Crossley said. "It would remove Samuel from Lady Hadley's influence."

The Pastor's wife looked around cautiously and in low tones said: "Do you think they are having an affair?"

Miss Crossley moved closer, "I would not like to be accused of making such a suggestion. But I have noticed she hangs on to his every word and action, much in the manner of a brooding mare."

The pastor's wife said, "There are rumours emanating from Brunton, which suggest Samuel sired the Hadley's offspring."

"Tut-tut," Miss Crossley said severely, "We must be extremely wary of malicious gossip. The person I feel sorry for, is young Timothy."

He moved away, dismayed and embarrassed by the thought of the family having become embroiled in the subject of gossip. He felt stigmatised and tainted by it all.

He came upon father and mother in conversation with Doctor Markham. He crept close enough to hear, but without them seeing him And standing to the rear of them at a discreet distance was the Squire and Lady Hadley taking note of the conversation.

"Have you heard the news, Rebecca, that Samuel is on the verge of proving that manned flight is possible." doctor Markham said.

Timothy cringed; they had yet to prove the effectiveness of the propeller in flight. And how come the doctor had got wind of their latest kite; the written agreement between father and Fanshaw stipulated the kite must be constructed under a cloak of secrecy, and to be handed over on completion without father carrying out any public displays.

"Samuel is capable of many feats, doctor Markham." mother said. "Though I strongly suspect others will take credit for his aerial experiments. Just as the officers who took the honours for his bravery when he served with the colours."

Father did not stir; he stood beside her, erect, silent.

"As you are well aware, he served with distinction in the African campaigns." she continued. "When he made that daring and courageous mission to rescue troopers and their officers from being beheaded or boiled alive. His reward for such gallantry – a brief mention in the London Gazette."

"A matter of carrying out my duties." father reminded her quietly.

"Quite so – quite so." doctor Markham remarked. "Modesty is the key quality of a gentleman, Rebecca. Be grateful and proud that you have such a fine man as a husband."

Determined as ever to have the last word mother said, "That may be so. But it is not justice where justice is due."

Father coaxed her to move on, exchanging a sly wink with the doctor as he did so and which was exposed by a sudden train of explosions and flashes of light that momentarily lit up the entire gathering on the back lawn. The explosions and flashes continued and marked the finale of the annual fete with the traditional firework display. The night sky reverberated, flashed and shrieked to the searing passage of rocket and firecracker, streaking in all directions, bursting red, blue, green and orange stars against the black wall of the night sky. Great cascades of coloured sparks rained down, melting into obscurity before reaching the ground.

Timothy had heard tell that some strategists were considering the use of more powerful flying projectiles as a source of weapon in battle. Many argued it would bolt the horses. He found himself pondering on the use of rockets to power a machine into the air, a notion inspired by the coloured missiles hurtling apace up there before him. A hand came to rest on his shoulder and he turned to find father at his side, "Your mother has expressed a wish for us to return her to Brunton in the trap." he said.

"Why not to the cottage with us, father?"

"The time is not yet ripe for that, my boy. Kindly respect my judgement and take one step at a time."

Timothy left him and made his way up the slow, winding hill to the cottage, pausing occasionally to turn and watch the continuation of the firework display. On reaching the top of the hill he whistled to Paddy to come to the gate of the paddock. His dark, limbering shape materialised obediently. An obedience that quickly changed to reluctance when he discovered what was intended for him, the distant flashing reports adding to his unease. Fetching a hand across his muzzle and delivering some hefty slaps to his hind quarters, were necessary to get him to wear a bridle and into the shafts of the trap. Something that Timothy was loath to do but which father had taught was the only way of demonstrating to certain mounts, who was in charge.

In an odd way Paddy shared a similar temperament with mother: forever fretful and determined to put his stamp of authority on the wishes of others. To the very end he lunged and backed whilst Timothy fixed and lighted the lamps on the sideboards of the trap. He quickly moderated his behaviour when he sensed father was approaching. The loitering dogs growled and withdrew at the imminent presence of mother who appeared over the brow of the hill with father.

"Are we ready, my boy?"

"Yes, father." He turned to mother. "Would you object to the dogs riding with us, mother? After all they are part of the family."

"Providing they do not soil my dress."

He called to the dogs who made a wide berth of mother before they leapt into the trap and sat obediently with their fore paws draped over the lip of the front board. Father helped mother embark and gave her a rug. Then he let Yorkie out the paddock, ordering him to follow up in the rear. In the darkness Timothy grinned appreciatively; for the first time in two years they were united as a family and he felt jubilant and secure.

They moved down to Four- Mile Cross and Timothy relaxed the reins a little. Paddy broke into a trot with Yorkie following at a safe distance to the rear. Dark, low-slung shapes of the heath land passed by on either side: silent witnesses to the romping motions of the trap, the jingling noises of the traces and the steady beat of Paddy's hooves on the packed earth of the highway.

An avenue of trees enveloped them for a time. Paddy groped his way through the shadows. But on emerging from the tunnel of foliage he resumed his steady pace. Timothy dared himself to think that mother might be undergoing a change of heart, where her relationship with father was concerned. But from the sparse conversation taking place behind him he did not build his hopes too high.

He reined in on arriving in Brunton. The small town reposed in a sleepy, dark silence, the inhabitants having retired for the night. Father urged him to keep Paddy's pace as slow and quiet as possible on the cobbled streets. After a number of directions mother told him to rein to a halt. She patted him on the back and thanked him for the safe journey.

Timothy said: "I am looking the other way if you should wish to make your farewells." He secretly hoped it would help them to patch up their differences.

On getting no response he turned to find father holding her hand. Timothy caught her smiling in the dim light of the lamps; she possessed a rare brand of beauty when there was a hint of laughter in her soul.

"Good night, Timothy."

"Good night, mother. Thank you for your visit. I trust it will not be long before we meet again."

He sensed his last remark touched her deeply. She stepped down from the rear of the trap with father's help, came around and briefly touched his arm, and walked away toward the dark form of an unlit dwelling. He lost sight of her and father for a time. The impatient Paddy registered his objection by clomping noisily on the cobbled street and snorting rudely.

At last father returned, clambered wordlessly aboard, and Timothy turned Paddy around in a clatter of hooves and headed homewards.

Eight

Hadley and the surrounding lowlands lay dormant beneath floating ribbons of early morning mist whilst the summits of neighbouring hills swam clear to view, above the mist, like a succession of mole hills.

A distant clanking and clattering echoed in the breathless silence. The Carltons' motorised carriage staggered over the peak of Pritchards hill and moved more easily as it descended the winding highway leading to Four Mile Cross. It disappeared at times beneath the draping veils of mist. Mr. Robert sat at the steering wheel, dressed in a long leather coat and flat cap, peering eagerly through his goggles for runts and hollows in the highway surface that he sought to avoid by deft movements on the steering wheel.

On reaching the level ground at the base of the hill he moved a small lever on the steering wheel column. The spluttering engine faded to a whimper. Each hand moved to a larger lever on each side of his seat; he pulled the one to his right and held it, and juggled the other lever with his left hand: the carriage lurched and jolted in the sound of grinding metal. He adjusted the lever on the steering column – a loud retort – and the carriage surged ahead with renewed vigour, improving its speed slightly each time he juggled with the levers to change gear. As they approached the turning at Four-Mile Cross he worked hard at the levers to change to a lower gear and thus slow the carriage. And each time he did so the engine gave a rebellious detonation that could be heard many miles distant.

It turned off the highway to begin the long steep climb to the cottage its pace slackening and being reduced to a jerking motion as it ascended. Mr. Charles vacated the carriage to lighten its load, and helped its hesitant motion by putting his weight behind it. The engine misfired and detonated noisily in its struggle to cope, and began to destroy the peace and tranquillity of the infant day.

Yorkie and Paddy, grazing quietly in the paddock, were suddenly bombarded by the startling noises. They took to their heels and hid behind the solid oaks as protection from the approaching evil, noisy monster.

Timothy heard the distant volleys of sound as he prepared breakfast. He laid a table for four. A pot of porridge simmered on the range and, as the carriage drew closer, he put strips of bacon onto a hot plate. Father came in from the outside earth closet followed by Sniffy who shot between his legs to shelter beneath the kitchen table from the threatening detonations of the approaching carriage. Jeppy, accustomed to the frequent explosive discharges of a 'shoot' accepted the discord of the carriage more rationally. He lounged before the unlit hearth, an ear cocked, an eye trained on the front door, possibly waiting for the order to 'retrieve'.

The carriage arrived outside the front gate of the cottage, lapsing into silence after a frantic chain of misfiring. Father greeted the brothers and they came in smiling, rubbing their hands and commenting on the tasty smell of the grilled rashers. Timothy took their caps and coats, sat them at the table with father, and served the porridge and, later the bacon and eggs and toasted bread and jam. He sat throughout the meal on a stool listening eagerly to them and father discussing the imminent trials with the kite.

Father said he would only attempt short hops with the kite if it should exhibit any desire to get on the wing. He felt it vitally important for him to get the feel of the control levers and to fully acquaint himself with the handling of the engine. The brothers agreed with him wholeheartedly and urged him to ignore Fanshawe's demands that the kite be handed over within the next week with, or without proof, it could take to the air. Timothy quietly fumed on hearing the name of the little fat man mentioned. On a more pleasant note, however, it pleased him to know the brothers were rallying behind father.

He refilled their mugs with tea and left them continuing the conversation, father lighting his pipe and the brothers a manikin cigar, to go and dress. He pulled woolen stockings over his breeches and up to the knee and trod into ankle boots. He slipped a waistcoat over his blouse and tied a muffler in the collar. He proudly put on the flat cap father had presented him with, and which he used exclusively for the kite experiments. He heard the men stirring and he nipped into the paddock and fetched the horses to the back of the cottage and tethered them loosely to tie rings on a wall. The idea was to blank off their view of the kite and at the same time stifle the noisy monstrosity of an engine.

The sun hung like a blazing shield resting on the horizon and shimmering in the mist. They wheeled the kite from the stable to the paddock, to position it in a corner that faced out across the longest stretch of open space. Timothy put the blocks before the wheels. The brothers clambered on to the centre section to attend the engine, and father followed his ritual of going around the kite, generally checking that it was in order, inspecting the calico for sponginess, the struts for security, the tension in the rigging wires, the wheels, the skids. The brothers checked the engine for having the correct amounts of fuel, oil, and water for cooling.

Father took his seat at the control levers. Mr. Robert crouched beside him, ready to give advice on the operation of the engine controls. Behind him his brother knelt, the cranked starting handle to hand and which he began to turn over on an order from his brother. The kite rocked and sprung upon its undercarriage of skids and wheels. Mr. Robert shouted: "Switch on!" And father tripped a switch on a small panel to the left of his seat. Mr. Charles cranked the engine more vigorously and when it did not respond after a number of seconds Mr. Robert reached across in front of father, fractionally moved a small lever on the same panel and slightly turned the top of a small valve. The kite shuddered from nose to tail in the sudden bursting, roaring sound of the engine that suddenly died and, as quickly picked up again and continued this frustrating habit till Mr. Robert made more adjustments on the small panel and valve. It settled down to a steady crescendo of sound, its long, shuddering, copper exhaust pipe shouting defiance to the world. Birds fled in terror from nearby hedgerows and rabbits, nibbling grass further along the paddock, scurried for cover.

After allowing the engine to get warm and for father to obtain more demonstrations from the brothers on how he should regulate the engine, they left the centre section and father signalled to him to remove the wheel blocks.

At full power the kite got under way, attaining a certain pace that it was unable to improve upon. Father made a dozen attempts, trying with different combinations of the control levers to coax the kite into the air. He only succeeded in lumbering across the paddock, making brief attempts to clutch at flight and which consistently ended with him and the kite slumping back to earth like a fledgling being tipped from its nest for first solo.

During a respite at midday to take refreshment the men discussed all the possible reasons for the failings that morning. Father suggested he might have erred by increasing the span of the wings. His theory that the extra span would increase lift was instead adding to the weight and drag. The brothers tactfully said his choice of a solid wooden propeller might also be adding to, rather than subtracting from, their problems.

Timothy, however, was certain as to where the real problems lay, and the remedy so simple he felt it would belittle father if he mentioned it in front of the brothers. He crept out of the cottage, leaving the men in deep discussion, and took a scythe from the rafters of the stable. Within minutes he was scything the unruly grass of the paddock over the hundred pace wide strip they had used that morning. The grass was very high in places and there were dense tufts on which he had frequently stumbled during the experiments with the first kite. He pulled the tufts out by hand.

Very soon he sweated from the urgency of his labours. Father, on emerging from the cottage and learning of his reasoning, congratulated him in the presence of the brothers. He offered to lend a hand and Timothy said: "Prepare the kite father. I only have another fifty paces to complete." he continued weaving the scythe from side to side.

He had returned the scythe to the stable and was dousing his sweating face with water from the garden pump when the engine of the kite broke into life with a noisy gusto of sound and ran relatively smoothly. He got back to the paddock to see the kite moving with more alacrity on the shorn grass. He smiled triumphantly to himself. The brothers stopped trotting by the wing tips as it pulled ahead of them, frequently showing wider gaps of light beneath the wheels each time father got it off the ground. About two-thirds along the paddock the engine switched to low revolutions, the kite lost way, the rudder went over hard and, with a surge of power, it swung around and came limbering back along the paddock.

On his second attempt father had it bouncing much higher and covering greater distances in the air until the engine died yet again and the whole construction succumbed to the invisible forces of gravity.

Back at the start point, in the sound of the spluttering engine, father raised his goggles, massaged his eyes, pulled his cap down more firmly, replaced the goggles, thrust an arm forward and reached blindly for the engine switch. The engine note rose dramatically in unison with the screaming revolutions of the propeller. The kite lunged forward, wings rocking, the juddering wheels, axle and skids echoing through the taut calico of the wings. Father did not hold back this time. At two hundred paces the kite pulled itself away from the brothers running at the wing tips. It careered on toward the opposite boundary without a chance of stopping. It passed the half-way point of the paddock still firmly earthbound. Timothy watched with bated breath, biting his bottom lip; he had visions of it smashing into the boundary hedgerows, possibly catching fire and seriously injuring father.

Suddenly...the kite scrambled into the air, barely clearing the bushes, and went staggering out over the surrounding countryside, rising and falling precariously before ascending cautiously against a background of rolling hills and blue sky. Mr. Robert and Mr. Charles hurried to Timothy, eyes bright with excitement, their moustaches stretched wide in smiles of celebration. They shook hands with such breathless congratulations they found it difficult to speak. Then they stood on each side of him, a hand on his shoulder, and watched incredulously the continuing magic of the kite's suspension in the air, without any visible means for its support.

The dogs, thinking the noisy brute had finally taken its leave, raced into view, leaping over the paddock fence, and came to bark their gratitude and whip the air with their tails in celebration. A state of euphoria that rapidly changed to panic when father turned the kite and headed back and the sound of the engine reached the ground like a swarm of approaching hornets. The dogs immediately fled the scene competing with each other to get over the paddock gate and race for the shelter of the cottage.

Father made the final turn and switched to low revolutions. The kite floated down, the sunlight giving prominence to the white calico and the skeletal ribs and framing beneath it. To Timothy it flew with an immense pride of what it had achieved; it sank through the air with a poise and dignity and as it drew closer it announced its arrival by sounding out a steady gush of air over the wings, and whistling through the rigging. It slipped over a line of Elderberry and Hawthorn, leveled out, whispered past and fell to earth, its tail swinging from side to side.

Father delayed their congratulations until he got back to the cottage end of the paddock. He stopped the engine and jumped down from the centre section. They gathered around him slapping him on the back and shouting their praises. Timothy never ceased to marvel at his modesty; here was a man, his father, having conquered what many eminent persons said was an impossibility, and all he could do by way of celebrating was to light his pipe and suggest a mug of tea would not go amiss. Perhaps a glint in his eye and the hint of a smile gave a clue to his extraordinary feat. That was all. At no point did he make any claims to victory, make any declarations of triumph or make boast of his resounding scientific achievement.

The reasons filtered through that evening when, having dispatched the brothers after suitably rewarding them with several jars of ale for the reliability of their engine, he went and sat on the brow of Hadley hill and lighted his pipe. For a considerable time he stared into space, his pipe clenched between his teeth.

"Is something troubling you, father?" Timothy said, thinking of Fanshawe's recent demands and the recent shock disclosure by mother regarding the origins of the Hadley infant.

He turned slowly, removing the pipe from his mouth. He faked a smile and the reflection of the sunset depicted every crease and wrinkle about his eyes and mouth and a tension high upon his cheekbones. "It concerns me, " he said. "That the kite will not carry two persons unless the engine is made to produce more power."

"Surely that would over-tax the engine, father, and put the kite at risk of another fire."

"That is precisely our dilemma, my boy."

Timothy said, "As I perceive it there are three options available to us. As a first step we could clear a path through the boundary hedgerows to give you a longer run for the launch..."

"That would require the permission of the Squire who, I regret, is not well-pleased with me at the present time."

Timothy did not have to think twice that it was to do with mother's devastating visit. He said: "You also overlooked the fact there was no wind today, father. Might you have escaped the earth in a shorter distance had you launched into wind."

Father massaged his eyes with his fingers, "Very true. But rarely will it blow as and when we want it." He got to his feet, stretched his arms wide and just managed to stifle a yawn with the back of a hand. "If you will excuse me, I am turning in for the night. I have had enough for one day."

Timothy followed his trudging figure back to the cottage. "We could try using either of the other two propellers, father. They may make for an improvement in the kite's performance."

"May be so, my boy. May be so. At the moment all I want to is get my head down."

Timothy spent the remainder of the evening experimenting with the sycamore blades, studying them more closely as he threw them up. And they rotated leisurely back to earth. The present propeller fitted to the kite had a coarse twist to its blades and had been chosen on the premise it would exert a stronger push on the air. Now, as he studied the descending sycamores, he was prompted to think that a less acute twist in the blades might accelerate a broader mass of air and, in so doing, improve the velocity of the kite. Of course it was only a theory and the only way of proving it was to experiment.

By eight of the clock next morning, leaving father still sleeping fitfully, he was down in the village rousing Mr. Cutler. Mrs. Cutler received him cheerfully and he stepped inside her home, ducking beneath the oak beams of the low-slung ceiling. "I apologise for imposing on you so early, Mrs. Cutler. But I need to speak to Mr. Cutler as a matter of urgency."

She showed him through a small back door, leading to a wooden outhouse where he found the old man pottering about on his workbench. He apologised for his intrusion, and said, "I would welcome your advice on how I am to change the propeller on the kite, Mr. Cutler."

To his relief the old man saw through his plea something more than advice. "I think I had better come and lend 'ee a hand. Hang 'ee by till I get a few tools together."

He put a mixture of tools in a hessian bag, led the way back inside his home and shouted, "I be nipping out for a bit, mother."

Mrs Cutler, unseen in an adjacent room called, "And mind yee be back in time for the Sunday meal." She appeared and came to see them off and something that had puzzled Timothy for a long time suddenly came to him. She was past her three score years and ten, evident as it was by her grey hair and shrunken frame, and yet her face did not portray a single line of age. It was if nature had given her a mask of eternal youth to compensate for her advancing years and was only marred by a small brown mole, sprouting three hairs, on the lower, left side of her face.

"Will yee see to it he only has one jar of ale, Master Timothy?"

"Still thy tongue, mother. If 'ee be good I might fetch 'ee a tipple of wine." And before she could comment further he hurried Timothy to Yorkie waiting in the shafts of the trap."

By ten of the clock Mr. Cutler had changed the propeller for him, and Timothy returned him home with a stone jar of ale and a flask of Elderberry wine for his wife.

When he got back to the cottage father was up and about. He did not take kindly to the news of the change in propeller and Timothy said, "You say we must not remove the hedgerows for a longer launch run, father. Neither do we have any wind to help us. So we have little choice but to experiment with a different propeller."

Father said irritably, "I suppose I must accustom myself to the fact you have inherited some of the traits of your mother."

"What has mother got to do with it, father. And what are these traits to which you refer?"

"You could be branded as too head strong and too cocksure of yourself."

" You delude yourself, father." Timothy laughed. "If I have inherited any seeds those seeds are from you and grandfather Willy. Why else would I concern myself with the propeller and the kite."

After a long pause father said, "Since you have got the bit firmly between your teeth we will see how clever you are when it comes to you starting the engine without my assistance."

The sun shone brightly and warm. To the west a layer of cloud was thickening and spreading, suggesting it was driven by a wind in the heights. Down in the village the church bell tolled an invitation to the Sunday morning worshippers. After much cranking with the starting handle, and what seemed countless adjustments to the engine controls, the engine stumbled into uncertain life. Father, having watched him from a distance, came to the centre section and shouted, "Give the valve another turn, advance the ignition by two notches, and switch to high revolutions."

The engine note soared, rising still more when father tapped the ignition lever and asked him to unscrew the fuel valve another turn. The engine roared steadily without an interruption to its beat. "Now!" he shouted above the crescendo of sound."Switch to low revolutions!"

The roaring engine diminished to a point where it turned the propeller over in hesitant revolutions and the exhaust spluttered like a candle flame caught in a draught of air. "Always make the adjustments before you trip the switch. That is the secret of keeping it alive. Now, keep an eye on it whilst I fetch my cap and goggles."

Timothy gave the engine a quick clean in his absence, wiping away small haemorrhages of oil whose drips and bleeding had already stained the surrounding centre section with black blotches. He was beginning to enjoy the vapoury smells of the life-blood of the engine, the spirit which father was now referring to as the fuel. Its fumes blended with the engine oil and the calico and, combined with the clattering and roaring tone of the engine and frantic propeller, it all made up a wonderful atmosphere of manned flight. It filled him with a sense of importance and of living in a man's world.

Father hauled himself up on the centre section and settled at the control levers. "Right, my boy. Jump down and remove the wheel blocks when I give the signal."

Timothy waited, leant against the leading edge of the lower wing that trembled constantly at the mercy of the vibrations of the engine, shuddering upon its thick rubber mountings and the jarring revolutions of the propeller. Up between the wings the diagonal runs of piano wire twanged and fluttered faintly to the fingers of an invisible musician. Father finished making the fine adjustments to the engine controls and waved the blocks away.

After a struggle Timothy got them free. The engine bellowed to the world and the kite moved off at a stiff trot, gaining pace better than ever before with the wings flexing and bending to the motions of the stiff undercarriage on the sun-baked grassland.

Timothy chased it for a time, revelling in its sense of dash and, what was to him, the gleeful call of the engine. At two hundred paces it gained on him. At three hundred the tail was up and it bounced up and down and made tentative attempts to get on the wing. At four hundred paces it rose clear of the earth and hung there: a sight that thrilled him to the core. Never had he savoured so rich a reward and been overwhelmed by such a sense of achievement, flavoured as it was by his decision to use a different propeller.

He found his thoughts drifting back through the frustrations, the exasperations and the disastrous fire that had led up to this unforgettable moment in time. He recalled the long, cold winter nights, the hours bent over the boiling cauldron steam-bending the lengths of spruce into the shape of the wing frames, the oceans of time carving the multitude of wing ribs and producing the necessary shapes for the horizontal tail and the rudder. He remembered how his fingers ached when helping Mrs. Pettifodder stitch the calico to the frames and ribs. Neither would he forget those laborious, tiresome moments walking back and forth and the endless clambering up and down a ladder with father to check and adjust the rigging to obtain the correct sweep and inclination of the wings. An attention and dedication that father also gave to calculating the precise balance of the kite.

As Timothy watched father take the kite out over the sunlit hills and dales the many irritations and sacrifices, associated with its construction, paled into insignificance. There was something strangely unreal about its suspension, something glorious about the manner in which it floated serenely before the face of the Heavens, something quite supreme in its determination to prove that manned, powered flight was possible. It was a pity mother was not there to see it – to witness history in the making – and being made by none other than her husband. He could not imagine her apologising to father for her scornful comments about his capabilities to take to the air. Mother never, ever apologised.

The kite headed back for the paddock; its engine note slackening as it approached. It swept around on another turn that had it descending toward the paddock. Timothy prepared to run after it once father got it down. But as it drew closer the engine switched to high revolutions and it levelled out and passed slowly overhead distinctly showing the ribs through the calico. In many ways a somewhat ungainly collection of wood and cloth defying the laws of universal gravitation. And which derived its motion from a noisy, cumbersome contraption called an engine, and a frenzied propeller.

It made another circuit of the paddock and came back to earth the harsh rumbling of the wheels and axle echoing through the hollowness of the wings. Father brought it back to the cottage end of the paddock using the blip switch. He screwed down the fuel valve, retarded the small ignition lever, the engine died and the propeller jerked to a halt. He draped his goggles around his neck, slid down from the centre section and lighted his pipe.

"How went it father?"

"We are nearly there, my boy. But not quite."

"Not quite! You took to the air as graciously as never before, father, and completed two circuits of the paddock with great aplomb."

"Quite so. However, we have yet to prove it can carry two persons aloft, as Fanshawe stipulated as a condition of us constructing the kite."

"What are we waiting for, father?"

Father patted him on the head, "Not so hasty." he said leading the way back to the cottage. "I must determine if your weight will greatly affect the balance."

By the time he had completed the calculations and munched his way through a plate of bread and cheese the sky had darkened behind a layer of grey cloud and the air was alive to a steady breeze.

"We will need to keep an eye on the weather, my boy. I think we are in for bit of a blow." Father said as he settled in the wicker seat of the kite and Timothy crouched behind him in readiness to crank the engine. "We will need to start the launch from the other end of the paddock, father, if we are to take advantage of a headwind."

"Begat Grandfather Willy!" father said raising his eyes to the heights. "This boy is one step ahead of us, yet again."

"Switch on!" Timothy called and pulled the handle over with both hands. After three energetic turns the engine kicked back, coughed loudly and barked into life. It struck him, as always, as rather magical in the way it transformed the kite. Moments previously it lay upon the earth like a dormant moth. Now it bustled with action and noise and a vibration that pounded the wings and struts and buzzed through the rigging to the tempo of the clattering engine.

He walked alongside a wing tip to the other end of the paddock, helped haul it around to face the wind, clambered up on the centre section and settled himself on the cushions exactly level with father's seat: the spot determined by father's calculations.

"Ready?" he shouted.

Timothy nodded. The spluttering engine surged to its high revolutions. The kite staggered at first. Then gathered pace, bumping and jolting on the grassland, moving more eagerly when father raised the rasping tail skid by moving the fore and aft lever forward and checking it. A movement that had them pitching upon their seats and skipping from side to side as the kite appeared to want to break out from the clutches of the earth. The boundary hedgerows began to bear down on them at speed. The shocks from the thumping undercarriage petered out. They were off. Not quite! The kite struck ground and clambered into the air. Down they went again with a slam that sent a multitude of tremors through the complete construction. Father made small hurried movements on the control levers; the dazed kite bounced back into the air – paused – and after some fraught moments of indifference collected itself and rose clear a hundred paces from the boundary hedgerows.

Timothy sighed and trembled with a mixture of relief and excitement. The world unfurled before and beneath the wings in the fashion of an unrolling map. He revelled in the sheer magic of it all and looked around for the sources of what was holding them aloft. As usual there was nothing and the mind boggled. His unprotected eyes smarted and watered from the draughty airstreams that also swept against his ears, as did the battering sound of the engine. Almost continually they bumped through the air, the wings dipping from side to side as they met the wind off the surrounding hills. With equal frequency they rose and fell. Father steered the kite around gently and headed back for the cottage; their passage became more stable. They passed over the cottage and Timothy spotted the dogs barking up at them. Nearby he saw the horses shuffling their hindquarters and wrenching at the tie rings, so nervous were they of the alien shape of the kite and its menacing engine. Father took the kite down over Hadley hill, following much the same trajectory they had used for the gliding flights with the first kite. They gave the manor a wide berth but flew over the needlepoint spire of the church – the trout streams – and over the cattle grazing on the slopes. Occasionally the boisterous antics of the invisible air streams tossed them about and rocked the wings as if challenging the audacity of the kite to challenge their aerial territory.

Just how vulnerable wildlife was from the air was demonstrated by the sight of a hare bounding across open ground in full view of any flying predator.

Father headed for Pritchards hill and they spotted the afternoon coach and six from Brunton making its way up to Four-Mile Cross. Timothy wondered if Yarpy had made it yet to the driver's seat of such a powerful team of mounts when, in fact, he should be setting his sights on motorised transport. The Carlton brothers claimed that it would replace horse transport within the next decade or two. And thinking of Yarpy and the Post Haste service made him consider the possibility of delivering the mail by air. Suddenly he had to increase his grip on the strut and father's seat when the kite hesitated under a flurry of blows and shakings that had it flopping about in the air like a wounded mare. He had yet to learn it was caused by the wind racing off the hillside, spinning into space and reaching the kite as tiny violent vortices that wrenched at the large areas of wing and snatched at the struts and rigging. Father acted superbly at the control levers, battling gamely with the invisible enemy who eventually gave up its struggle and retreated, leaving the kite to resume dignified flight.

They ascended very slowly to reach the cottage. The paddock came to view; father adjusted the small ignition lever and fuel control valve and switched to low revolutions. In the ensuing silence they listened to the persiflageous overtures of the air over the wings and struts and through the rigging and used it to gauge the inclination of the wings and their pace through the air. Father repeatedly reiterated the importance of avoiding the 'drop'. At one point it appeared they might strike ground before reaching the paddock. Father switched temporarily to high revolutions that had the effect of checking their descent. In the last two hundred feet he switched back to low and they floated down over the hedgerows – levelled out – and hung on the air until its energy to support them faded and they rumbled noisily and solidly back to earth.

By way of a change in the routine father decided not to return the kite to the stable. They roped and staked it down and lashed a rick cover over to protect it from the elements. And when Timothy returned the horses to the paddock he made certain they went to their usual place under the twin oak trees.

Then Timothy followed father who stripped naked, lathered up with soap and took a good dousing under the garden water pump, not a very warming experience for the time of year and whose discomforts Timothy hid from father for fear of being branded a wimp.

Suitably refreshed and attired in clean garments they put Yorkie in the shafts of the trap and journeyed north to the Carltons' residence, a distinctive property that featured lattice, bay windows which peered out from a mass of red ivy. In the grounds to the rear a low-slung building accommodated the construction of their motorised carriages.

An old man servant answered the door, and was insisting the brothers were not expecting any visitors when the voice of Mr. Robert called, "Who is it Joseph?"

"A Mr. Herby and his son Timothy, Sir..." and before he could say more the door moved further ajar to disclose Mr. Robert.

"Samuel and Timothy. Welcome!" he beamed, offering a hand in greeting. "These guests of ours, are to be admitted at any time, Joseph. Kindly bring a tray of drinks to the study and, perhaps, a plate of sandwiches."

Before they were ushered in Timothy requested a pail of water for Yorkie. Mr. Robert nodded to the manservant to oblige.

By the time he got back from watering the horse he found Mr. Charles had joined the throng in the study and looked most suave in his quilted smoking jacket. Rarely was he without a burning cigar, a good quality one that lent quite pleasantly to one's sense of smell.

As was to be expected the conversation revolved around the kite for the entire evening. What father and he had achieved that day and, of special interest to them, how their engine had performed. The more father convinced them of the success of their brainchild, the more the alcoholic beverage flowed. Timothy was left out of the conversation for long periods; he was not dismayed. He spent much of the time looking at an interesting display of model motorised carriages set upon shelves in a glass-fronted cabinet. Some, he observed were driven by a steam engine, others followed the lines of a horse carriage with the shafts removed and an engine slung between the wheels. A certain model was in the shape of the brothers' present carriage whilst another, sleek, low, and streamlined carried the label of, Futuristic.

Another cabinet displayed the components that made up the workings of their engine. On the wall above it a large drawing gave a sectional view of the journals, the crankshaft, the connecting rods, the pistons, the valves, the spark plugs, the magneto, the fuel/air mixer. Timothy looked at it hard and long and much of which had puzzled him in the past, now came to him more logically and with greater understanding. From time to time he overheard snippets of the men's' conversation. Fanshawe's name cropped up on more than one occasion. It heartened him to hear the brothers voicing their continuing support for father.

A little after midnight he and father took their leave from their pleasures of the evening and father had him take the reins for the journey home. Father lounged in the back of the trap, his arms draped over the sideboards. They drove steadily, dodging between spots of rain.

"What now with the kite, father?" They were moving down Pilley's Ridge, and Yorkie's hind quarters were pushing into the brake strap to check their speed.

"The Carltons have agreed to convey another letter to Mr. Fanshawe in which I have requested to retain the kite for a further seven days."

"What purpose will it serve, father, when he has already warned you he will take possession of the kite this week, with or without proof that it can take to the air?"

Pilley's Ridge rose up behind them as they reached the flat and Yorkie broke into a stiff trot. Father said, "If he should refuse, so be it. But I am determined for you to take the kite aloft, alone, before the transfer of ownership takes place."

Timothy suddenly felt very humble. Father putting so very much at risk to give him the honour of flying the kite on his own. The burden of responsibility came to rest on his young shoulders. It needed only a minor mistake on his behalf to cause damage to the kite and Fanshawe would jump at the opportunity to instigate legal proceedings against father for numerous breaches of the contract between them. Yorkie moderated his pace before reaching Four Mile Cross and, without prompting, made the turn that led to a ten pace wide track that rose steadily to the cottage. Timothy smiled; the mount paused briefly to get his breath and find his step, then moved up the hill at a sprightly pace not faltering once: all in sharp contrast to what Timothy had seen of the Carltons' struggling, lumbering motorised carriage.

On reaching the cottage he sent father onto bed, and took Yorkie out of the shafts, gave him a rub down and a bag of feed, rugged him up, and saw him into the paddock and clear of the kite. By this time the rain was falling steadily. He could not resist a quick visit to the kite. It stood in silence apart from the patter of raindrops on the rick cover under which he sought shelter. He ran a hand over the smooth taut calico, up and down a glossy, varnished strut, and plucked at a rigging wire that sent a deep bass note through the entire kite. He could smell the fumes from the fuel tank, mixing as they were with traces of the oil, wood and cloth: a combination that made up the character of the kite and lodged permanently in the mind.

It was curious to think that it had soared into a world previously known only to the birds. Yet here it now stood resting on the palings of the earth smugly hiding the secrets of its conversation with the air and, apart from father's assistance, refusing to yield what means it had actually employed to conquer the forces of gravity. He arrived at the centre section and looked up at the dim shape of the control levers, the wicker seat and the bulk of the engine. "I trust you will be as kind to me, as you were to father." he murmured and, slowly, made his way to the cottage.

Nine

The following week was filled with mixed fortunes. On Monday a farmhand was gored and killed by a bull, the same day that Harry Griggs's father succumbed to the inevitable destiny of his long-suffering illness.

On Tuesday the body of a man was found hanging from a tree in the woods on the estate. Jake Howson was known only to a handful of employees. And Timothy had good reason to sit up and take note because the name had cropped up when mother confronted Lady Hadley on the origins of baby Samantha and named Jake Howson as her source of information. Timothy got wind of Jake's death down at Mr. Cutler's whilst having Yorkie and Paddy shod and Michael Shotter, a stable lad from the estate, brought in a strawberry roan mare for new shoes. Michael told him in a whisper that there was a lot of gossip going on amongst the grooms and farmhands who were questioning the suggestion that the notorious poacher had committed suicide. There was a general opinion that Jake had been put down by the hands of others: a suspicion based on orders given by the squire on the day following the annual fete. All estate employees were ordered to apprehend every poacher found trespassing on the estate and to use whatever force was necessary to secure the capture of any villain. The squire condoned the use of weapons.

Timothy hoped father would throw some light on the matter. But he never did. And Timothy did not attempt to prise him because he would have to name Michael Shotter as his informant and that would lose the lad his job for originating gossip that was private to the Hadley Estate. Timothy, however, was in no doubt that Jake's death was connected with mother's revelation at the manor on the day of the annual fete.

On Wednesday of that week father let him loose with the kite, telling him to practice operating the engine, and to try a few hops with the kite. He was to delay sustained flight until another day.

By luck or judgement, he was not quite sure, he set the fuel valve and ignition lever, cranked the engine and after about ten swings of the handle it roared with laughter into life and settled down to low revolutions, spluttering through the long copper exhaust pipe. He settled in the seat, checked the feel and movement of the flying controls as father did before each flight and switched to high revolutions to get the kite under way out of the long grass and onto the strip he had shorn with the scythe. He prided himself on remembering to note the direction of the wind. As it was there was little or nothing to contend with. He swung round at the cottage end – took a deep breath and switched to high revolutions – the kite toddled forward, converted to a brisk walking pace – to a canter – into the steady rhythm of a gallop. He moved the fore and aft lever forward, as father had demonstrated, to raise the tail. The kite veered off course. Too late! Before he had a chance to switch to low revolutions the kite had swung him around to face the opposite end of the paddock. It happened so quickly that it humbled him a little.

On his second attempt, in anticipation of the swing, he pressed a foot on the rudder bar an instant before he went through the motions of getting the tail up. It worked, though for a time he found himself doing a sort of tap dance on the rubber bar to keep the kite running straight. They bounded along, jolted by the rigid undercarriage, the pitching of the wicker seat, the thundering wings on either side of him and in the sound of the frantic buzzing of the engine and propeller. He drew the lever back – a pause – the pounding and rumbling stopped suddenly and the kite lifted from the earth. He drew breath at his detachment and would have liked to carry on. But out of respect for father instructions and the risk of legal proceedings by Fanshawe, were he to damage the kite, he switched to low revolutions. His oversight in easing the control lever forward, before doing so, sent him and the kite sprawling back to earth rather heavily. He very nearly ran into the hedgerows on the boundary in the process of getting back to earth. He decided it was enough for one day.

On Thursday the farmhand, gored by the bull, was buried.

On Friday a horse-drawn cart, carrying the body of Mr. Griggs in a plain wooden box, moved slowly through the village trailed by an entourage of mourners, comprising children and adults. They walked in silence, tolled by the chiming lament of the church bell. Harry, upright and grim-faced, held his mother by the arm and led the procession. Behind him Timothy and Marie walked arm in arm, followed by 'Spindle Baker and Becky Redshaw, and 'Podger' Cracknell who was too shy to take the arm of Molly Langdon. Benjamin Hampton ambled alongside 'Cryer' Popham. Behind them the wife of Ottie, the shepherd, and their two daughters, Petal and Rosey. Apart from the very aged and infirm most of the village turned out to pay their respects including several men who forewent a day's wages to attend.

The cart drew up before the churchyard gate. Four burly men lifted the box onto their shoulders and transported it amongst a gathering of mounds and headstones to a waiting cavern of earth and the Reverend Peach. A passing cloud blanked out the sunshine for a time, marking the sombreness of the occasion. And a mischievous bout of wind plucked at the Reverend's white surplus and attempted to lift it above his head during his reading of the last rites...ashes to ashes, dust to dust. Then that awful, helpless, clutching moment when the box is lowered into its earthy recess and as it disappears it releases a spate of memories of the deceased. The manner, in which Mr. Griggs spoke and behaved, the clothes he wore, the pale ashen face, the dull eyes...figures collect handfuls of earth and sprinkle it into the grave and hear it patter on the lid of the box.

As they filed out of the church gate they shook hands with the mourning widow who is attended by her courageous, pale-faced son. He stands, receiving their condolences, an arm about her hunched figure. If tears there are, they are stemmed and held at bay by the support of Harry who has loyally supported her throughout the years to cope with the many difficulties in her life.

Some mourners took up the offer to travel back home on the cart. Others chose to go on foot. Timothy and Marie took Harry and his mother, in the trap, to their home; a humble but scrupulously clean abode set amongst a row of terraced cottages and unusual for village folk a warm, red carpet covered the sitting room floor. Marie told Timothy later that her mother had obtained a small job for Mrs. Griggs up at the manor, cleaning and dusting, for a small wage to compensate for her ailing husband. During the annual spring-cleaning the manor discarded the carpet and Mrs. Griggs gained permission, again through Marie's mother, to take it home where a good wash and scrub revived it for further use'

It did much to enhance the comfort of the room, brightened as it was by a collection of polished brass ornaments that reflected the light from the solitary window in the room. A small fireplace, smartly shining from a coat of blacking, was attended by a brass fender and a small portable gantry that suspended a brass-handled brush, a small shovel and a poker. Timothy left Marie talking to Mrs. Griggs and followed Harry into the small scullery.

"If there is anything I can do or something you desperately need, Harry, you need only give me the word." he said.

Harry turned from putting a small pot of water on a wood-burning stove and said, "I could be doing with a sack of 'taties, and a bit of flour to make bread, Timmy. Otherwise we be doing all right. Lady Hadley has promised ma some extra hours up at the manor. And old Cutler has offered me a bit of paid work till I join the colours next year."

"That is good news, Harry. Very good news."

Harry carried on arranging cups and putting nettle leaves in a strainer, "How is yer dad's new flying machine? They say it kicks up a real racket and can be heard all the way down in the church."

"Oh, it is going on very well thank you Harry. You won't hear the noise much longer. My father has constructed it for a man who lives over at Brunton."

Harry said: "Ever since you and I started school I remember you chasing flying creatures. Do you remember you netted a butterfly and made a drawing of it, and studied it under a magnifying glass, and made a lot of notes about it? I often wondered what you was about." He paused. "And what happened to that song thrush you had caged in the garden?"

"Father wanted to compare the spread of its wings and tail to the size and weight of the body. He reckoned it had some bearing on why the bird has an easy access to get on the wing. Not long after the thrush he found the skeleton of a blackbird up in the woods. And when we had a good look at it we discovered the bones of a bird are hollow."

"So, what do you make of that."

"Father thinks it makes for less weight for the bird to lift with the strength available to the beat of its wing."

"I heard tell your mother kicked up bit of a fuss about you keeping that thrush in a cage."

Timothy was amazed by Harry's sharp memory. "Yes," he laughed. "She threatened to imprison me and father in the stable for a week to sample the ordeal of the thrush."

Behind them the boiling water in the pot billowed up a cloud of steam. Marie came in quietly and steeped the nettle leaves in the water and presently strained them, smiling to herself at overhearing Harry telling Timothy about his latest pet mouse. Another invention of his that used two elastically operated cotton reels, which caused the mouse to nod its head and shake its tail when in motion.

Timothy said it must frighten the ladies for sure. Harry confirmed, with a chuckle, that it did and, what was more, it scared the family cat. At this point Marie politely interrupted and reminded them that Harry's grieving mother was in need of their company.

Later that day, after nightfall, Harry opened the door to let the cat out and found two sacks and a cloth bundle containing 'taties and flour, and a collection of clothing. He did not have to think twice who the good Samaritans were, and who considerately and tactfully made the delivery under the cloak of darkness without the need of his appreciation or recognition for their act of kindness. They were good sorts were the Herby and Sawyer families.

On Saturday Timothy got aloft with father with the intention of him taking it alone later in the day. They were a little harassed because father's recent plea to retain the kite for a further seven days so infuriated Mr. Fanshawe he put the matter in the hands of his solicitor. Father had received a legal document that morning summoning him to deliver the kite by Wednesday next, at noon, the latest. Or face the distress of having all his worldly goods impounded by a sheriff officer to pay for the monies lost by Mr. Fanshawe in the breach of the written contract made by him and father.

Timothy was also chastened by his attempts to fly the kite that day. In the days of his gliding flights he had built up his experience of flying by listening to the airstreams fluctuating in pace and sound around the wings and through the rigging just as father had taught him. But with the powered kite the noisy engine overwhelmed the sound of the airstreams and robbed him of all capability to fly by sound. Father said he must get used to the idea of flying by feel and sighting the angle of the wings in relation to the earth in order to avoid falling victim of the 'drop'. It was easier said than done. His hands and feet responded slowly, hesitantly on the controls, not unlike a mount at the mercy of an incompetent rider. And returning to earth with finesse and a measure of accuracy deserted him. On three successive occasions he would surely have pitched them onto their noses had it not been for the saving graces of the skids, and father's hasty intervention on the control levers. The day ended in defeat and with little prospect he would ever succeed. But father was very supportive, "Do not lose heart my boy. Tomorrow is another day." he said when they retired for the night.

Timothy lay awake for most of the time, his thoughts dwelling on his difficulties with the kite, and father's dilemma with the solicitor. The boy thought the crisis could be resolved by him admitting to father he would never master the kite, and it would be best all round to hand the kite over to Fanshawe without further delay, thus sparing father from all the legal repercussions.

He must have dozed off for a spell because the next he knew was father rousing him and daylight had yet to come to the window of the room, "I have important matters to attend to up on the estate, my boy."

"Shall I come with you, father?"

" No-no. It will not be necessary. A couple of estate hands are all I need. But you can prepare the kite for when I return." He walked to the door, stopped and turned and smiled, "I think the kite will be kind to you today."

Timothy got up shortly after, to watch him depart on Yorkie. And most unusual for father he had a spade strapped to the saddle of his mount. Timothy puzzled over the need for the spade for a long time. To eventually come to the conclusion that it would be used to bury the carcass of a dead animal; it was not unknown for individual sheep or cattle, nearing the end of their days, to desert a flock or herd to find an isolated spot and die in privacy.

Samuel met up with George Sawyer and two estate hands driving a brown mare in the shafts of a flatbed cart. Greetings were exchanged in quiet, sombre tones, George insisting they move into the shelter of the woodland without delay. Samuel had a good look around as they moved off the highway, and hoped desperately their clandestine meeting would go undetected. Shafts of light from the rising sun pierced the gaps in the foliage of the trees spot-lighting features of the woodland: the craggy bark of an oak, a cluster of flowers, the trickling journey of a stream, an insect rising joyously in the embracing warmth of a light beam.

They reached the centre of the wood and George Sawyer said: "A suitable spot, do you think, Samuel?"

Samuel nodded, filled with grave misgivings about the whole purpose of their visit, and deeply suspicious about the circumstances in which the notorious poacher had died. He dismounted from Yorkie and using the spade scribed a rectangular shape measuring eight feet by four on the ground in a clearing. He removed the first few inches of top soil then stepped aside on George's orders and the two estate hands removed the earth in earnest, digging until they were nearly lost to view.

"That is enough." George said and pulled them out of the pit in turn. "Now, get along and fetch the corpse from the cart."

In their absence Samuel and George looked at each other unable to speak. They diverted their eyes to looking down at the gaping hole and the surrounding mound of earth, possibly besieged by similar memories of the poacher who had long worked the estate. But was never challenged because he confined his purloining to rabbits, hares, foxes and the odd deer: all of which would have wreaked havoc on the farm crops had Jake not kept them in check. The fact he sold some of his spoils at market to keep a roof over the head of, and clothes on the back of, his wife and children showed the man had a bit of gumption. Jake had also kept Samuel and George informed of villainous elements that ganged up to invade the estate and steal food resources in huge quantities. Forewarned by Jake they were able to forearm and counter the raids before they really got started.

The two estate hands returned carrying the stiff corpse in a shroud. Ropes were arranged around it and at a nod from George it was lowered to the depths of earth. A robin flew into the clearing to perch on the top of the mound of earth and looked at them curiously, its red-orange breast distinctive against the rich, black soil. George lowered his head, clasped his hands – all hats were removed – and he offered up a short prayer. He concluded by suggesting the final resting place for the poacher could not be more appropriate, since it was an area where Jake had spent most of his working life and which was as well known to him as the palm of his hand.

The robin rose to the branch of a nearby tree and George nodded for the grave to be filled in. Somewhere down the wood the stammering call of a magpie reached them. Samuel worked busily with the spade helping the estate hands fill the hole. He thought it ironic that Jake had not died as a result of his illegal poaching activities but, in reality, a loose tongue had caused his death. Had he not mentioned the indiscretion he had witnessed on the banks of the trout streams Rebecca would have been deprived of the verbal ammunition on that fateful day in the nursery of the manor. Samuel too had scruples about Jake's death; had he confined the liaison with Claire to the manor, which she preferred, and not rode into the countryside and been observed, Jake would still be alive, today.

It also unsettled him to think who was responsible for the poacher's untimely and sinister demise because nobody could convince him that Jake had taken his own life. He had been murdered in revenge for the smear he had unwittingly brought on the reputation and name of the Hadley family. George had it from the squire that Jake's father died in similar circumstances, several years back, on Squire Edgecombe's land twenty miles to the east of Haley. It would therefore be reasonable to assume there was a mental disorder associated with the medical history of the family and led the two men to take their lives. But Samuel did not believe a word of it.

"How best, do you think, Samuel we might help Jake's widow and children." They were making their way back to the highway and the cart carrying the estate hands moved several paces ahead of them over the uneven floor of the wood.

"I think it would be wise to invite them to set up house in Hadley to get them away from the gossip and speculation in Brunton. There is an empty dwelling close to that of the Griggs family. It would allow the two widows to share their grief."

George said, "I am given to understand that accommodation has been allocated to Tommy Cox and Sarah Hodge who are to be wed in the next few weeks." He hesitated. "And do you think the Squire would really approve of the Howson family moving here when a member of their family has so enraged him."

"George!" Samuel arrested him by an arm. "You and I know, and many of Jake's friends know that Jake did not take his life. I feel certain there will be some form of retaliation. You and I have a duty to the Squire to cover his tracks and we can do this by confusing the potential conspirators in Brunton. It is my opinion that we can do this by bringing the family to live in Hadley."

"Killing two birds with one stone, as it were?"

"You could say that."

George regarded him with a sympathetic smile. "Do you mean to tell me that you are willing to protect the squire at all cost, when he is making plans for you to be removed from Hadley. Sending you abroad I am reliably informed."

Samuel said: "I can understand his reasons. It is to remove me from the focus of attention where the parentage of the baby Samantha is concerned. Given time and my absence and persons will forget that I had anything to do with the child. And let us face it fairly and squarely I did make mistakes. I exposed him and Claire by taking her away from the manor that evening. He had always been under the impression we spent the evening at the manor, out of sight, out of mind. I have much to answer for George, make no mistake about that."

They continued walking and presently moved out of the woodland to be greeted by the warmth of the rising sun. Fallow deer, five in number, glanced across the track ahead of them, narrowly missing the cart, and charged amongst the gorse on the heathland. The curdling call of a horn reminded them of the early morning stage from Brunton . They spotted it mending its way up Pritchards hill.

Before they caught up with the cart and before the estate hands could overhear their conversation Samuel said: "When I have gone George I like to think you will muster all the support you can for the Squire. You will need to organise a bodyguard to escort him wherever he goes, on and off the estate, and that person should be discreetly armed with a pistol."

George assured him he would do as he requested and they hurried to the cart that was waiting to join the highway. George heaved himself in reverse on to the lowered tailboard and the cart set off following the bottom road to the manor whilst Samuel mounted Yorkie and made his way up the long straight hill to the cottage. He rode slowly, riddled with guilt at what he had just done, carrying the weight of the world on his shoulders, and encompassed by a heavy, grey cloud of regret.

His gloom and the burden of his thoughts began to ease a little when the stuttering and clamour of the kite's engine broke through the stillness of the youthful day. He grinned; he had visions of Timothy trotting the kite back and forth across the paddock, tempting and briefly triumphing over gravity. But as he reached the brow of the hill the kite flew over his head and moved northwards.

His concern for the boy's safety and the fact he had gone against his wishes gradually dissipated as the kite rode the air steadily. It filled him with an immeasurable pride and joy, for was this not evidence of the strains of an aerial pioneer coming up through yet another generation in the family. Willy Herby had not died in vain.

The kite made a gentle turn to come around and follow a course parallel to the eastern boundary of the paddock. For Samuel it was the very first time he had seen the kite in full and sustained flight, from the ground. He thought of all the scientific personages who claimed manned flight was not possible and argued that the universal laws of gravitation would forever remain the obstacle. He grinned agreeably; he had proved their theory to be grossly in error, as was his son at this very moment. To the south of the cottage the kite made another turn, its wings as delicate as the membranes of a moth lured into the light of a candle. The rising sun made the wings look transparent and its brilliance glinted on the polished brass and copper fittings of the engine.

Samuel lit his pipe; returning the kite to earth was never the same on each occasion. A slight misjudgment of height and speed could make alighting into something of an ordeal, as he knew only too well. Timothy switched to low revolutions; the kite came floating down, occasionally tilting its wings but seemingly under control. Suddenly it plunged out of sight on the other side of the hill. Samuel tensed; he had experienced it himself on more than one occasion: a giant hand reaching up from the lowlands and dragging the kite down with breathless velocity. And it had been more by luck than judgement how he had recovered from it. "Switch to maximum revolutions, my boy." he murmured, hoping desperately Timothy had not forgotten it amongst the many flying instructions he had given him over the months.

The top wing appeared first above the summit of the hill, followed by the struts, the rigging, the bottom wing and the skids and wheels. The kite remained aloft at the generosity of the caressing air streams and the salvation of the power from the engine and propeller. It made enough height to clear the boundary hedgerows and slumped to ground. Samuel tethered Yorkie to a gate and went in the paddock to meet it. Timothy trotted it to the cottage end, turned it into wind with rudder and a burst of engine and stopped. He retarded the ignition and screwed the fuel cock closed. The engine died and the propeller juddered to a halt. He lowered the goggles, father's goggles, and jumped down from the centre section, "I trust you will forgive me for going against your orders, father. The truth is I could not resist it. You might say it was a bit of Grandfather Willy coming out in me."

Samuel shook his hand vigorously; "You did exceedingly well my son. You are to be congratulated."

Timothy frowned heavily, "Are you not angered, father?"

"Not at all. Many miserable moments have I had in recent years. But today your flying skill and gallantry has compensated for each and every one of them." He put an arm around the boy's shoulders. "Let us attend to the needs of the mounts and dogs and then celebrate the occasion by taking a late breakfast.

After midday the Carlton brothers paid their weekly visit. Not long after Marie and her parents arrived unexpectedly. Mr. Robert decided he would like to sample a journey to the heights and Mr. Sawyer was as keen as ever. Timothy and father were preparing the kite for flight when Mr. Pook and Mr. Cutler and their wives stopped by. Followed shortly after by Mrs. Pettifodder and her husband. Evidently father had extended an invitation to them all, at the beginning of the week, to come and take a last look at their work of art before it was delivered to its new owner. Timothy fetched a couple of wooden bench seats from behind the cottage for the elderly couples to sit on and watch the proceedings. He thought the Squire and Lady Hadley would not put in an appearance. He suspected mother's revelation about the origins of their child had well and truly made them distance themselves from father.

It turned out to be another memorable day. The face of the weather was that of bright, warm sunshine tempered by a gentle breeze. The elderly visitors were plied with ale and wine by Marie and her mother whilst the kite made its comings and goings in the sound of its noisy chattering engine. Father took Mr. Robert first, making a wide sweeping turn over Pritchards hill, drifting south to the trout streams and making another wide turn to head back for the paddock.

The aged Mrs. Pettifodder whose dim sight and deafness denied her much of the spectacle of father's flight was given a running commentary by her husband who fared little better than her as far as his sight was concerned. He pointed to a bird claiming it to be the kite. Marie tactfully pointed out his error to him and, on showing him the exact whereabouts of the kite Mrs. Pettifodder shelled an ear with a hand in the hope of hearing it. She heard and saw nothing and was about to return to her seat, using her black gamp as a parasol, when father flicked to high revolutions and flew low overhead. The noise startled her and she would surely have missed her seat had Marie not assisted her.

"I never thought I would see the day." Mr. Pook exclaimed at the sight and sound of the passing kite that seemed to hang there in the emptiness of sky with nothing visible to hold it up.

Mr. Culture agreed with him and added: "How does your father do it, young Timothy?"

Timothy said, "He could never have done it without the help of you all. You, Mr. Pook, with all you're help and guidance on the carpentry. Mr. Cutler, for your advice and help on the metal work. Mr. Robert and Mr. Charles for your supply of the engine and their instruction on how to operate it. And, of course, Mrs. Pettifodder's great contribution with her needle and thread."

"What say he?" Mrs. Pettifodder shouted.

"He say you did a grand job on the stitching." her husband said aloud in her ear. His tone indicated she was testing his patience by making him repeat everything he spoke to her.

The smithy, carpenter and Mr. Charles moved further out in the paddock to watch the kite make its final turn and approach in preparation for alighting. Mrs. Pook and Mrs. Cutler were content to sit in the warmth of the sun and sip at their goblets of wine. The dogs crouched, looking through the paddock gate and, long before any of the mortals, they heard the kite approaching in the sound of the air swishing over its wings and whistling through the rigging. They deserted the scene at great speed and joined the horses tethered on the other side of the cottage.

The landed kite moved back to the spectators. Mr. Robert jumped down from the centre section a distinct glow attached to his countenance and a triumphant glint in his eyes. It so inspired his brother Charles he decided he should sample the experience. He clambered up beside father and the kite moved off to turn into wind. The rumbling wheels and the drumming wings were lost in the rising clamour of the engine. The kite trotted – cantered – galloped and broke earth just over half way up the paddock, father's skill and competence growing by the minute. He followed the same route as his previous flight and came back over the paddock with Mr. Charles waving his cap to the spectators.

When it alighted this time Mr. Sawyer swapped places with Mr. Charles on the centre section and off again went the kite, always appearing a little clumsy on the ground but posing rather calmly once it reached the freedom of the heights. Marie served Mr. Robert and Mr. Charles with another jar of ale. In the diminishing sight and sound of the kite Jeppie and Sniffy came back again to look through the bars of the gate. Mr. Pettifodder was forced to repeat another comment to his wife. Mr. Pook and Mr. Cutler accepted a cigar from the Carlton brothers.

Father ventured much further on this flight with Mr. Sawyer, Timothy noticed. It seemed to him that father did a complete aerial tour of the estate, ranging as far east as the sheep country. Then it moved around to the south and out to the west, seen as not unlike a bird circling over the slopes of the hills. He was gone for a good twenty minutes of the clock before he headed back, the noise of the clattering engine breaking through the warm bright stillness of the day. Timothy, on looking for the whereabouts of the dogs, noticed a gathering of villagers at the paddock gate who had chosen the route up Hadley hill for their Sunday afternoon stroll. Father brought the kite in over their heads and there was a lot of excited laughter and chatter. He came back along the paddock and turned into wind with use of the rudder and engine and a helping hand at the wing tips from the Carlton brothers. Mr. Sawyer slid down from the centre section looking rather pleased with himself, and father beckoned.

"Come – take the levers, my boy." he shouted above the stuttering noise of the engine. "And take Marie aloft. You will need to make haste; Mr. Fanshawe is on his way up the hill."

Timothy took his place in the wicker seat and donned his cap and goggles. Father lifted Marie onto the centre section and told her to hold fast to a wing strut and the back of the wicker seat much as she had on the first kite.

"Off you go, and take care." he shouted in farewell.

Timothy unscrewed the spirit valve a turn and advanced the ignition lever two notches and flicked the engine switch. The kite edged forward, rumbling, drumming and shaking on the uneven grassland and in the shattering noise of the frantic engine and propeller. Before long, with the tail raised, the grass passed beneath his feet as a green blur. Then came that thrilling, spectacular, triumphant moment when a steady pull on the fore and aft lever freed them from the shackles of the earth. And the trees, hedgerows and the coloured patchwork of fields and pastures fell slowly beneath the wings. He glanced down to his left to see Marie's laced boots protruding over the front edge of the wing, her long skirt rippling to the opposing flow of the air streams and her long fair hair streamed from the back of her head. A glow of excitement painted her cheeks and like their first flight together she was possessed with a sense of adventure.

He had made his first turn just short of Pritchards hill and was flying with the wind on the tail when a scourge of misfiring beset the engine. He reached blindly for the spirit control valve, unscrewed it a turn, and advanced the ignition a couple of more notches: all of which father had taught him during the many rehearsals in the stable. But the engine failed to respond. Its disputing grew more frequent until it was reduced to spluttering feebly, and eventually snuffed it. For brief moments his thoughts wandered about in confusion. He had visions of crashing to earth and being consumed by the horrendous fire that had destroyed the first kite. He thought of the grief that it would bring to Marie's parents were she to perish under the wing of his responsibility.

"Should you have doubts concerning the engine." father had told him many times. "Screw down the spirit control valve, fully retard the ignition lever and glide back to earth as you did with the original kite."

Timothy acted accordingly, also remembering to keep the kite in a steady descent to avoid the 'drop'. Father had not, however, told him it would be necessary to sink at a stiffer pace to compensate for the weight of the engine and the dragging effect of the stilled propeller.

"Steer close to the paddock boundary." more of father's words came to mind. "And ensure there is adequate height before you make the final turn."

The experience of his gliding flights with the first kite came to his rescue; he found it easier to make judgements and decisions without the distracting clatter of the engine. He turned early and higher onto the approach to the paddock; at all costs he must keep clear of the down draughts that sought to wrench him from the air during his morning flight. The kite floated down, talking to him through the sighing, wailing, shrill whistling orchestra of the streams of air, which caressed the wings and plucked at the struts and rigging.

Samuel was standing in the middle of the paddock with the Carlton brothers when they heard the serious interruptions to the steady buzzing of the engine. They watched the kite lurch and stagger for a time before the engine lapsed into silence. Samuel prayed fervently for the boy to know what he must be about at this critical time in the flight. A grin crept on to his face and he exhaled a loud sigh of relief as the kite kept on the wing and commenced a controlled descent. The boy had learnt well, he decided. Either that or he had the traits of previous Herby generations coursing through his veins. He performed with great courage and coolness of thought, sliding the kite in closer to the paddock boundary with plenty of height in hand to make the final turn. His only obstacle now was to get it safely back to earth.

Timothy watched the groups of spectators rise up, the persons by the gate, those seated on the bench seats and a threesome standing in the middle of the paddock. He weaved the kite from side to side to dispense with the excess height, a trick father had taught him on the original kite. He saw the horses tethered to the back of the cottage and the dogs running from the paddock to join them. At a couple of hundred feet the kite made its customary shy at the closing proximity of the earth, giving the impression it would prefer to stay on the wing. In the last hundred feet it glided down in hesitant steps. Then the pace quickened. They glanced over the cottage, the hedgerows. Ease the control lever back – pull harder as the grass rushes up for the wings – check the hold of the lever – they hang on the wing – the rushing air streams fade away – his feet rise up before him – a moment of hesitation – the kite deserts the air and is met with a jolt and the rumbling undercarriage and rasping tail skid in greeting.

Ten

Overhead the stars were still in place but fading. Far to the east a pale yellow beacon heralded the birth of a new day. Timothy arose before father. He let the dogs out. Went to the outside earth closet and emerged minutes later to douse his face with cold water from the garden pump. He dried off in the cottage and set about preparing breakfast of oats, toasted bread smeared with butter and damson jam and mugs of nettle tea laced with honey. He had not slept well, and neither had father he suspected. They were parting company with the kite within a matter of hours. The previous evening had been spent checking it thoroughly and replenishing the fuel tank, the oil reservoir and the cooling water of the engine.

Father came through, wished him, 'Good morning' and went out the back door to the earth closet. He too used water from the garden pump to wash and dried off with a towel in the scullery. Timothy served up and they made their way through the food in silence. Through a practiced routine they washed and dried the dishes, and togged up with the apparel they used for their flights. Timothy brought the mounts from the paddock and tethered them to the cottage and gave them a bag of hay. He gave each of the dogs a boiled rabbit.

By the time he got to the kite father had removed and cleared the rick cover and taken the ropes and stakes from the wings. They started the engine and moved off along the paddock to get in position to turn into wind. A pause to tighten their caps and pull their goggles down. The stuttering engine suddenly opened out to high revolutions and they began to bounce and surge along the grassland that gleamed in a covering of early morning dew.

The mail coach lumbered over the crown of Pritchards hill and started to increase its pace down the south side, its carriage pitching and swaying on the groaning suspension. The lead mount attempted to check the pace against the weight of the carriage pressing forcefully through the shafts and harness. This part of the incline of the hill was steep to say the least. The rest of the team tried to change step with him, scornful as they were of the driver's reluctance to use the brake. "Move on! Move on!" he commanded irritably and slapped them with the reins, and lashed the leader with the whip. They had been delayed at Brompton for nearly an hour of the clock to change a broken snaffle and a split leather trace and to replace a lost shoe of number three in the team. He was trying to make up for the lost time.

The team of six was familiar with the route but it was in shadow because the sun was not yet high enough. And owing to the blinkers they wore they were cautious of running into ruts and hollows, and earth slips, which often appeared at short notice on the surface of the highway particularly after a fall of rain. At first the leader ignored the stinging strokes of the driver's whip and by means of telepathy signalled to the rest of the team to follow his pace. But he had no sooner done so when his whole spirit detected, over the thundering noise of their hooves and the trailing crunching, crushing, squealing wheels of the coach, a sound that was totally alien to the communications of the animal world. The strange noise had a menacing note about it and his senses told him it was approaching from the rear, drawing ever nearer and rising frantically in pitch. Visions of a predator diving from the air flashed across his mind and in an instant he was driven to think he must escape at all costs if he were to survive. With no immediate shelter in view his only choice was to run for his life. He relayed his concerns to the rest of the team and they bolted.

At first the driver grinned; he had disciplined the team; they were doing as he commanded; at this rate they would make up much of the lost time. Then his satisfaction changed to deep concern when he realised they were approaching Four Mile-Cross, to snatch the mailbag from the pole, at too stiff a pace. He mustered all his strength to rein them in and slammed a foot against the hand brake. It had no effect. And at this very moment a large winged shape passed low overhead and the demonic noise it made drowned out the pandemonium of the charging coach. It fled past Four Mile Cross with the driver and his companion gripping the rails of their seats with what little anchorage there was and fearing the worse as the terror-stricken team of mounts careered madly out of control.

Timothy saw nothing of the drama passing beneath the wings; details of the earth were in shadow. It was as much as he could do to keep the faint trace of the highway in sight to aid his navigation. Nearby woodland was seen as dark, bulbous shapes. He spotted the silvery trace of a river. Occasionally ribbons of mist floated into view. Ghostly spirits drifting home after a night of revelry.

Fanshawe had insisted they deliver the kite to a certain stretch of land on the outskirts of Brunton with great discreetness and where he could take ownership of the kite in secret, on the assumption no mortals would rise early enough to witness the clandestine flight. For Timothy it was bad enough to be making his last flight in the kite. But more so he loathed the little fat man for what was, in effect, stealing father's knowledge and expertise and which, for certain, he intended to appropriate to his own advantage and claim the credit and honours that rightfully should go to father. It was nothing short of theft and dishonesty.

The rising sunlight pierced a gap between the hill ranges and lit up the heath land on each side of the highway. Father had given him the honour of taking the control levers for the last flight, and to give him a taste of aerial navigation. To the left the wings, struts and rigging bathed in the gold colour of the dawn. To his right father sat in the second wicker seat they had fitted that week and which was in accordance with Fanshawe's stipulation in the contract with father. Behind them the engine and propeller clattered and whined without an interruption to their industrious cycle. For some reason it reminded Timothy of the failure of the engine during his last flight with Marie and the folly of not ensuring the fuel tank had sufficient contents for the needs of the engine. He had considered it an unpardonable error at the time and said so to father. But father overlooked it and preferred to insist that he had done an admirable job in getting the kite back to ground without harm.

Details of the earth came to view in the growing daylight. Mother Nature put on her chequered dress and jewellery, a river of diamonds around her neck; silver bangles adorn her wrists, her ankles. A tiara of flowers crowns her wheat-coloured hair. She holds close to her bosom a gathering of dwellings and so too she plays host to an abundance of wildlife that she nourishes with her fertility. She stirs slowly and smiles up at the growing warmth of the sun and the freshness of the cool, blue morning sky. The view made Timothy aware of the fact that earthbound mortals were never honoured with such spectacular, and so breathtaking, views in the dimension of life that flight had to offer. There is a profound taste of freedom – of having escaped. The petty irritations of the earth float away in the infinity of space. This new life, this New World, has a peaceful serenity and ethereal quality about it.

Was it, he pondered, the search for freedom and the hope of finding a new life out beyond the impaling forces of the earth that compelled Mr. Lilienthal, Mr. Pilcher and grandfather Willy to embark on their quest for flight. Or were they simply men imbued with the pioneering spirit destined to venture into the unknown to catching a fleeting glimpse and, perhaps, gather a sprinkling of knowledge of what hitherto had been secured behind a wall of ignorance. Their brief experiences of flight had allowed them only small opportunities to express what they had discovered during their experiments. But for certain these gallant men died in the cause of attempting to open up new avenues of knowledge.

Much of what they wrote and observed was inconclusive and erroneous. But it was enough to inspire those who followed in their footsteps. Father, for instance, had learnt a great deal from Mr. Lilienthal's misconception that stability and weight distribution was the key to the safe conduct of flight. Father had proved beyond doubt that whilst balance and stability were important it had to be complemented by a system of control. Grandfather Willy had erred in not having control surfaces on the wings of his craft and contradicted himself by having a horizontal tail that he operated by stirrups. But as Timothy well remembered, Grandfather Willy was correct in likening the air to a sea, an ocean. And it was this comparison that had prompted him to get father to fit a rudder to the kite. The rudder not only provided directional control; it was also used to stop the lower wing slipping forward in a banked turn.

Father drew his attention to Brunton forming in the distance; a church tower and two tall chimneys stood guard over the small rural town. He consulted a hand-drawn map tied to his thigh with twine and pointed to a stretch of open ground in the suburbs, half in light, half in shadow. They spotted a low-set wooden building as they drew closer. By the side of which a motorised carriage and three personages lingered. Timothy felt the ire rising in him again at thoughts of the loathsome Fanshawe waiting down there and who could not wait to get his hands on the kite – their kite. Father broke into his thoughts to tell him to make the final turn and switch to low revolutions. And as he did so Timothy savoured those precious remaining moments on the wing. The kite spoke to him in cheerful, jerky movements on the control levers, renderings given support by the invisible orchestra of air that sighed and rushed about him in equal measure. A river, overhung by coils of misty bunting, passed beneath the wings. Out to the right a row of terraced dwellings overlooked the field. Trees of adjacent woodland rose ever closer clutching for the wings. Then they were gone and the kite was sinking apace. He drew a deep breath and eased a lever back a fraction to check their descent. The kite levelled out – floated a short distance – went very quiet – and fell gently to earth. Only when they were down did he notice the ground sloping down toward the building where figures were waiting for them. He kicked the rudder bar hard over and blipped the engine twice and had the kite turned about before they reached the front of the building.

The engine had barely stopped and they had vacated their seats when Fanshawe, without so much as a greeting or compliments of the day, gave hurried orders for the kite to be pushed inside the building, out of sight, and for the doors to be closed. Then he whisked father aside, held a brief exchange, during which a package changed hands, and then he instructed a figure to return the visitors to Hadley in a motorised carriage.

The chauffeur looked very much the part in his grey uniform, his cap and goggles, and large brown leather gauntlets. But his lack of knowledge and confidence in handling the motorised carriage displayed itself soon enough when the engine stopped three times during the first two miles of the journey. Father's experience gained on the Carltons' engine came to the chauffeur's aid and prevented them from being stranded. On the third occasion father restarted the engine and before they set off he finely tuned the fuel control valve and the ignition lever through a combination of settings that had the engine chugging evenly. The chauffeur looked on, bewildered and embarrassed by his own helplessness.

They got under way without further interruptions and passed through the countryside at a stiff walking pace. The growing heat of the rising sun drew vapours of steam off the tops of the hedgerows and drew attention to a colony of spider webs strung along the sides of the hedges. Timothy compared the glittering silver structures of nature to an array of miniature jewels as he bounced upon his leather seat in the sound of the creaking suspension and a clanking sound that accompanied the trotting note of the engine. To his way of thinking the motorised carriage had yet to find a more suitable suspension and acquire means to improve on its slow, ambling turn of speed. The passage of the journey compared not at all with the rhythm of riding a horse with a good saddle, or a well-sprung horse-drawn carriage, or his graceful journeys to the heights with the kite.

They passed through an avenue of trees and were traversing a curve in the highway and beginning to straighten up when the chauffeur stopped the engine and reached out with both hands to pull the brake on. Timothy found himself colliding with the back of father's seat and returning sharply to his seat in the sudden halting of the carriage. There before them on the highway, obstructing their way, was a scene of great sadness and confusion. A coach lay sideways in a ditch its wheels overhanging the highway. Two of the mounts were trapped by it. The other four were on their feet trembling nervously and showing great restraint by not moving. For had they done so they might have injured their trapped companions still more.

He and father found the driver and coachman to the rear of the coach, sat disconsolately on the grass verge bemoaning their sorry state of affairs. Father quickly determined they were unharmed and reverted his attention back to the trapped mounts. He undid the traces of those standing and had Timothy lead them clear and feed them with handfuls of grass. Then he squatted down by the other two, patting and talking to them whilst he debated on the best way to get them clear of the shafts and tangled harnesses.

Timothy helped him free the topmost mount first. They cleared away the harness, raised one of the shafts and with a pull on the head collar the mount scrambled awkwardly to its feet. Dazed and not quite believing in its regained freedom it walked round in circles several times before shaking itself vigorously and being led away by Timothy to join its other companions.

The final mount had taken the full weight when the coach toppled and a tip of a carriage shaft had punctured the gullet. The pitiful beast lay still, eyes closed, barely a movement showing on its nostrils, so feeble was its breathing. Father burrowed beneath the mount's shoulder and shouted for Timothy to remove the shaft. The blood flowed freely from the wound. It was Timothy's first experience of witnessing a mount fighting for its life. It looked out at the world with large sad eyes, and he was compelled to put a hand on the mount's brow and keep it company in what he thought to be the closing moments of its life.

Father left him kneeling by the mount and summoned the driver, his companion and Fanshawe's chauffeur to help him upright the coach. Several minutes were to pass before they succeeded and, apart from father, they needed to sit and take a breather from their exertions. He went around the coach ensuring it was fit to travel. Then he checked the harnesses and traces of four of the mounts, made a number of adjustments and backed them into the shafts and shackled them up. He tethered the fifth mount to the rear of the coach. It took considerably more of his persuasion to get the driver and coachman to take their places on the driving seat.

"Use more of the tongue," he called up to them. "And less of the whip and the mounts will serve you well."

The round, ruddy complexion of the driver's face creased into a grimace in the shadow of the brim of his top hat. "That all be well and good, sire, if my guv'nor did not keep on warning me to keep to time or be thrown out of work."

Father said: "Your haste today cost you dear, did it not?"

"No, sire. We were making good time until a weird contraption passed overhead and bolted my team of mounts. He clicked his tongue several times to move the horses on and the coach pulled soberly away and disappeared around the curve of the highway. Timothy smiled in amazement; not once had the driver or his companion offered a word of gratitude to father for his initiative in up righting the coach and reviving the mounts. That was added to by the chauffeur who complained at length about the time he had lost and of his soiled and creased uniform caused by his labours of helping father get the coach back on the road.

Timothy was sorely tempted to remind the inconsiderate fellow of father's invaluable help with the problems of his motorised carriage. Before he could do so father said: "Feel free to take you leave, my man. My son and I will continue the rest of the journey on foot."

Moment's later Timothy was fighting to disguise his mirth at the chauffeur's many failed attempts to crank the engine into life. His face turned red with rage. He tore off his grey tunic and threw it into the back seat of the carriage. Once again he returned to cranking the engine. And the more the engine refused to yield to his demands the more he cursed and swore. In a fit of frustration he left the starting handle and vented his fury by giving a wheel of the carriage a hard and mighty kick with a boot. In a trice he collapsed on the ground nursing his painful injury, shouting, aloud, another train of unsavoury words.

Father ignored him. He made a couple of adjustments to the engine, cranked the starting handle for about six turns and the engine came to life. The limping, disgruntled chauffeur took his place at the steering wheel to be posed with another dilemma: how to turn the carriage about to make the return journey to Brunton? The Carlton brothers had yet to design a reverse form of gearing. Father checked to see the carriage was not in gear and that the brake was off and with the chauffeur steering he and Timothy pushed the carriage back and forth until it was facing in the opposite direction. Without so much as a 'thank you' or a wave of the hand in farewell from the chauffeur the carriage set off along the highway in jerking movements and periodic detonations of its engine.

"We must pray he makes it safely back to Brunton." father said.

"We may do better by praying for him to dispense with his appalling manners, father."

Father laughed, "Do not be too hard on him, my boy. Not long past I was as ignorant as him about the mechanical workings of the carriage." He moved and knelt by the fallen mount and ran a comforting hand up and down its face. It made feeble motions of stirring, struggled to lift its head, issued a painful whinny and the head slumped back to ground. The eyes were large and fearful and its laboured breathing came through yellow clenched teeth.

"Is there nothing we can do, father?"

"Nothing at all, my boy. Except that we go to home farm and collect a cart to remove it from here."

They walked along the highway in the hot, bright sunshine, leaving the mount in a growing pool of blood and a swarm of flies gathering around the open flesh of the wound.

It turned out to be a long day. A day filled with mixed emotions. They eventually arrived back at the cottage at six of the clock in the evening. They stood naked by the water pump, lathered up with soap and tipped a pail of water over each other to rinse off. They attired in fresh apparel and hatched up a meal of two potatoes each, baked in their jackets, and filled them with butter and sour cream sprinkled with salt and pepper and chives. Timothy felt cheated by all that had happened that day; they had done so much and had nothing to show for it. Fanshawe had literally grabbed the kite and sent them on their way as if they never existed. And his chauffeur was just as bad. Not once had he acknowledged father's skill at getting his engine going for him. A most unpleasant fellow? Then Timothy found himself smiling,' at recalling the chauffeur giving the wheel an energetic kick and being rewarded with an injury that threw him to the ground in agony. 'Well deserved, sir!' Timothy remembered thinking at the time.

The crew of the coach acted little better and had father not assisted them when he did they might still be waiting to be rescued from their plight. Timothy looked across the table at father. He was such a benevolent, patient and undemanding man. Nothing was ever too much trouble for him. He helped all and sundry in distress, never expecting a favour or reward in return. And in times of crisis he displayed a cool, steady nerve. Just as he had that afternoon when they returned to the stricken mount with a cart and Mr. Coley, manager of the farm on the estate, spared the mount from furthering suffering by putting a pistol shot to its head. They levered the carcass on to the cart with lengths of timber; he had brought for the purpose, and transported it back to the estate. Where it would be butchered, some of the meat is used to feed the dogs and the rest going to the tables of the poorest families in the village.

In the days after the delivery of the kite to Fanshawe Timothy helped his father clean and organise the stable to accommodate the mounts for the forthcoming winter. The big black cauldron was pushed into the open. They dismantled the fire pit and converted the area back to flooring. They tidied an assortment of wood calico and piano wire in the loft and restocked it with hay. Remnants of nails, screws and odd pieces of metal were stored in a small trunk and stored in the outside earth closet. They cleaned and polished all the horse tack and hung it in their rightful places. They returned the tools; they had borrowed from Mr. Cutler, Mr. Pook and the Carlton brothers. Timothy was left in no doubt that their days of taking to the air had come to an end. Father made a last entry in the journal that dealt with all their flying experiments and stored it in a closet of his sleeping quarters.

For a number of days thereafter nothing of note happened. Then, at short notice, father travelled to London for reasons he did not reveal at the time. He was away for seven days and within hours of his return Lady Hadley put in a surprise visit to the cottage under the cover of darkness. Timothy was sat at the table in the scullery working on a model of a single wing craft which was equipped with a propeller driven by a rubber band, an idea inspired by Harry Griggs's principle for giving motion to his cotton reels. Anchored near the tail of the model the rubber band was connected to the propeller at the front. The propeller was wound through a great number of turns. When released the rubber band unwound and rotated the propeller at speed. Which in turn propelled the model through the air. Timothy had, as yet, to get the model correctly balanced, and to adjust the control surfaces to cure its habit of pulling to the left in flight. But he enjoyed the challenge; it gave him something to occupy his mind in the loss of the kite to Fanshawe.

"I trust all went well in London, Samuel." he heard Lady Hadley remark to father in the adjacent room.

Father said: "Shall we say, I now know I am to embark on a passage to North America. But in what capacity I am to serve, when I arrive there, I have yet to be told."

North America! Timothy's mind cried out as he was reminded, from his geography lessons at school, that the Americas was on a huge continent situated many thousands of miles away on the other side of the vast Atlantic ocean.

"Is Timothy at home?" she said before he had a chance to dwell upon the possibility of father making the passage alone, thus breaking up the family entirely. Father called to him and he moved slowly to the other room.

"Good evening, Timothy."

"Good evening, Lady Hadley." The dramatic change in her appearance shocked him. She looked so pale, aged, and extremely worried. There was a hint of greying in the gold colour of her hair which also lacked grooming. A red rawness around her eyes suggested she had gone without sleep or that she had been weeping.

"What I am about to relate to you," she said hoarsely. "Must be treated with the utmost confidentiality. In other words, Timothy, you must not breathe a word of it to another living soul. Is that understood?"

He nodded; notwithstanding he was not quite sure what was expected of him. It was compounded by her visit so late in the evening, unaccompanied, and her mood of consternation. He was suspicious of her need for secrecy.

Father, sat in his rocker, an index finger curled around the stem of his pipe, said: "I think Timothy is quite aware of his duties and loyalties to the Hadley family. Is that not so, my boy?"

"Yes, father."

Lady Hadley fidgeted with her hands, her head lowered. "I fear the squire and I have been made the victims of a conspiracy," she said. "A treacherous and evil conspiracy that led the squire to make rash decisions and, in so doing, perpetrate a grave miscarriage of justice." She paused and raised her head to look at them, her eyes more enflamed and she was fighting back the tears. "Do you recall when the squire said he could not aid you with funds to build the powered kite because he was laying out his monies to purchase a motorised carriage from the Carlton brothers?"

Timothy nodded as did father.

Lady Hadley said: "I regret you were misinformed. The truth is: the Squire received an anonymous letter threatening to expose many irregularities on the estate were he to continue to fund any more of your experiments at flight. There was mention of unpaid taxes and illegal claims to the boundaries of land on the estate. The family solicitor established there was an element of truth in the claims and advised us to abide by the wishes of the correspondent." She sighed heavily. "Regrettably it was not the end of our troubles .."

"As a friend of the family and a trusted employee, why was I not told of these threats." father demanded.

Lady Hadley said: "Chambers, our solicitor, ordered us not to mention it to anyone. There was, and still is, a suspicion that a person in the employ of the estate leaked certain information to the blackmailer. How else could the wretched culprit have obtained the information."

Father paused, thoughtfully for a time. "No doubt Rebecca is included in your list of suspects," he said at last. "After all she is the wife of an estate employee, had access to certain confidences, and left the estate as an embittered and wounded woman."

Timothy frowned; he found it extremely difficult to believe what he was hearing. Conspiracy, treachery and blackmail, as he knew it, only ever happened in the newspapers and most certainly not in Hadley.

Lady Hadley said: "The truth is Samuel we received the anonymous letter some weeks before Rebecca made the visit to the nursery that day. Also Chambers is convinced the letter is in the handwriting of a male personage. And strangely enough it arrived shortly after your first kite perished in the fire."

Father moved forward on his chair, his face pained, anguished, "Tell me then, Claire. Why the slaying of Jake Howson. It was well known the poor fellow could neither read or write."

Before Timothy could grasp what he was hearing Lady Hadley cried: "Samuel! I beg of you not to haunt me with that evil tragedy. Believe me it has aged the Squire and me well beyond our years and continues to rob us of our sleep. I can only assume we were so desperate to get our hands on the blackmailer that when Rebecca mentioned Jake Howson bandying about the origins of Samantha the Squire and I clutched at straws and unjustly drew the wrong conclusions." Tears began to well in her eyes. "Believe me, Samuel." she cried. "I am at my wits end." She threw her hands out to him. And father moved and lifted her into his arms.

Timothy debated on what he should do. There was a time he would have been embarrassed by such a scene, father embracing the wife of a fellow man. But on this occasion he had reason to think there was something gallant in his response to Lady Hadley's genuine distress.

Eventually her emotion calmed a little and she stood comfortable in father's arms, her head resting against his chest, her eyes closed.

"I find it rather odd," father said quietly. "That the Carlton brothers, nor I, have been threatened during the construction of the kite for Mr. Fanshawe. And yet you and the squire were threatened not to help us. I would suggest there is a link here, Claire."

Timothy did not have to be told where father's conclusions were leading. He had never trusted the little, fat man and he was surprised how long it had taken father to arrive at the same opinion. Fanshawe was an out and out fraudster, stealing other personage's designs and ideas and claiming the credit for the idea and invention as his. Oh, yes, he had paid father for the kite but to Timothy's way of thinking that was nothing short of bribery and corruption. Very soon it was most likely Fanshawe's name would feature in the headlines of the Brunton News as being the first to achieve manned flight in a heavier than air flying machine. And Fanshawe would be awarded all the credit and honours for this magnificent achievement. There would be no mention of father, or the Carlton brothers, Mr Pook, Mr. Cutler or Mrs. Pettifodder who between them had constructed and perfected the kite to take to the air.

Lady Hadley looked up at father, "Are you suggesting, Samuel, that the fellow Fanshawe or his agents sent us the anonymous, threatening letter?"

He looked down at her in the fold of his arms. "Shall we say, at this moment in time, a number of clues point to it."

She stirred, "If what you say is true, what are we to do?"

"I regret there is absolutely nothing we can do. Except to let justice take its course."

At one time Timothy would have accused him of giving up without a fight, just as mother had. But in recent years father had shown he had a sound philosophy, and true to form justice did take its course during the weeks following.

They were sat, quietly, of an evening in the cottage. The evenings were drawing in, and in the light of an oil lamp father pored over the plates of an atlas. Timothy sat opposite in mother's rocker perusing through the book on mathematics she had sent him at Christmas. He was attempting to unravel the mysteries of algebraic equations and found it heavy going. Out the corner of an eye he saw the ears of the dogs go up a moment before they stirred and slipped through to wait at the front door. Presently, a chain of distant reports interrupted the deafness of the evening – the dogs stood and wagged their tails – the reports grew louder and combined with the continuous clanking of the Carltons' motorised carriage. It stopped by the front gate and after misfiring several times lapsed into silence. Timothy went to the door to greet them, father vacated his chair to organise seats for the visitors who appeared with solemn faces and were far removed from the jovial characters he and Timothy had got to know. And when Timothy was asked to get jars and ale from the pantry, when he returned he too had never seen the engineers look so downcast and depressed. They overlooked the handshake in greeting and collapsed heavily on their chairs with an audible sigh.

"We are the messengers of tragic news, Samuel." Mr. Charles remarked his gaze fixed on the pit of the hearth.

"Gentlemen!" father laughed. "My life is nothing but a train of failures and disappointments. I lose a good woman in Rebecca. I lose the kite to Fanshawe because I do not have the funds to construct it myself. In recent weeks I learn my employment upon the estate is to be terminated and I am to move to another continent many miles across the sea. I can think of little else to add to my trail of misfortune."

Mr. Robert said: "The kite has perished."

Father frowned over the bowl of his pipe as he put a lighted match to it, "How so?"

After taking a swig of ale and taking a light from father for his small cigar Mr. Charles launched into giving an account of what happened:

Evidently, over the weeks, Fanshawe had been experimenting at flight by making short hops across the field with the Carlton brothers in attendance at his request. They had little choice but to oblige because he had ordered a second motorised carriage from them, and also convinced them he had three associates on the verge of placing orders.

During his brief hopping flights he had shown great flair in controlling the engine, but less so in controlling the kite. Time and time again he came back to earth in a series of bouncing and clutching motions and luckily missed colliding with the trees and hedges around the field. It was a credit to the kite's robust construction that it was spared from structural damage.

However he did manage to increase his time on the wing and actually made hesitant turns a few feet above the ground within the confines of the field. But unlike father's banked turns he slewed the kite around by the sole use of the rudder with the result the inner wings lost way then dropped dramatically pulling the whole kite earthwards. Only in the nick of time and through a stroke of good luck did he manage to right the kite and avoid dashing it to ground.

The fact that he avoided a calamity obviously led him to think he had acquired sufficient experience and it was time he put his flights on display to the world and collected the credit and honours that went with such a feat. He sent out invitations to a newspaper editor and a number of local dignitaries to come and officially witness his flights.

They arrived just after midday of the previous day, Mr. Charles pointed out to father, the editor, a reporter and a photographer from the Brunton News and the mayor and two officials from Brunton town hall. Fanshawe had them all transported in by a Carltons' motorised carriage. They congregated by a table from which Fanshawe's chauffeur served a choice of ale or wine. The kite stood nearby its copper and brass fittings glinting in the sunlight, its calico clean and white except for a number of blotches of oil in the vicinity of the engine. It rocked occasionally from the playful antics of a breeze. The photographer moved around with his large camera on a tripod and hid himself under a black cloth to take pictures intended for showing in the Brunton News. One picture featured the mayor, wearing his chain of office, stood beside Fanshawe who was attired in a brown tweed suit and waistcoat, brown leather gaiters, gauntlets, and a large flat cap and goggles. Another picture was taken of him stood with the editor before the kite. Then, as a finale, the whole gathering posed before the kite with Fanshawe in the middle.

Moments later he clambered on to the centre section of the kite and invited Mr. Robert to join him to wind the starting handle. The photographer, seized by the thought of capturing another historic moment in time, rushed his equipment into position and took a picture of Fanshawe sitting in his revolutionary craft of the air. And when the engine clattered into life he took his apparatus to the rear of the kite to take a clearer picture of the lumbering engine and revolving propeller. Mr. Robert left the centre section and joined his brother in removing the blocks before the wheels. Fanshawe threw a salute at his spectators blipped the engine switch and got the kite under way and made his way to the other end of the field which Mr. Robert thought was three times longer than the paddock.

The chatter amongst the spectators faded when it reached the distant boundary and swung around to face them. A pause, then the engine switched to maximum revolutions. For a time the kite appeared to be stationary. Then very gradually movement was discernable – it was on the move – trundling – it came prancing across the field wandering from side to side – growing larger in size, reaching for the air many times but failing to get on the wing. And each time it struck ground the drum-tight calico boomed out its protest over the noise of the engine.

At the very last moment when the demonstration of manned flight seemed doomed to failure the kite clambered awkwardly clear of the earth and clawed at the air as it passed over their heads. Exclamations of disbelief followed it and some shouted their congratulations! The mayor and his followers thought it nothing short of a miracle. The newspaper team regarded it as a scientific triumph: at long last man had defied the laws of gravity and won; no longer was the air reserved exclusively for the flying transportation of the birds.

Moments later their celebratory shouts and exchanges were dashed by a single devastating blow. Fanshawe had made two jerky circuits of the field, flying fifty feet in the air, and was making the final turn of the second circuit, to approach the spectators, when the kite made a breathtaking plunge and crashed to earth with astonishing abruptness and severity...

Mr. Charles paused in painful recollection of the last moments of the kite. Father poured him another jar of ale and, quietly, posed him with a number of questions: Were the wings tilted before the fatal dive? – Did any part of the construction break off in flight? – Did the engine falter?

Mr. Charles, plagued by despair, threw his hands up aimlessly, "I cannot say anything with reasonable accuracy, Samuel. It happened with the speed of lightning. So much so Fanshawe was trapped under the weight of the engine which burst into flames. And by the time we arrived on the scene the heat was so intense we could not get to him. I can truly say it was the most horrific sight I have ever witnessed."

At first light the following morning Timothy awoke to the sound of father's voice telling him to get dressed and give him a hand to put Yorkie in the shafts of the trap. They journeyed to Brunton, to the scene of the disaster or what little there remained of it, an area surrounded by a rope cordon guarded by the uniformed figure of a police constable. A solitary wing strut had survived the furnace. It stood amongst a pile of wood ash; a length of piano wire still attached to it. The bulky shape of the engine lay half submerged beneath the ash and a few paces away the horizontal tail and vertical rudder were visible as charred skeletons. Father made to step inside the cordon to be immediately arrested by the voice of the constable. "The cordon is there for a reason, sir." he shouted gruffly.

Father said: "I will have you know, Constable that Mr. Fanshawe was well known to me."

"Be that as it may, sir. I have my orders."

Father did not argue further; he walked on around the cordon looking in at the grisly remains trying, Timothy thought, to find clues to the cause of the tragic accident in which Fanshawe met so violent a death. Timothy trailed behind him, certain in his own mind that Mr. Fanshawe's lack of knowledge and experience had taken the kite to its untimely destruction. On more than one occasion he had overheard father telling the Carlton brothers of his invitation to Fanshawe to go aloft with him before he took ownership of the kite in order to familiarise himself with the flying controls and the engine. But the offers were always rejected for the usual reasons Mr. Fanshawe had more important matters upon his time, rather than admit it was beneath his pride and dignity to take advice from so a humble a personage as Samuel Herby. The folly of refusing such an offer had led to his unnecessary and premature demise.

Father led the way back to the trap; head hung low, glum faced, deep in thought. Timothy guessed he was affected by the loss of the kite and was thinking of the many hours laboured on constructing and perfecting it to take to the air. Now, it was nothing more than a scorched lump of metal, a few remaining burnt bones of wood and a covering of ash that would gradually disperse at the hands of a light wind. It did not pay to think about the shrunken, charred black body in the local mortuary.

They were making an exit from the field with Timothy at the reins when a figure stepped into view from behind a hedgerow forcing him rein short quickly to halt the trap. Mother's sudden, unexpected appearance struck them both dumb.

"Good morning." she greeted them brightly. "Would you care to join me for breakfast.

After overcoming his surprise father said: "I think not, Rebecca. I am not in the best of spirits."

Timothy felt the tensions of late creep between them, the fear of putting a word out of place, father's mistrust of her intentions. He grinned when mother brushed father's excuse aside and said, "Then that, Samuel Herby, is all the more reason you should partake of a nourishing start to the day."

Timothy nodded to her discreetly in agreement.

Father said, "Did you by chance witness the disaster here, yesterday?"

"A brief glimpse, perhaps. It happened so quickly that it was over and done with in a trice. Now tether your mount and allow me to lead you to my abode."

Father overlooked her cunning, Timothy thought, in his pursuit to learn more about the doomed kite. Whereas she had offered the information as a carrot to lure father to breakfast. Parents could be strange people at times

Within minutes they were seated in her quarters which overlooked the field of the kite disaster. Her abode was similar to the cottage in size but in contrast was elegantly furnished with a carpeted floor and soft easy chairs. Burgundy coloured paper ingrained with a gold pattern dressed the walls. Fine lace curtains covered the windows, sided by thick, velvet drapes. A mantelpiece displayed a black china antelope in flight, an impressive chiming timepiece and a model soldier in scarlet uniform with his sword drawn. Timothy could not help comparing the tasteful setting of her home to the Spartan simplicity of the cottage. Might it have been one of the reasons why mother took her leave of him and father?

An attractive, embroidered cloth covered the table and was set with polished silver cutlery and fine china crockery and serviettes. Mother bustled around them serving food. Grapefruit slices came first, a fruit Timothy had never tasted before and which came over as a trifle bitter until mother sprinkled sugar over it.

Cold sliced ham and poached eggs followed. Pursued by plates of toasted bread smeared with butter and a layer of orange jam. Liquid refreshment came in the form of what mother described as tea from India that could be taken with milk and sugar. Timothy thought its smell and taste differed greatly to the nettle tea he was accustomed to drinking. He looked around the room as they ate in silence, feeling deeply happy at the three of them being together again. Never had he seen mother smile so regularly. She fussed around them serving and removing dishes and plates of the respective courses. And carried over from her time at the cottage, no matter what time of day, she was always well turned out. A black skirt covered by a multitude of long, thin beads fell from the waist to the ankles. A white silk blouse covered her ample bosom and was fashionably billowed at the sleeves. Cuffs and collar were a snug fit, the left wrist wearing a gold bangle. A cameo brooch adorned the throat of her blouse. Her hair, a rich jet black in colour, was coiled up on the back of her head and held in place by a gold comb. She was indeed a beautiful woman and even moreso when she was smiling.

The meal had come to an end and they were sipping tea when she said: "What do you propose to do to counter the loss of the second kite, Samuel?"

Father frowned heavily, "Were you aware I constructed the second kite for Fanshawe?"

"Not really. Only that I happened to arise early on the morning when the kite arrived here. And I spotted you and Timothy with it." She pointed to a telescope on a sideboard. "That little instrument told me everything."

When father failed to comment she said: "What is more Samuel, I am certain that had you been steering the kite the disaster would not have occurred."

Once again father was stuck for an answer, as was Timothy. The radical change in her interest in their flying experiments was in complete contrast to times past when all she could do was scorn father's dreams and aspirations to take to the wing.

"Do you plan to construct another?" she said eagerly.

Father lowered his cup to its saucer. "There is no chance of that whatsoever. You see, Rebecca, Timothy and I are on the verge of leaving Hadley to start up a life elsewhere."

"Leaving Hadley." she gasped, her smile vanishing in an instant.

"Yes. We are to be dispatched to the North Americas."

Father's revelation struck deep in her. She clenched her hands tightly and the knuckles stood out clearly against the stretched paleness of the skin. Timothy found himself comparing her gathering distress to the grave look on father's face that day when she took her leave of them and boarded the coach for Brunton.

"Why so far away?" she pleaded, almost in a whisper. And for the first time in his life Timothy noticed tears springing from her eyes.

Father said gently, "It is hoped that my removal from the estate will take the focus of attention off the Hadley child and the truth of its origins."

Mother said hoarsely, "I suspect it has more to do with my disclosure at the fete. And for it I am to be punished by distancing me ever further from my husband and son."

Timothy considered it quite ironic that she should mention the separation from him and father when, after all said and done, it had been her decision, and her alone, to abandon him and father.

"The truth is, Rebecca," father said. "I am more than a little happy to be leaving Hadley. So much has changed it is not the place I once knew. And I see nothing of a future here for Timothy."

Mother fought hard to blink back the tears and retain her dignity. "What position will you hold in North America, Samuel?"

"An official in London hinted at the possibility it may be connected with the Colonial Office."

The timepiece on the mantelpiece chimed out the hour of eight. Timothy sensed that mother had been pushed into a corner and was praying earnestly for help to extricate her from the perils of her predicament. An excess of personal pride prevented her from making the first move. She said humbly, "When do you actually embark for the voyage?"

"In some six weeks from what I gather."

She sat very still looking down at her hands. Then father, ever considerate, ever gallant, reached across the table and placed a hand on her, "If you can find it in yourself, Rebecca, you are welcome to join Timothy and me in this great new adventure."

Her head drooped lower. Two tears fell as damp blobs on the tablecloth. She began to tremble uncontrollably and before she collapsed upon the table father hurried to her, lifted her into his arms, and the weeping became a flood of tears. Timothy, feeling their need to be alone, made a hurried discreet exit from the room.

She moved back to the cottage a week later. And happily joined them in making the many preparations for their departure. Father took her to London to confer with his new employers and to include her in the passage by sea. Arrangements known only to the Hadleys, the Sawyers and the Carlton brothers.

Nobody else on the estate or in the village were aware of their pending departure. Life for Timothy had not been so complete for a long time. Mother and father were making a determined effort to make a success of their reconciliation. They laughed and joked and, as frequently, he caught them unaware in an embrace reviving a lost affection.

The Carlton brothers arrived with two motorised carriages to collect them one morning just as the sun was coming up. The second carriage would carry their luggage. Timothy looked at the cottage for the last time and recalled the visit to Marie and her parents the previous evening; the family had agreed to take over the care of the dogs and horses. Father stood alone on the brow of the hill and in a strange way cut a figure of importance. The rising sun depicted him as a statute commemorating a deed, a feat that furthered the progress of mankind.

"It is indeed a tragedy, Timothy." mother said softly.

He turned to her, "Tragedy, mother?"

"Yes. A great tragedy my son. That great man, your father, standing there has made history. But fate has decided he shall remain unknown to the world."

It pleased him greatly to know she had, at last, come to recognise father for what he was. Suddenly his thoughts were with father on the brow of the hill, reliving those unforgettable moments of their early flights. Those taut, breathtaking rumbling journeys down the hill face. The awesome confrontation with the fathoms of air that lay over the lip of the hill and where a plummeting death stalked if a control lever was wrongly placed or the kite buckled under the invisible and unknown pressures of the air. His early solo flights came to mind and the great loneliness he felt, at times, suspended out there in the void that did not yield readily and easily to a mortal's desire for knowledge but, since time began, had compromised with the flight of the bird.

Most of the time of a flight was taken up getting accustomed to the language qualities of the air, and understanding the changing note of the air streams. The hissing, whistling, wailing, moaning, groaning overtures around the wings and against the struts and rigging and which, at times, were heavy enough to make a spar or rib creak and shriek.

The powered kite had brought with it a need to learn another language entirely. A language made memorable by the smell of hot engine oil, the gaseous tang of the combustible liquid spirit that gave life to the noisy engine and in conjunction with a mixture of air sustained its chattering cycle.

But in equal measure there were moments on all of the flights that were rich with reward. In particular that glorious, spectacular, triumphant moment when the kite is coaxed to break free of its earthly tentacles, and take to the wing and fly. Every sight, every sound and every smell is indelibly imprinted on Timothy's memory.

Father came and interrupted his thoughts by apologising for delaying him and mother. He helped mother into the carriage and joined her on the back seat and Timothy climbed onto the front seat beside Mr. Robert, a seat of honour, father jokingly remarked. Mr. Charles cranked the engine and after he had started the engine of his carriage they set off in convoy for the docks laying some fifty miles distant.

By late afternoon they were aboard, and standing at the rail of, the mighty iron steamship, looking down at the Carlton brothers waving to them from the quayside below. A freshening southwesterly wind drove fragments of dark cloud along beneath a lighter grey overcast. Occasionally they felt spots of rain. Father stood to the right of Timothy dressed in a dark business overcoat and a black bowler hat. Mother stood to the left wearing a fashionable pelisse. She looked out from the shadows of the hood, a smile dancing about her lips, a look of eager anticipation in her eyes.

Timothy accepted their new life abroad would require various personal adjustments – meeting new personages – new scenery – perhaps a different culture. But it was made less daunting by the unity and renewed strength of their small family. He cared, and wanted, for nothing more. It mattered little if their accomplishment of manned, powered flight went unrecorded to the world. Most important was father and mother being together again. Father, he felt sure, was content to rest in the knowledge that he had proved what he had set out to do and which served as a fitting tribute to grandfather Willy who had died so valiantly in his quest for flight...

The ship began to ease away from the quayside, aided by tugs. They waved their final farewells to the diminishing figures of the Carlton brothers and, as the ship moved deeper into the channel and through a curtain of rain father said, "If we make haste we can pen a short letter to our friends and have the pilot take it ashore."

Timothy hurriedly led the way down the decks to their cabin, suddenly realising how much he had forgotten to tell Marie.

****

Typeset, printed and bound by Hobbs the Printers Ltd, Brunel Road, Totton, Hampshire